MW00814690

Watson & Holmes: The Twisted Blackmailer
by
T. L. Garrison

First edition published in 2016
© Copyright 2016
T L Garrison

The right of TL Garrison to be identified as the author of this work
has been asserted by her accordance with the Copyright, Designs
and Patents Act 1998.

All rights reserved. No reproduction, copy or transmission of this
publication may be made without express prior written permission.
No paragraph of this publication may be reproduced, copied or
transmitted except with express prior written permission or in
accordance with the provisions of the Copyright Act 1956
(as amended). Any person who commits any unauthorized act in
relation to this publication may be liable to criminal prosecution
and civil claims for damage.

All characters appearing in this work are fictitious or are used
fictitiously. Except for certain historical personages,
any resemblance to real persons, living or dead, is purely
coincidental. The opinions expressed herein are those of the
authors and not of MX Publishing.

Paperback ISBN 978-1-78705-024-2
ePub ISBN 978-1-78705-025-9
PDF ISBN 978-1-78705-026-6

Published in the UK by MX Publishing
335 Princess Park Manor, Royal Drive,
London, N11 3GX
www.mxpublishing.co.uk

For Jim, who's there for me,
Nana and Grandpap, who said I could do it if I worked hard,
Warren Scheideman and all our Saturday talks,
and other people who helped along the way.

Chapter One

My world crumbled hyperbolically before me on a misty November morning, the week before Thanksgiving.

The word around the halls had been two words, really. Mostly consisting of "new girl." Will Murray had seen her in the office registering for classes (without a guardian present), and Michael Stamford had been in her first class, where she'd pitched a fit about astronomy being of no relevance to her being, then stormed out, back to the office.

This did not bode well. I had the last locker in the Junior hall, since my last name began with a W. That wasn't true. I didn't have the last locker. I had the last column. Locker 221A, which meant New Girl would have the locker below mine.

Not only was I unused to sharing, but students changing schools mid-semester, nay, mid-week was a tipoff that the rest of my school year was going to either be awkward or hellish. Students didn't do that unless they'd been tossed out of another school. Ever.

I'd received texts from Will and Michael just as Mrs. Hall dimmed the lights and began repeating word for word choice bits of the narrator's monologue from the video on cell reproduction that we were watching.

The texts detailed the further adventures of New Girl Drama, which were a delightful change from Mrs. Hall's monotone reiterations that always made me wish she'd make up her mind as to whether she was giving a lecture or letting the video do the work for her.

Before I could copy down the bit about blood and platelets and plasma into my notes, my phone buzzed in my pocket. I slid it out as quietly as possible. I didn't look around to see if I'd been noticed; Mrs. Hall would have ripped the phone out of my hand by now.

Marybeth Hunter, soccer buddy and occasional person to copy homework from, had sent a message that read more like a warning than the morning's fast-flying gossip. Three words: *Coming your way.* That wasn't foreboding. Not at all.

And then it happened.

The door swung open, light shot in from the hallway into the darkened classroom, and then there was a tall, thin figure in dramatic outline, the hall lights outlining her like some holy body.

Easily six feet, thin and angular, I thought at first the silhouette must have been a teacher. But she moved into the room smoothly with a sheet of paper in her hand. I could see her better now, and she was no less imposing than when she had been a shadow, just a few seconds before.

Caught in the light from the video, she was much more defined--the stern, unimpressed cut of her thin lips, the strong Roman nose and the disaffected arch of her brow. New Girl was like a statue in a museum: pale, chiselled and perfect.

As Mrs. Hall read over the schedule, New Girl adjusted the strap of what looked like an old but expensive leather satchel on her shoulder. My heart leapt from anticipation to misery to a tangled and knotted in my stomach. Other than 'trouble,' I had no initial instinct regarding her.

I was curious, of course. Writers were supposed to be. But I was left with a dread of not only having a locker column-mate, but also a new lab partner. I'd been sitting at this table by myself blissfully since late August, and I was not emotionally prepared to share, much less share with New Girl, who had been obviously expelled from another school, and who walked around as if nothing really mattered. Maybe if I'd had time to prepare.

Knowing it was coming, I pulled my backpack off the table and put it under my stool, like a polite and decent human being. I still had the phone in my hand, so I held it under the table, sending a group message to Marybeth, Michael and Will.

It has begun.

I slid the phone into my back pocket as the stern figure of New Girl passed around the perimeter of the room, sizing everyone up with cold eyes, past the rows of tables, past my favorite jocks, and the Veronicas. Apparently one of the requirements for being on the cheer squad was being named Veronica. Hence I stuck to soccer and intramural rugby. Well, and I had no actual gymnastic ability. I was built like a pit bull, so I kept to my strengths.

They were all staring, of course. I had no idea why Mrs. Hall didn't just pause the video and introduce New Girl properly, but nothing the woman did made sense. Apparently, plasma reproduction was such hot stuff that not a single second of the DVD could be spared, not even for a new classmate.

New Girl looked even more stern up close, as she sat on the stool next to me, ignoring me completely. Expensive Oxfords, long black trousers and a crisp white shirt under a black sweater vest, finished off with a severe and tight bun low on the back of her head. I'd seen detention teachers that were more festive than this girl.

She pulled a leather portfolio out of her bag, set the bag beside her, and then opened the portfolio to a blank sheet of paper, thick wooden pen gripped tightly in a fist, kind of like a shank, showing she had no intention of taking notes.

It was entirely outside the bounds of social allowances, but I kept stealing looks. Everything about her wardrobe was on the bespoke side, and she didn't have a single hair out of place. She was a little too put together for someone who had been tossed out of another school. Maybe she really had just moved here.

At least this was interesting. Nothing of note had happened at this school since September when Warren Siegel had been suspended for having pot in his locker… in a hollowed-out apple. That had been the talk of the town for weeks. I bet we could get a whole month out of a new girl who looked like she'd stepped off of a television set.

New Girl might have sensed me staring, but she never looked over or acknowledged that she was being gawked at like a zoo animal. She just sat there, watching the rest of the video. Attentive though she was, there was a palpable disdain coming off of her, and I wondered if we were going to have another scene like in astronomy. In some ways, I was kind of hoping for it. Molecular Biology was a dirge of a class and a verbal lash-out by the new kid would be the most amazing thing that could happen on the week before a holiday. Or ever, really. Stuff just didn't happen here.

But the video played on without incident.

When the lights finally came up, Mrs. Hall spoke a minute or two on antibody production in white blood cells, because god forbid anything get in the way of human biology. Eventually her reiteration of video contents played out, and she gestured to my table.

"We have a new student." She searched the paper on her counter for a moment. "Sherlock Holmes?"

New Girl nodded once.

"Sherlock?" Mrs. Hall asked again, incredulous that someone could be called that. But the world view in this school was especially small; there were three people in the class named Veronica, after all.

"Old family name. It means fair of hair."

The expected snickering from the rest of the class never came.

Mrs. Hall stared at her blankly for a second, then seemed to catch up. "I'll have a book for you tomorrow. And a syllabus. We're working on a group project this term. Jo, I am going to pull you from Tyrone's group and you can work with Sherlock."

Which was fine with me, in theory. Tyrone was smart, but his father was the favorite linebacker of the city's football team, so he thought that made him the instant lead of every group project and the center of all attention. It would have been easier to deal with him if he didn't actually have the intelligence to back it up. Apparently modesty was a lost virtue. He grated on me...a lot.

Of course, now this meant working with this completely unknown factor, Sherlock Holmes. Obviously wealthy and with the attitude that she thought she was better than all of this, so the project could go either way. This didn't suit me at all. I had grades to maintain for scholarship purposes.

"Sherlock?" Mrs. Hall seemed to have trouble with the name. Was it really any different from all the designer names running around this school? My own name was boring, but at least spellable. "Ms. Watson can catch you up on the blood typing presentation before next Monday."

Oh god. In addition to actually having to interact with New Girl, I was going to have to tutor her on a month's worth of class information. I hadn't thought about that. Of course I had to be sharing a presentation project and a locker space with someone who had not so much as given me a second glance.

I closed my notebook, swallowing over an uncomfortable lump in the back of my throat. I didn't want life to be interesting in this particular way. I just wanted some big fit or something in the middle of class. "I'd be happy to."

Mrs. Hall nodded and headed back to the front of the room to shut off the AV equipment. This was going to be…interesting. Mike and Will's barbs and constant joking aside. I could deal with Laurel and Hardy if I didn't have to actually stress out about working with someone I didn't know, of questionable ability and enthusiasm level for the actual project.

Mrs. Hall blathered on about the project to the class in general. Page length, presentation time, how she was going to grade on individual presentation. As if she hadn't said all of this before. Multiple times.

To avoid staring at my new partner, I took great interest in the 1950s industrial-style clock on the wall, just above the teacher's head. Each second ticked away audibly, bringing me closer to the end of class.

I might be able to get another essay for the school's literary journal out of this, if I could turn it into a proper story. And change all the names and places to protect the guilty. Without being entirely obvious that I was talking about the only thing to happen in this school since September.

No. It was a terrible idea. I'd have to think of something else. Maybe Will would let me write about that time where I did something stupid and he saved me from drowning when we were ten. That sounded appropriately dramatic. They'd liked the anonymous stories about my brother coming home from the marines, and his subsequent troubles, and the one about the flood in our basement that had pretty much wiped out all traces of my mother's existence by destroying all memorabilia associated with her. Even her birth certificate. People liked those sad things, I supposed. Sherlock Holmes was interesting, but hardly sad drama material.

Then again, I still hadn't worked on the project with her. The situation could go from awkward to sad very quickly.

One of my ambitions in life (I had many) was to be a real writer. But I felt like I would never get there. Especially if I wasn't even willing to sign the few things I'd submitted to the school newspaper and literary magazine over the last few years, due to fear of embarrassment. And all my other writing consisted of melodramatic fan fiction written under an ageless, sexless pseudonym on the Internet.

Given the circumstances, it was a blessing I was good at math and science because fanfic and anonymous personal essays were not exactly bestseller material.

Just when I was two clock ticks away from moving directly from self-pity to maudlin despair, the bell put me out of misery. Everyone stood up, grabbing their bags and notebooks, shuffling like zombies toward the door. The slow moving kind. The ones that got you from persistence, and not from speed or skill. That was how I was going to die someday. Probably.

I also rose, grabbing my bag from the floor. Maybe I'd read the new girl wrong. One could hope. "So, uh, I guess we're working together."

The new girl made a dismissive grunt at my obvious statement. She slung her amber-colored leather bag over her shoulder. "It is simple blood typing and discussion of plasma and platelet production. I can have it, and the presentation completed by tomorrow. You don't need to worry about it. And then we will not have to worry about engaging in tedious social interaction."

I had been expecting the worst, and was somehow blown away. "Look, I kind of want to learn this stuff. So can you indulge me? And do the project with me anyway?"

The girl sighed. "Studious. I would congratulate you, but it is trite. Just take the easy A."

I clenched my jaw, grinding my teeth. "Look, I need to learn this stuff if I am going to get into a decent pre-med program next year, ok?" I flung my own bag onto my back with angry intensity. It hit hard and I winced, almost stumbling forward, into the new student. "Ugh. Sorry."

Sherlock Holmes squinted at me with those sharp, cutting grey eyes. "You blew out your knee in rugby last spring," she stated, completely unprompted. "You thought it would be healed by now, but it required ACL surgery and physical therapy, and since then you have been curiously off balance. You chose not to play soccer this season in an attempt to not allow a bad performance to ruin your chances for a scholarship, and you hope to stage a comeback next year."

"What?" I asked, taken off guard.

She smiled tightly. "I find you to be acceptable."

"Gee, thanks." My lips pressed together tightly.

"I mean, I can work with you."

That didn't make me feel any better.

The girl reached into her satchel and pulled out a small silver case, opened it, and presented me with a simple white and black business card.

Sherlock Holmes
Consultant Examiner of Facts
sws.holmes@gmail.com

I flipped it over, waiting for the punchline. "What kind of name is Sherlock anyway?" It wasn't polite, but I was out of things to say.

That tight smile pulled at the girl's thin lips again. "It's an old family name. As I said before. Of little concern."

That said, she turned on her heels, marching out of the room with a purpose normally reserved for the military and not a mid-morning trip through the halls of a public high school.

I flipped the card over and over in my hand, mind rushing with everything and nothing. Questions, mostly. No answers.

"Ms. Watson?" Mrs Hall asked, one eyebrow arched as members of the next class began the slow march toward their tables. "Don't you have somewhere to be?"

I gave her a dazed shrug, then went back to looking at the card in my hand.

"Watson, that's my seat." Someone from the football team, I couldn't remember who, said it as he pushed past me. I'd complain about jocks being the reason we couldn't have nice things, but according to many, I was counted among their number.

Tapping the card twice against the table, I looked up at the other student. "Sorry. I'm out of here."

Walking out, I almost rammed into two tables as I looked the card over again and again, even though it continued to reveal no new information. I caught my shoulder on the door as it opened, and I almost walked into someone else coming into the classroom.

Stepping aside from the door, I missed the chaotic flow of the hall as I stared at the thick, shining black print on the card, wondering just what the hell I was getting into.

Consulting examiner. Of facts. That wasn't even a thing. What a pretentious...

My phone buzzed twice in my pocket, and I was about to reach for it, but the bell rang again. Great, and I was now late for my next class.

Portents of the future. Again, hyperbole. But just barely.

Chapter 2

I didn't have a chance to text the guys back until I had snuck into English class, homework had been collected, and the class itself was well on its way. By then, I had gotten two texts from Manisha from the soccer team, who was offended that a junior was in her senior history class, to which I responded with deepest sympathies.

Manisha tended to be unimposing and quiet, both on the field and off, but there were hidden depths of resentment and hatred for everything and everyone in the school. Which I certainly appreciated. And might have done some things to foster. School was school. Everyone acted like it was an entire lifestyle, but it was a means to an end, and while I had to play the game, I didn't have to like it.

It gave me more information to pass to the boys. A name, a few classes in the schedule. It made me popular with Mike and Will for all of about two minutes. In the intervening class period, Will had been trying to figure out which lunch period she was in, and Michael was convinced that this was the most interesting thing to happen since Allison Kaminski had climbed onto the school roof and had unlocked the doors last year before a band festival because the band was locked out of the school. I was still holding onto the pot thing. He just loved Allison because she had broken into the school with the band director's permission and blessing.

Other than the senior privileges being revoked after a dead catfish was left in the courtyard, this was about all we had going for us as far as something new and exciting.

When Michael's fifth message about New Girl appeared, I slipped the phone under my binder in an effort to not get caught. I hadn't had detention for excessive phone usage since freshman year, and I wanted to keep it that way. I did have an academic record to uphold for scholarship purposes, after all.

The district wasn't necessarily large, as far as student size went. But it covered a large swath of land in the county. It was sort of diverse. Mostly economically. That was something you never forgot in this place. There were the haves, the have less, and the rest of us. I was a river rat. One of the kids from the boroughs near the river and railroad tracks, at the bottom of the hills where pretty much the rest of the school district lived. It was a working class area. The farther you went up into the hills, the more expensive and the more rural the houses became. Professional football players, retired baseball players, and new money from business people and politicians took up the lower parts of the hilly area, all in modern glass houses with three pools. And on the tops of the rolling hills were the old houses. The old money, tied up in land and farms and hundred-year-old companies. Most of those kids went to boarding school, or to one of the fancy private schools named after old philanthropic white men who'd been dead a hundred and fifty years or more.

I was definitely of the less-than middle class variety. Dad was an officer with the borough police department. It was just the two of us, living in an old Victorian row house which was far longer than it was wide. Dark and gloomy on the inside due to insufficient windows and lighting (and electrical outlets) that had been retrofitted into the house during some long-forgotten renovation before we'd owned the house. I'd grown up there, and if I made it through medical school, I would probably still end up living there, mostly because it was all I knew.

I said 'if' because nothing was for certain. I didn't really have the chances or opportunities afforded to the kids who lived up on the hills. Hell, Tara Gill was taking classes in the afternoon at one of the local universities, and her grades were no better than mine. But her parents were willing to ferry her back and forth, and had the money to pay out of pocket for tuition for a part-time student. My dad paid out of pocket for a neighborhood art class once. We lived vastly different lives. Which gave me all the bad feelings about this Sherlock Holmes, who was very, very much from the top of the hill.

Maybe I just needed to stay positive, right? Some self-help book said that one received the energy back that one projected into the universe. Maybe if I were really nice, I'd end up with something at least cordial in return.

Then again, after about seven books' worth of reading, I'd long ago come to the conclusion that self-help books were garbage. And a racket.

I was probably doomed.

##

When I got to my locker, Sherlock was already there, crouching as she put a book inside. The setup wasn't at all convenient, but with a sudden spurt in student population a few years ago, they'd run out of room for full-sized lockers, and had switched to these rows of mini lockers that almost resembled something you'd find in a bus station. It was crummy and no one liked it.

I hesitated, trying not to watch her too closely, but it was difficult. She was taking up all the locker space at the moment. "Hi," I muttered, like some sort of awkward duck.

God, that wasn't me at all. "Are you having a good first day so far?" That was better. A bit of small talk couldn't hurt. And it was polite.

"I will reserve judgement until the day is completed." Sherlock rose, brushed lint off of her trousers and straightened her sweater vest. "E-mail me. I will pencil you into my schedule for this terrible project." The girl walked off, hips swaying ever so slightly as she departed, with just the barest hint of annoyance somewhere in the movement. It must have been her natural state of being.

As I pulled open my own locker, I watched her go. This was going to be a very long school year if I couldn't find a way to make peace with Sherlock Holmes.

Shaking my head to clear it, I dumped my books, and grabbed my drawing pad, taking off toward the art hall. I had absolutely no talent for it, but I'd been informed at the end of last year that there were a required number of electives in order to graduate.

Weaving through the freshmen congregating in the middle of the hall, I barely made it into the Drawing and Painting room before the bell rang. Ms. Novak was really harsh on late arrivals. Apparently, people thought her class was a blow-off class. Well, I had. But that lasted about 12.2 seconds until I read the syllabus with the required number and types of projects due at the end of the term.

Dodging supplies and half-completed projects sticking out of every storage space along the wall, I made it over to my usual table, which was as far in the back of the room as I could get, away from the teacher's critical gaze. Holding in a sigh, I put my pad on the table and looked down at my new table mate. "We meet again." I tried to sound jovial, but somehow, even I couldn't keep a crisp dryness out of my tone.

"I was informed that I am required to have a certain number of non-core classes, and I am not eligible for orchestra, since I have competed at the state level." Sherlock Holmes seemed as excited about a drawing class as she was about everything else in the school -- meaning *not.*

"Tell me about it," I muttered. Life was suffering, The Buddha had said. Wasn't that the truth?

I pulled out a chair and sat on the short end of the table, opening the drawing pad to the page I had been working on the day before. Checking the pocket of my jeans, I winced, pulling out a blue disposable pen I'd stolen off of a teacher's desk not even a week before. I'd forgotten drawing pencils...again. Ms. Novak was going to rub this into my face so hard my kids would have graphite stains.

But then, a pencil dropped onto my paper. "I expect it back before the end of the class," Sherlock Holmes said, entirely displeased with the situation.

"Uh, thanks?" Maybe we were kind of moving towards some sort of rapport?

The girl closed her leather bag and waved a hand dismissively in my direction. "It's nothing. By the hunch of your shoulders, I can tell that borrowing a pencil from the instructor is not the most productive use of anyone's time."

As much as I wanted to argue, I couldn't. It was flawless logic, if a bit cold. "Anyways, thanks. I really appreciate it."

The other girl shrugged, taking out a medium-sized hardbound drawing book. She opened it to a page in the middle, and began sketching something very lightly.

"Hey, you came prepared, didn't you?"

"I always have this with me. It hardly counts as preparedness." Her pencil made soft sweeping lines along the edges of the page.

"Oh. Well. Ok." I pulled out the baby food jar of linseed oil that I'd been trying to draw for several days and turned it until it was in the correct position. I got it close enough, and started doing my interpretation of drawing. Tiny lines that formed the notion of a jar, and maybe someday would actually look like one.

It was boring work, though, and I found myself watching Sherlock instead of drawing. Heavy lines were starting to take form and it looked kind of like a puzzle. I was about to ask about it when someone kicked my chair and Sherlock's pencil gouged into the page.

"Watson! Move it in!"

I tucked my chair in and Chris Neeley slid past me. "You could try asking before kicking."

"You take all the joy outta life," he said, hand on his heart, covering the logo of the school's football team on his polo shirt. "Who's your friend?"

I wouldn't go that far.

"Sherlock Holmes," she said absently, not looking up from her page.

"Sherlock, this is Neeley--uh--Chris Neeley. Neeley, this is Sherlock."

"Cool, cool. Cool." He nodded in time to something only he could hear. "Welcome to the hardest easy A you'll ever have, New Girl. Also, if you need anything, do not hesitate to ask. I am available for tours, individual tutoring, and dates."

Sherlock glanced up at him then. "Don't make me punch you in the throat."

I bit my lips to keep from smirking.

Neeley held up his hands in self-defence. "No offense intended. I just want to make your transition to a new school as easy as possible. I'll leave you to your... floor plan. Or whatever it is. But if you need anything, you know how to look me up, princess."

As soon as the word 'princess' was out of his mouth, I kicked him in the shin. The girls' soccer team had been trying to beat the patronizing behavior out of him for over a year. Obviously, we weren't beating him hard enough.

"No offence, no offence," he said coolly. "Just trying to help someone out. I'm done, I'm done." Instead of turning and walking off, he backed away, his hand still on his heart and making tiny bows.

I rolled my eyes, taking an eraser to the unattractive scribble I'd managed when the chair had been kicked. "If you do punch him in the throat, I just want to be there to see it. And possibly take video." Neeley wasn't the worst of the football team by far, parts of it were probably all an act. But he was more annoying than some of them.

Will would have been one of the worst, the way he talked about girls sometimes. Fortunately, I knew he was too terrified of actual, live girls (I didn't count) to do anything about it. And he knew better than to be too skeevy around me. He'd gotten enough two-knuckle punches from me to know better.

Neeley sat down at the table next to us, high fiving one of his friends. "Sorry," I muttered. "This school is full of idiots and jerks."

She continued on with her drawing. "Yes... yes it is."

18

Even though I'd said it first, I felt oddly insulted. I hated this place, but I had reason to. This stranger had been here a couple of hours and was passing judgement?

I ground my teeth for a moment. "So, where'd you come from, before you ended up here? Any place I've ever heard of?" I imagined some boarding school in Switzerland, or some equally exotic place. Like Canada.

Sherlock's head tilted to the side. "Willowford Academy."

"Huh. Really? What brings you here?" See, I knew it.

Sherlock sighed. "Yes, I was expelled. It was a...basic misunderstanding."

"Over?"

"The dean was sleeping with a professor. The professor was embezzling."

I squinted. "That... doesn't really seem like a misunderstanding."

The girl shrugged. "I thought something should be done about it. The board thought nothing should be done about it. Other than I would be expelled for bringing to light a shame on the hallowed halls of Willowford." She pursed her lips. It sounded like a very sore subject.

"How'd you get into that situation, even?" That seemed kind of... far-fetched, really.

"One does not just stumble across a set of circumstances like that. One goes seeking them out."

"Oh-kay." I didn't have anything more thoughtful to contribute to the conversation at that point. "Um… Welcome to Foxhollow?"

"It'll do," she said with that stuck-up air of hers.

"Uhh, ok. Enjoy your time here?"

"Right." Sherlock went back to full concentration on her drawing.

Neeley had been right. It did look a bit like a floor plan. I watched it take shape, interior walls and doorways appearing with the sharp motions of her hand, circles and squares for furniture appearing in the developing rooms.

Somehow, the silence was killing me. Actually, it was making me anxious. "So, uh, planning a renovation?"

"You're extremely talkative," Sherlock pointed out with a dryness I was getting used to.

"I'm trying to be friendly." I scowled.

Sherlock actually did bother to look up at me this time. "Why? So we can be friends?"

I looked around the rest of the room, wondering if anyone was paying attention to the exchange. They weren't. "Would that be terrible?" I wasn't shooting for actual friendship. Just amiable human interaction.

The girl put down her pencil with precision, lining it up evenly with the top of her drawing book, then crossed her arms over her chest. "I don't think that you should presume that we are friends simply because we share a locker row. Nor should you presume such simply because we are forced to sit near each other in multiple classes. You are under no obligation to befriend me, or like me, or tolerate my existence."

I took a deep breath. "Alright, then." Not daring to try again, I invested myself fully in the baby food jar. Which was looking as bad as my previous two attempts. There was hopeless, then there was me. I'd taken woodworking and basics of sewing in previous years. I could cut the smallest angles out of the center of wood. I could make barely noticeable stitches in fabric. But I couldn't draw a straight line to save my life.

##

Sherlock was not at 221B when I got to my locker. It was a relief and a disappointment. I had to spend the entire art class actively avoiding looking at the person sitting across from me. And Neeley had kicked my chair one more time for good measure. I kept hoping that someone would accidentally give him a cleat to the face at some point in his sports career. Violence was wrong. But someone should smash his perfect face. Very wrong.

Of course, that had actually happened to one of the Olls brothers and it had smashed his face so badly he'd needed reconstructive surgery and now he looked suspiciously like Tom Cruise. Young Tom Cruise. Not Crazy Tom Cruise. Maybe I didn't wish for anything that harsh to happen. Just that karma would catch up.

Grabbing the bagged lunch off the top shelf of my locker, I wove through the freshmen (they were always everywhere, huge backpacks taking up all the space between them and loitering like cows chewing their cud) on my way to the cafeteria. At first when Sherlock Holmes had told me about the injury and the sports I'd played, I figured someone else must have told her. But now that I thought about it, I had huge doubts that anyone would willingly tell someone like Sherlock anything at all. The girl was....abrasive.

Exhausted and still having four more classes after lunch, I tumbled out of the massive crowds and into the lunchroom, toward one of my usual tables. Some people were staunch supporters of routine. I sat with who was the least annoying (and whomever I was the least annoying to) that day.

I didn't see Marybeth Hunter or anyone else from the soccer team around yet, so I flopped into the corner booth where the Tweedles would turn up shortly.

Unwrapping my sandwich, I took a healthy bite, keeping track of Michael and Will, my Tweedles, as they made their way through the lunch lines.

When Michael got to the register, I had to look away. The Great Ketchup Fight went on nearly every day. The school allotted two packets of ketchup to each student, and Michael had decided that this was the hill he wanted to die on. Searching for just about anything else in the half-full lunchroom to distract myself with, I, of course, set eyes on Sherlock. Who was sitting with no lunch, a book on the table in front of her, and her hands folded very properly in her lap.

I tried to figure out whether I would hate myself more for staying in my seat, or for getting up. Gathering up my lunch bag and sandwich, I walked over to the table with the lone occupant against the wall. "I was thinking."

"I hear people do that sometimes." Sherlock turned the page of her book. It was filled with hand-drawings and lithographs of mushrooms. Sherlock studied each one, focusing on it intensely, as if there would be a quiz later on the material.

"You can sit with me and the guys, if you want. Sitting alone is kind of social suicide around here."

"I'm reading."

Fidgeting from my bad knee to the good one, and back, I tried again. "I just mean -- if you want to meet some people..." I sighed. "Look, I am trying to be friendly. You don't want that, ok. I get it. Anyways, there's an open

22

invitation to sit with us if you want it. If you can drag yourself away from…" I squinted at the header on the page. "Poisonous Plants of North America? And what the hell is a fact-finding consultant, anyhow?"

Closing the book, she grinned, suddenly coming alive. Pulling out the chair nearest her at the round table, she patted the seat with the most energy she'd expressed all day thus far. Her hands waved in front of her face dramatically. "Sit, sit. Let me tell you all about it."

Chapter 3

Sherlock Holmes took out one of her own business cards and stared at it for a moment. "I'm the only one that I know of. I saw a need, and I chose to fill it."

I looked at the card as Sherlock turned it over and over mesmerically with her long, elegant fingers. "You really need a better title. But is that like… an online thing? Like a massive multiplayer game, or LARPing or something?"

Sherlock looked at me, eyes completely devoid of any sort of idea as to what I was talking about.

"Live Action Role Play. Uh, nerds do it? Which means my friend Michael is there every weekend?" Not that I had never been guilty of creating the occasional vampire character here and there and running off for a weekend in the woods around the school, basically having nothing but red soda for two days. I had a jock reputation to uphold.

Still showing no signs of recognition, Sherlock continued. "No. It's an actual thing I do."

"So, people actually… consult you? Is my wife cheating? Like that? And you… tell them?"

She shook her head. "Not at all. They come to me with their problems, I listen. One of two things happens: either I give them advice and they leave, or I look into it myself. Either way I pocket my money at the end of the exchange."

"You really don't look like you need… supplementary income."

She smiled tightly. "You would be surprised how tight of a leash I am on."

"But you're in high school. This is not an anime. You can't just go off having a side business. I think you're pulling my leg."

"Your locker smells of dried grass. Dried grass only adheres that heavily to cleats after a game played on a freshly cut, wet field. This is more likely to happen in the spring. You favor your leg, even though you don't realize it most of the time." She looked down at my t-shirt, where it overlapped my jeans. "You've put on at least ten pounds since you stopped training with such intensity. This tells me you were injured in the spring, and that you are not playing this fall. Therefore the injury was rugby-induced, and required surgery."

I tugged my hoodie more securely over my muffin top. "So you're psychic now too?" I laughed uncomfortably.

A naughty little grin graced that normally hard face. "This is not my first rodeo. People often have questions -- very similar questions, in fact, as to all of the tedious intermediary steps that I can see in flashes, in less than a second, which brought me from watching you stumble to concluding that you required ACL replacement due to athletic injury, and the type of injury and sport."

Blinking, I tried to think of some way to contribute to this conversation. "You're… kind of creepy."

Sherlock shrugged it off playfully. "I've had worse accusations leveled at my person."

"I bet." How often had she been accused of being the perpetrator, for having too much knowledge about someone, just based on their appearance.

"And you're completely not… just an aspiring detective or an amateur who likes to Monday Morning Quarterback the police, right? You get out there and do it?"

25

"I don't get out there unless I have to. But believe me, I read the papers and the news blogs. I 'Monday Morning Quarterback' the professionals as well."

I smiled. "You probably have no idea what a Monday Morning Quarterback is. Ok, what kind of stuff have you solved? I mean, besides the thing that got you expelled." This would probably be the part where her tall tale dissolved into unimpressive chatter.

Sherlock grinned, her eyes alight with enthusiasm as she explained the cases she had solved. "Besides the case with the dean, I have done loads of stuff. The anonymous tip that solved the Barring double murder that you may have heard about on the news?" I hadn't. "That was me. The police missed a small strand of terry cloth towel that had caught on the bit of fencing the murderer jumped over in order to evade arrest. Oh, yes, and I solved the giant rubber duck theft. But that was just me showing off."

It really did sound like something out of a TV show. Who just went around... solving crimes? Unprompted, and unasked for? I squinted, reexamining Sherlock, as if seeing her for the first time. "Is this like... an after-school job?"

"I'm far more committed to--" She nodded at something over my shoulder. "You have admirers."

I turned slowly with a groan. The Tweedles stood there, both with expectant grins on their faces. "Sherlock, this is Michael." I gestured to Tall, Wide and Bestbuy (it was all the blue shirts, really), then pointed to Short and Gothy. "That one's Will, they come as a matched set. Sort of. Guys, this is Sherlock."

"Hi, New Girl!" they exclaimed simultaneously.

My head slipped into my hands. "They're not allowed out in public without supervision very often."

Sherlock nodded to each of them, which they apparently took as an opportunity to set their trays down. I had a feeling that was not what Sherlock had intended. "Ugh. I would have been over in a minute. You didn't have to come hunt me down."

"We wanted to see what you were doing." Will pulled out a chair, far too interested in what was happening.

I was not that cool. They wanted to have an excuse to bother the new girl. "I'm talking to Sherlock. It's girl talk. Very secretive." Neither of them budged, both far too enamored with the existence of a new human being in the school, and the fact that I seemed to have an in.

I scowled at them. I really wasn't in the mood for them to be interrupting constantly with inane things. Like ketchup. I was so over ketchup. In fact, I was turning against it simply due to the excess amount of discord it seemed to cause in the lunchroom. "Go. Or I will tell her how you two spent last Tuesday night."

Both of them jumped back and made a face. "God. You are a bad person," Mike muttered, taking Will by the arm and dragging him two tables down, to the usual spot.

Part of me wanted to apologize, but It personally wasn't my fault those two were the way they were. "They're an acquired taste," I explained, hoping that was more palatable for both of us.

"Apparently," Sherlock noted in her usual dryness, as she observed them at the table in the far corner, arguing about ketchup packets.

Glancing back, I shrugged. They were… well… them. "So you solved an actual murder? Like really? With a bathroom towel? That's crazy!"

Sherlock scoffed. "Commonplace. It's science, Watson. It was not difficult at all to place the husband at the scene of the crime after that small detail arose, possibly because he'd done it in a fit of rage -- not my problem. But anyhow, shoddy local police work is mostly what that came down to. I solved it in a mere four hours, once it came to my attention."

She shrugged. "The photographs from the crime scene show the bathroom mirror with the slightest traces of fog around the edges. The shower curtain is pulled back, I could infer from the shine on the tub that it was still wet. A stranger does not take a shower before killing someone. He may afterward, which is what the police thought, but there was that bit of towel on the fence. That placed him as evading the police through the back of the house, not the front as they had supposed. I simply alerted them to the strands of terrycloth towel on the fence and where they could find footprints in the leaves. The less-than-skilled nature of the getaway is what leads me to believe it was a crime of passion and not conviction. But, as I said, I don't care."

I mulled it over for a moment. "So, his minimal efforts of throwing the police off worked, because they just weren't looking for him. It all makes sense when you put it like that," I answered dreamily. This really was interesting. I crossed my ankles in front of me, and put my elbow on the edge of the table, resting my chin on my fist. "Tell me about the giant duck."

That was something I had heard about. Everyone had. The four-story duck that was meant to launch the early autumn river festival had gone missing the night before the opening. It was enormous, made of sheet metal, and nearly impossible to move without a crane. But it had disappeared.

"Give me your ketchup," Michael grumbled loud enough for me to hear several tables away.

Will dodged and eventually slapped his hands away. "No, it's *my* ketchup. Just quit fighting with the lunch lady and give her fifty cents for more ketchup." Will's upper lip curled to one side in disgust.

"No, that's giving into the fascist lunch lady regime. I am not playing into their hand."

I rolled my eyes. "No, you're just going to fight with them every day. Bring some from home," I called back behind me.

"I shouldn't have to bring--"

Sherlock got up suddenly, shaking her head in exasperation. Walking across the lunchroom in long strides, she went to the door that led to the kitchen, disappearing from sight for a moment, then reappeared with a box slightly larger than a shoe box. Again with lengthy steps, she made it back to her table in a matter of seconds. The boys approached with wide eyes, wondering what the hell she was doing, until she dropped the box on the table in front of Michael.

Will's jaw slowly rose upward, and he licked his lips. "You are a god," he said in wonderment.

We all looked at the ketchup for a moment. She had done what no one had ever dared to do: enter the lunchroom kitchen.

Sitting back down, Sherlock crossed her ankles again, the picture of languid uncaring. "Anyone can do it. You can walk through just about any door if you do it with purpose. Go directly to what you are after, and leave swiftly. Speak to no one. That is all." She folded her hands in front of her, having issued her wisdom for the day.

Michael opened the box. It was filled with packets upon packets of ketchup. "Dude." He ran his fingers through it, like a miser with gold.

Sherlock waved him off, then folded her hands on top of her closed book, ignoring the boys and focusing her full attention on me. "So, the duck. They didn't come in the middle of the night and snatch it with a crane and truck. It was much simpler than that. The thieves, from a fraternity. Aren't they all? This is like the cases of Bob's Big Boy statue thefts in the 1980s. You should read up on them. Amusing in a juvenile sense." She waved her hands excitedly in front of her, the piano-player fingers flying in front of her face like a paper fan. "So simple. They launched it into the water."

I shook my head. That was so not right. Even I could see the plot holes in that story. "There are enough lights down there that even in the dead of night, no one is going to just not notice a seven-ton yellow duck floating down the river."

"Wait, you were part of the duck thing? Was it just a publicity thing? My mom thinks it was a publicity thing."

Sherlock looked up at Michael without saying a word, nor did she blink. After seconds building on seconds, Michael's shoulders slumped and he broke eye contact, grabbing the box of ketchup. "Fine. I'm going to eat my fries before someone steals them."

Will scrunched up his nose as he walked behind his other half.

I shrugged a silent apology.

"I didn't realize ketchup was such a commodity here." Sherlock nodded to the guys approaching Michael as soon as he got back to his table. "One could make a tidy sum off of the rationing practices at this school."

I wasn't thinking at all about the ketchup situation. I was still stuck on the duck. "So. Duck. Middle of the night," I prompted. My dad was with the police, and he had great stories about people getting caught doing embarrassing things, but I wanted meat and potatoes.

Sherlock turned her chair, edging it closer to me. "No. That is the best part...they actually thought this through. Quite well, actually. They were from RMU, which has what?"

I shook my head, having no idea where this was going.

"The best theater department in this half of the state. So, they untie and make off with enough black velour curtains--and someone actually did the math on this and calculated the square yardage needed, so I admire their dedication to a prank... bringing them in several F-150s to the site of the launch, which is unprotected and unguarded, because who is going to steal a giant duck?"

"Oh my god." Everyone had thought the thieves had driven off with the duck because of the tire tracks on the park grounds. But they hadn't carried it by land at all. "So, they cover the thing, and the velour has enough shine that it'll blend in with the lights on the water, and they float it to wherever they're holding it hostage." And yes, a ransom note had been sent to the city. "Holy crap." It was really clever. Really.

Sherlock nodded solemnly, but I could see the unbridled joy in her eyes. "And then, those talented children folded up the curtains, took them back to the theater department and rehung them before the matinee performance of 'Peter Pan.' They only made one mistake. And there is always a mistake."

My eyes went wide with anticipation. "Yeah?""

"The bottoms of some of the curtains were wet in the morning."

I leaned forward, nearly sliding off the front of my seat. "Holy crap."

"Everyone at the theater thought it was strange. In fact, they were looking for leaks, and checking temperature and humidity levels in the auditorium. Which is how I caught wind of it."

"You know a plumber or a climate expert?"

She smiled. "No, I follow social networking. Closely. I had it sorted by the end of the day, and they were able to launch the duck the next morning." She tugged her sweater unnecessarily. I supposed it was for dramatic effect. "They would have gotten away with it, if they had pointed the top of the curtains toward the water. No one would have been the wiser, not even me. But they'd use the ropes on the top of the curtains to tie them together to cover the duck, which left nothing but the bottoms to hang down toward the water. Clever--the bottoms of the curtains are weighted, so they'd have no problem with the wind revealing their pinched prize. But one solution created another problem. And now they've been expelled from the university. I'm almost sorry to see them go. Perhaps they will go on to a life of crime and I will meet them again."

I laughed at the absurdity. "You actually want them to resort to a life of crime?"

"If nothing else, their endeavors would be interesting. I get bored easily."

"Wow, I didn't know the criminal element existed solely to give you something to do."

Sherlock waved a hand in front of her face again. "No, no. The history of the world teaches us that crime will always be an appealing or necessary path for certain people to travel down. But since it's bound to happen anyway, with or without my existence on this planet, I ought to at least keep entertained by the criminal element while I am here."

Ok. So, Sherlock was bonkers. And I kind of liked it.

Chapter 4

I ate my sandwich while watching Michael and Will attempt to shove the box of red gold into a backpack. First Michael's, then Will's. First with books included, then without. Sherlock was watching them too, amused. Probably like watching a monkey play an accordion, but at least she was kind of smiling. She was just so uptight, when she wasn't excited about crime and punishment.

"I swear," I said, after they finally ditched the box and dumped the packets into Will's gym bag (eww; I knew what lurked there). "They're actually smart. They program phone apps in their spare time and stuff. They just… um…" Have issues? I really wasn't sure how to describe their codependent nature that somehow lowered their IQs once they got together. "They've just been married for approximately thirty years."

That tiny smile cracked at Sherlock's lips again. "Yes. I can see. Stamford knows you from…" She squinted, as if she had some sort of clairvoyance and could look directly into the past. "Well, since you were very small. He doesn't feel the need to look at you for your approval or opinion; he is secure in the knowledge that you will continue to be friends with him no matter what. And Mr. Murray… he is a bit more recent of an addition to your entourage."

Blinking, I sat back in surprise. "Dead on. Wow." It shouldn't have been so shocking. Sherlock had shown just how quick she was in the last twenty minutes. "I met Michael the first day of school." I did not tell her that we hadn't understood how playtime was supposed to work, we'd been too scared to go to the bathroom, and had mutually wet our pants together in the back of the kindergarten classroom. We had never spoken of it then, or since.

"Will and I had a brief brush with stupidity and almost drowned. You can't *not* be friends with someone who saves your life. There's some kind of rule, I'm sure of it."

Sherlock's brow arched. "And yet you are not the one currently showing off your disgusting gym bag full of ketchup packets."

I shrugged. "I don't know. We ride the same bus, and we live a few blocks from each other, and... I don't know. I get to be the normal one when I hang out with them." I had friends in other places, plenty from soccer and rugby. Manesha and Marybeth Hunter were great to hang out with. We all hated the same people, which was a good basis for a friendship.

On the other side of the lunchroom, money had just changed hands for ketchup packets. "I guess I am the keeper of the peace between the Tweedles."

"Yes, I did surmise that." She gestured for me to continue.

"Nothing to tell, really. Law. Order. Upstanding citizen, say the pledge of allegiance. Be in bed by the time dad gets home. That sort of thing." My life was duller than I had previously thought, when I said it out loud like that. I needed hobbies beyond hating people and writing anonymous stories online and otherwise. I had no idea what macramé was, but I supposed I could take that up.

"What's the biggest case your father was ever involved in?"

I wondered if Sherlock's interest was in me, or because my dad may have worked on a grisly murder or something. "I don't know. Some suicides. The gross ones, where they don't find them for days. That murder down by the river."

Sherlock shifted in interest. "Go on."

"Oh, I don't really know anything about it. But everyone in law enforcement in our borough and the others along the river were involved at some point, right? Before the state police got involved. One of the seniors was doing junior EMT stuff when the body was found. He would probably know more about it than I would." Another story that sounded cooler on the surface until I bothered actually talking about it.

"The one that is unsolved?"

"I don't know. But I know Dad stopped talking about it. Not that he talks about work that much. And I didn't see anything on the news about if they caught the guy--"

Sherlock's body language changed as she leaned forward, suddenly on the offensive. "Why do you assume that the killer was male?"

Wait, how did I end up being cross-examined? "I don't know. Killing someone with car stuff down by the river doesn't seem like a very girly thing to do. That's all."

Sherlock shook her head, and then glanced at her watch, an old piece with a new leather strap. "There are a lot of assumptions being made, Watson." She got to her feet and a clock tick later, the bell rang. She put away her book and slid the strap of her bag over her shoulder, then waited as the other students hurried out of the crowded room.

Will and Michael were among those that had filed out with the rest, without dragging me further into their ketchup hell, for which I was grateful.

I tossed my empty lunch sack into the nearest garbage can. Oddly, Sherlock was still beside me. "Going my way?" I winced on the inside. That had almost sounded like a pickup line.

"Perhaps. But I did want to follow up upon my former point about assumptions."

"Don't judge, lest ye be judged? That sort of thing?"

We headed toward the door as the herd thinned.

Sherlock held the strap tight on her shoulder, like the bag would get up and run away if she didn't. "By all means, judge. Harshly. I do. But be sure to have all of the facts to your line of reasoning. Car cables. Waterfront, strangulation. Gives the vague impression of maleness, does it? But you don't have enough data. If I said to you: rugby, soccer, injury, molecular biology, medical school... what would you think of? A male or a female?"

My pace slowed as my brain chewed it over. "Point taken. But are you saying some chick killed the lady down by the river?"

The other girl looked up, like she was asking for help from the heavens. "I'm not saying anything of the sort. What I am trying to impress upon you is that you do not have enough information to have a basis for those assumptions. Erroneous assumptions turn into erroneous conclusions. Or no conclusion at all. And then the case remains open for eight months while the local, county, and state police waffle on jurisdiction and nothing actually gets accomplished because the woman wasn't killed by the water."

I made a face as our pace slowed even more, nearly to a halt. "I think the county coroner would have figured that out. He's kind of smart. He's written books and things." I had read most of them.

Sherlock tilted her head back and forth. "Well, ok. Technically she was killed by the water. Whoever abducted her started her off at the abduction point. Grabbed her around the neck like this…" She pulled the bag off of her shoulder, stepping behind me and sliding the thin strap around my neck.

My fingers instantly went to the leather, hoping this wasn't going where I thought it was going.

"Cinched it," Sherlock continued, "and gave her just enough air to not asphyxiate right on the spot, then drowned her in the river. While she was struggling for air, she drowned."

I clawed at the leather strap around my throat, the airway suddenly constricted, but not enough that I couldn't breathe. A second later and I was panicking, wondering what that woman had felt, in the long, long minutes of extended strangulation until she was taken to the water's edge and finished.

Sherlock pushed forward, until I was bent in half, which made it even harder to breathe. I panicked, clawing at the leather around my neck.

Sherlock let go of the strap and lifted it over my head, then put the bag back where it belonged, over her shoulder. "That was the detail they left out of the media reports," she said in a steady voice, as if she hadn't just tried to strangle me. "She wasn't asphyxiated. She technically drowned."

The glass doors at the far end of the commons opened and Mrs. Turner, the librarian, came storming out. "Sherlock Holmes, what the hell do you think you're doing?" Her face was swollen and red, and she looked like she wanted to do more than just swear at impressionable school children.

With slumping shoulders, Sherlock sighed. "Illustrating a point to dear Watson, here."

I still had my hand on my neck, but mustered up a hopeful sort of smile that would show I was unharmed.

"Sherlock was explaining something to me." The librarian was unconvinced. "For homework," I added in a rush.

Mrs. Turner's eyes narrowed and her index finger found its way into Sherlock's face. "I have heard about you."

"Should I be flattered that my reputation precedes me?" Sherlock straightened her collar and flattened her sweater vest.

The middle-aged woman's lips pressed together, and I knew she wanted to say more, but her hand dropped to her side. Then her attention turned to me. "Joanna Watson. Don't you have somewhere to be?"

I shrugged. "Study hall?" I wasn't in the mood to scurry off to class with my tail between my legs. This was scary and dramatic and I wanted to see how it played out.

"I suggest you get there," the woman said with a threatening calm.

"Um, I want to show Sherlock where her classroom is. She's new here, you know." I acted like I didn't even understand the depth of trouble I was close to being in.

Mrs. Turner crossed her arms over her chest. "Oh, believe me, I know. I know what sort of reputation she's built up for herself at Willowford."

Sherlock turned to me, ignoring the woman completely. "Librarians talk, you see. They all know each other, no matter how wide or far apart they are. They're an interconnected web of gossip. Always be friends with a librarian. And a janitor. They have keys to places."

That bit of wisdom imparted, I tugged on Sherlock's whiter-than-white shirtsleeve. "Well, anyways, we need to be going. Class, you know. Thanks for letting me print out those articles from the British Medical Journal yesterday!"

I dragged Sherlock off into the nearest hallway before Mrs. Turner could say anything else to either of us or drag us off to the principal's office. How awful would that be? Being expelled on your first day at a new school? I didn't want to find out.

Once past the first row of lockers, I dragged Sherlock into the girls' bathroom. "Oh my god."

"What? So? I got a teacher bothered. It's nothing to be alarmed about."

I looked in the mirror, rubbing my neck. Other than some red marks, there were no other signs of asphyxiation-- redness of the face, or broken blood vessels around the eyes. I even tugged my eyelids up and down to be sure. "I have an idea, let's just illustrate some cold case murder in the exact middle of school during the change of classes so everyone can see. Why are we reenacting murders? How do you even know she was drowned and strangled? Seriously." There was something very wrong with Sherlock. There had to be.

Sherlock stared at my neck in the mirror, her face blank. "I just got excited."

"Over murder! Julius H. Caesar!" I was sharing a locker column with a serial killer.

My companion's shoulders slumped and her face fell in instant regret. "About someone actually listening to me," she mumbled. Head bowed, she turned and left, the door closing quietly behind her.

Chapter Five

I didn't come across Sherlock for the rest of the day. Michael and Will had been all abuzz about everything from ketchup to her super-expensive bag. I had kept silent, not really sure what I could or should say about the incident in the commons. I had no idea what kind of girl was already on teachers' radar on her very first day.

There were other questions, too, like what had really happened at her last school. Did I just believe she'd stumbled into some conspiracy that had ended in her expulsion instead of justice being done? Of course, I had lost my opportunity to ask Sherlock outright.

And to add another layer to the crap stack, it wasn't like I could avoid her either. Our lockers were stacked on top of each other, and we shared a lab table.

I made sure to go back to my locker after my remaining classes, in the hopes that I'd see her and could apologize or something (I didn't exactly have a plan). Every time I didn't see her, I panicked a little. I didn't know if it was guilt or fear, or something else. But it sat between my lungs and went straight to my gut.

I couldn't concentrate in class either. Usually, I was the last to be called on, since I was as far back as one could get. But I hunkered down, hoping that the teachers would just forget about my existence. I just wanted to… find Sherlock and do something about it. Even if it was just making sure that the other girl wasn't a mad strangler or budding serial killer.

We both had our macabre interests, I supposed. I liked to watch knee surgery and hip replacement videos on the

Internet after school. Was it really so bad or different that Sherlock was fascinated with crime?

My excuse was that I wanted to be a doctor. I wanted to help people. Who knew what Sherlock wanted to do with them?

Helping after they were dead was still helping, I supposed. I tapped my back pocket where her card was tucked. Maybe she really just wanted to be a detective. My dad wasn't even a detective and he had seen a lot of unpleasant things, like deaths that took days to find. The world was full of bad stuff. It wasn't a crime to be interested in it.

On the bus ride home, through the winding hills, down to my little corner of the world near the railroad tracks and the river, I decided it was guilt I felt, and that maybe I had overreacted. Normal was relative, after all. Before the bus got to my stop, I'd already pulled out my phone and sent an e-mail to the address on the card I'd been given.

Sherlock,

Sorry about this afternoon.
When is a good time to work on our project?

-Joanna Watson.

Before I could think better, I hit send and hoped for the best.

After that, there was just a lot of sitting at the kitchen table, staring at the phone, which was even lamer than sitting around waiting for a boy to text. Realizing this, I fixed myself a bowl of cold leftover pasta and grabbed a glass of orange juice.

As I stuffed spaghetti into myself, the phone vibrated on the table. I grabbed it and opened the message, but it was just a text from Will, asking why I hadn't reminded him to give me the updated version of the app he and Michael were working on.

I didn't answer.

Finally, I retired to the living room, turning on one of the dim lamps so that I could read by it. One binder and two folders were spread across the old wooden coffee table with the weird blue glass top. The thick AP history tome was in my lap, and I tried to read the assigned chapter, but there was nothing resembling learning going on. The book would have been much better with pictures. Most things were.

Slumping on the sofa, I nodded off. I wasn't prone to napping, but today had sapped my strength and left me tired and hollow. I was in nowhere near a comfortable position, and it wasn't like the furniture was meant for sleeping on, but I didn't resist when sleep tugged my eyes closed.

Somewhere, on the edge of my consciousness I could hear the back door opening, and then the refrigerator, and finally the microwave going. I rubbed my face and forced myself to open my eyes as my father entered the room. Instinctively, I snapped to attention to sit properly in front of him. "Hi. Fell asleep doing some stuff."

He yawned, scratching his bristled cheek. "Well, at least you were studying. Get your stuff put away and get to bed."

I started packing up, and in the other room the microwave beeped, signaling his food was done. Dad walked into the other room, his long legs rubbery after a night of work.

If I tried, I could probably get it done on the bus ride to school in the morning. I was tired, and I did want to go to bed. I forced everything into the straining bag and zipped it closed, then kicked it into the corner where it lived when I was home. "Good night, Dad," I muttered, heading for the stairs.

Foot on the first step, I turned around. "Dad, how do you know if someone is a serial killer?"

Dad chuckled as he propped his feet up on the table, sinking into the old sofa. "From what I hear, serial killers look like everyone else. So, if they're acting like a serial killer, maybe they're not? And if they're not acting like a serial killer, and you suspect them of being one, you should probably just check the freezer and back yard."

I stared at the hand-carved newel on the end of the banister, chewing on that information for a bit. "Ok. That makes sense, so if they talk about murder and stuff, they're probably not a serial killer?"

Harold Watson poked at his dried-up spaghetti. "Is this a generalized question, or in regards to someone specific?"

Dragging myself up two steps, I tried to shrug it off. "Nothing. There's just a new kid at school, and they're interesting, but kind of weird."

My dad grinned. "Does someone have a crush?"

"God, no." I made a face.

"Uh-huh." He sounded wholly unconvinced. "I was wondering when we'd cross that bridge."

"Nope. It is not like that. We're not crossing a bridge. We are burning the bridge. We are blowing the bridge up with C-4. But not burning-burning." The analogy had gotten away from me. "I still want to be friends. Maybe."

Dad was far too amused by this. I scowled at his goofy grin. "Alright."

"Good night."

"Good night, Joanna."

"Right." I scurried up the steps the way I had when I was a small child. Ducking into my room, I threw myself on my bed.

It was not like that. It was not like that at all.

##

No Sherlock at the lockers before school. No Sherlock in the cafeteria first thing in the morning. No Sherlock after first period. No Sherlock at the beginning of Molecular Biology. Was I capable of running another human being off?

But fifteen minutes into the class, and fifteen minutes into me staring alternately at the chair next to me, and the door, Sherlock Holmes came sailing in, as if it were perfectly reasonable to show up that late, like people did it every day.

She passed Mrs. Hall a note folded in half, and pinched between her index and middle fingers. Without waiting for the woman to read it, she walked immediately over to our table, sitting down and staring forward, like she'd been there the whole time.

I did my usual terrible job of looking while making it not look like I was looking. Sneaking a look at Sherlock's hands folded in front of her on the table, I saw she had no intention of taking notes regarding the lecture or the slides. A glance over at Sherlock's face showed her to be entirely impassive, staring at the front of the room, but eyes entirely unfocused.

Sherlock knew how to tune everything out. Not just the lesson, but me as well.

Focusing on the board myself for a few minutes, or at least trying to, I gave up and dragged a paper with a quiet carefulness from my binder. Setting my pen to it, I asked a question I was kind of dreading an answer to. Folding it, I pushed it into Sherlock's line of sight.

A moment later, my phone vibrated in my pocket. As surreptitiously as possible I pulled it out and looked at the message.

Sherlock: *Saturday afternoon at one.*

I hadn't expected so firm an answer, especially to a question Sherlock hadn't even read.

How do I get to your house?

An almost-smile touched Sherlock's lips. She went very briefly from a dour resting face to her lips pressed together in a straight line.

Sherlock: *I will send someone for you.*

It sounded ominous and stuffy. I wondered just how far up the hill she lived.

I guess. If you want to. Or my dad can drop me off. Or I can give you my address.

Sherlock looked at the front of the room, ignoring her touch screen as she typed. That was a skill that would have come in use for me, for all the texting I seemed to do during class time lately.

Sherlock: *I know where you live.*

My head swung around as I tried to judge if anyone was paying attention to us. No. They didn't care. I was having this weirdo conversation in cyberspace and no one else was privy to how strange my life had become.

My phone rumbled again in my hand.

Sherlock: *Relax. I am not stalking you. Your family, however, is highly Googlable.*

My family? I really hoped not. My family was a litany of black sheep, wolves in sheep's' clothing and outright constrictor snakes. I wasn't up to dealing with that via an amateur detective's inquiries. Hell, I didn't even want to run a web search on my family. I had seen the article in the weekly local paper from the time my drunk brother had managed to side-swipe four street-parked cars with his motorcycle and had somehow walked away from it.

Needless to say, after that, family tensions ran a little high. Especially since Dad had been the first law enforcement on the scene. He'd actually followed the breadcrumb trail of scraped and torn cars all the way to the sidewalk my brother was lying on, unconscious.

It was too much to hope that the Internet had somehow magically forgotten the incident and it wasn't the first result when my last name and neighborhood name were typed into a search engine. I was a realist, though.

Was it as exciting as you hoped it would be?

Sherlock: *You have an interesting background.*

Oh Hell. She *had* seen the article about my brother. And who knew what else about my mother. It depended on how far news archives went back.

Well, at least my family isn't boring.

Sherlock: *Everyone has skeletons in their closet. Some more, some less. Some are even goats and chickens.*

I had to put a hand to my mouth to keep from laughing out loud in the middle of class. The back of the room was prime real estate for doing things one shouldn't be doing while a lecture droned on, but I wasn't sure I could think up a truly valid reason why ketosis would be exceptionally funny. And, of course, I wasn't entirely sure that Sherlock had been meaning to tell a joke.

Hitting reply to the message, I almost did something like ask what was in Sherlock's closet, but I glanced at my table mate. Sherlock had already stowed away the phone and was absently staring toward the front of the room again. I pushed my phone under my notebook. Out of sight, out of mind. Or, at least, out of sight, less likely to be taken away by the teacher. Just when I had reached a point of absolute desperation with ketosis, the bell rang. People threw things into backpacks and shoulder bags, exiting as soon as humanly possible.

Both Veronicas were the first out the door, as usual. They were both blonde, petite, athletic gymnasts and cheerleaders. I couldn't tell them apart. Of course, when the cheerleading squad had their hair pulled into ponytails, I really couldn't distinguish any from the others. Even the Korean exchange student was blonde.

The weird kids from the junior football team (I was half certain they were part of a cult), Gregory, Anders, that kid who'd gotten his ears sewn so he'd look like an elf forever… they all filed out. My bag was packed and I'd slid my phone back into my jean pocket. I kicked in my chair, surprised that Sherlock had waited for me. "So, um… sorry about the thing? In the bathroom?" I tried to console myself by saying I was a writer, not a talker. But I still sounded awkward when I was on the spot.

Sherlock looked me over in scrutiny. "You are. I can see. But are you sorry for offending me, or for making yourself feel bad?" With a curt smile, she turned and headed toward the door, her long legs taking her faster than I could keep up.

Dodging between chairs and tables, I went after her. "Hey, you didn't even let me explain!" Saturday was going to go smashingly if all our conversations ended like this. "Look, I'm sorry I overreacted. I've never been in trouble before! I freaked out!"

Sherlock Holmes stopped mid-step and turned around. "You've never been in trouble before."

I caught up to her finally. People poured around us like water flowing around a rock. "I've never been in trouble with a teacher."

"At school. Ever." Sherlock Holmes, who seemed to know everything about everyone, looked skeptical. "In twelve years of school."

I shrugged. "Thirteen. I went to preschool too."

"Thirteen years."

"Well, there was the one thing in kindergarten. But we don't talk about that."

"Young children often wet themselves," she answered dismissively.

My heart lurched and my cheeks flared and burned. "I will *murder* Michael…"

Sherlock rolled her eyes. "He revealed nothing to me. Statistically, that is the thing most people do not wish to talk about regarding early school experiences. But I suppose if Stamford was involved, it could be considered a bonding experience that would cement a friendship."

I covered my eyes, as if that would somehow ease the embarrassment. Maybe if I couldn't see Sherlock, then she couldn't look into my eyes and divine all of the rest of my sins. "Please do not tell him you know about that. Please. For the love of god."

"I doubt the existence of God, but if you wish for me to, I will not. However, we find ourselves off topic. You've never been in any serious trouble not related to the maximum holding capacity of a child's bladder."

While fascinating, Sherlock Holmes was also kind of a prick. I'd only asked thirty seconds ago for it to not be brought up again. "I've never been in trouble. With so much as a late assignment. Ever."

Sherlock waved a hand in front of her. "Then, Watson, you are a rare and magical unicorn. Celebrate your uniqueness."

"Well, someone just ruined my record."

Sherlock turned around. "Nonsense! I was the one who got in trouble!" She headed off to wherever her next class was, leaving me standing around like an idiot. Checking the clock on the wall, I saw I only had about a minute and a half to get to another part of the building and took off running.

##

I didn't see Sherlock again, not even at our lockers, until lunch. Still feeling that odd guilt springing up, I'd even taken my time digging through 221A, putting my books away, shifting my coat for no real reason at all, then sliding my lunch bag off the useless top shelf.

In the cafeteria, the odd girl was once again sitting alone. an old cloth-bound book open on the table in front of her.

Did I say something? Was it pushing the boundaries of an already-tenuous relationship? I stood four tables over for far too long, clutching the bag to my side, wondering where to go from the morning's conversation.

Something big and wide slammed into my shoulder. I spun around, prepared to yell at someone, but it was just Michael. "Are you trying to kill me?"

Michael shrugged. "I dunno. Why are you standing here staring at your girlfriend all mopey-eyed and crap."

"She. Is. Not. My. Girlfriend." I punctuated each word by poking him in the chest. "I was wondering if I should invite her to sit with us," I continued sarcastically, even though it hadn't crossed my mind. It sounded plausible enough, though.

"Oh my god. Just ask her out or something. Or we'll sit back in the Man Cave, and you can sit with her. Or whatever." He blew a puff of air straight up, knocking the curls around his forehead.

I looked up. "Man cave?"

"It's what we call that booth when you're not there."

"Well, far be it from me to 'girl' up your man cave. I'll sit over here with her." Marybeth Hunter was here, so I could always wander over to that table too. Social butterfly, that was me.

He gave me two thumbs up and a smarmy smile, just as Will came into the cafeteria, nearly invisible as he filled in with kids twice his size. "Go for it! You can do it!"

"Yeah. Whatever. Maybe you two can do something with the app, while I'm over here?" I suggested by way of distraction. Without waiting for a response, I left, winding around the tables with strewn chairs acting as an obstacle course.

"Hi, maybe we can..." I thought up a list of possibilities. "Talk about the project? Or something?" That seemed fairly business-like.

"Don't the Tweedles want you to sit with them?"

"I don't sit with them every day, you know. They're working on some kind of... guy thing anyway." I winced. "I mean, they can take care of each other. I mean..."

Sherlock kicked out a chair in my direction. "Watson... sit down before you hurt yourself."

Chapter 6

I sat down, trying to think of something clever to say to bridge the gap, but mostly it had just turned into a series of awkward sighs on my part, while Sherlock read, and I consumed my lunch with far more care than usual.

About ten minutes into The Lunch of Awkward Sighs, (perhaps I had the title for a new anonymous biographical essay for the school newspaper) a few of the girls from the soccer team 'wandered' over to the table, under the auspice of saying hello to their former (and hopefully future) teammate. But it took all of twenty seconds before the topic of conversation turned from my healing leg to the new student.

Sherlock smiled tightly, but refused to make smalltalk. She'd explained where she had come from, of course, but didn't go any further.

Marybeth Hunter asked if Sherlock knew her sister, Violet, who had probably been a senior when Sherlock was a freshman. Sherlock shrugged, but I had a feeling that Sherlock had, indeed, known Marybeth's sister. Liz Schofield smartly asked if Sherlock had found Willowford too challenging, if she'd ended up at Foxhollow because she had bombed out. Well, she hadn't said that. But she'd certainly implied it. I loved them, and wanted to kill many of them. It was one of the most conflicting situations in my life.

Fortunately, Sherlock had not taken the bait and had just shrugged, then asked how Liz could possibly still be playing on the school team, given that her grade point average had obviously slipped below the school's minimum for participation in sports. Liz had backed off from the table in a huff, and I had to choke down a laugh.

That was how the remainder of lunch went. Sherlock explained how the purple marker smears on the girl's right hand, coupled with the new presence of someone else's school ring on a chain around her neck made it obvious her attention was not on her studies, but the GPA thing had just been a leap.

When she explained it, everything seemed logical, like I should have known, if I had just looked hard enough and thought hard enough about it.

By the time lunch ended, I found my fascination with Sherlock Holmes had been reinforced by those lectures about marker and locker note-writing. Sherlock had assured me that the notes were the mark of the infatuation stage of a relationship, as they were more personable than black and white texts in a standardized font on a phone screen.

I wouldn't know, of course. Sometimes there'd been a flirt here or there, maybe even a serious conversation, but they never seemed to amount to anything beyond that. Certainly not hands smeared with marker due to writing cutesy locker notes. I mean, I wanted to be. My father said I was just a late bloomer. I just never seemed to get out of the gate, to move things from the dugout to the on-deck circle. If I could abuse a baseball metaphor.

After the bell rang, Sherlock and I made our way leisurely toward our joint locker situation. Mrs. Turner seemed to be keeping an extra special eye on Sherlock. She suddenly appeared in the area outside the lunchroom and followed us with her laser-like librarian look of death (I liked alliteration; sue me) until we were well out of her range and hallway territory.

Getting our things for the afternoon out of our short but deep lockers, I paused a minute, resisting the urge to swing my bag onto my back, lest I accidentally behead Sherlock Holmes, which would probably reflect poorly on my permanent record. "Well, it's been an interesting lunch. Now I am going to be watching for marker-smeared hands and people shoving notes into each other's lockers. It'll be a good distraction for the rest of the year." She wasn't even looking up at me. I blushed, wondering if she was listening. "I mean, it's better than the 'which teacher or student is pregnant' game."

Sherlock did look up with that. Probably to explain how the game wasn't a game and just simple deduction, but before she could, I headed off to class instead. Was it bad that I could start imagining her protestations after only a few days?

I had no idea where this current course of vocation would one day take Sherlock. Anywhere from the heights of the detection profession to a jail cell. And all points in between. Minor celebrity and 'dead' seemed to be somewhere on that spectrum as well, but I tried not to think of it.

Instead, I tried to invest myself in my own routine. I needed to reconnect with the guys, check the status of their phone game app. I was their main cheerleader and beta tester. If I could play it without hang-ups, it was good. But I also had a magical ability to find every buggy bit of programming available. I had even gotten the aliens to turn on their own kind one time, which was certainly not how the game was supposed to be played.

Fortunately, reconnecting with the guys was as easy as explaining to Marybeth Hunter that I had to reconnect with the guys and couldn't go shinguard shopping. I didn't know if there was a word for going to the big sports shop at the mall and purchasing soccer accessories. Sports nerd? Sports shopping enthusiast? Probably something like that. Shopping enthusiast.

We would have had to stop in the hippie place that sold crystals and tie dye body wraps and constantly smelled of incense and dirt. I fully respected that Marybeth wanted to live in the mid-sixties and smell like she was covering over drugs she wasn't actually doing. It was a lifestyle choice. Mine was mostly hoodies, hiding my hair with really big hair bands and hiding my twin secret shames of fan fiction writing and anonymous biographical essay writing.

Marybeth said she'd drag someone else from the team. It was always a group effort to find her the right stuff. She had thick legs like me, but she was over a foot taller. My father once bought me a shirt that said 'I'm not short, I'm fun-sized,' so I was certainly below average. But Marybeth was built like me, a bulldog. Only she was taller than some of our teachers. Not Sherlock tall. Just… tall. If she was anywhere near the goal, you kicked the ball to her. It would hit some part of her body, and she could redirect it toward the net. She was a blessing to all who knew her.

As much fun as hanging out with another actual girl would be, I also wanted to dash Will and Mike's hopes and dreams of making their fortune from phone app games. Some part of me wanted to see them miserable when I managed, yet again, to break their programming.

I met them at the usual pizza shop after school. They sold pizza by the slice and French fries were actually reasonably priced.

Mike was waiting, already working on a basket of fries, a small plastic cup filled with ketchup in the center of his golden potatoes. Will came in as I was ordering. I didn't have much in the way of spending money, and he had less, so I got two slices of pizza. It was unspoken. I'd just give it to him; it wasn't worth discussion, or embarrassment, or any of the other weird things that happened when circumstances made you the poorest kid in the room. And if he wasn't in the room, it was me. Do unto others...

We sat down at the booth near the door. I always sat with my back against two corners, my legs stretched across the length of the seat. Once I'd heard that Wyatt Earp (or someone else, the details were unimportant) had been shot in the back of the head cause he hadn't been able to see the door. The statistical odds of being shot in the back of the head in a pizza shop were very low, but the paranoia had grown on me over time.

Mike and Will were across from me, staring. They leaned forward, hands folded in front of them on the table, taking on an air of concerned parents.

I sighed, ripping off some of my crust. "What?" I pointed the bread at them. "Out with it."

Mike's eyes lit up. "Where's your girl..."

"Shut up," I finished for him.

Bobby, the owner, ignored us, tossing frozen fries into the basket above the deep fryer and lowering it into the oil with a hiss from the vaporizing water. "We are sharing a locker row and are working on the bio project together. That's it. If you bring it up again, you *will* be in trouble."

Will winced. "Why are you so violent?"

"Why are you such a jerk"

He shrugged. "I play too many video games?"

"Video games are supposed to make you more violent," I corrected. "Wait, I'm violent because of video games. Why are you such a jerk?"

Michael and Will looked at each other. "Television?" they answered in unison.

I crinkled my nose. This is why Michael had been dumped by Megan and why Will couldn't get a date if his life depended on it.

Our food came, and I squirted ranch dressing all over my cheese pizza. It was quiet for a few minutes while we shoved food into our faces. Things were weird with us suddenly. It was the same old banter, but it was just... odd.

Will licked his thumb, thoughtfully. That was a sure sign of trouble. Pushing crumbs around on his plate, he avoided eye contact with me. "Have you made up with..."

I scowled. "Go on, say it."

Michael leaned in to his other half. "She plays video games. She's violent. Don't do it," he whispered theatrically.

"Look, man. I'm just saying. You two are awfully snuggly, you hear me?"

I pulled the band out of my hair, tugged on the tufts on top with sharp, angry movements, then bound it back up. "The topic of Sherlock Holmes is completely out of bounds from now until... well, when this stupid molecular biology project is done."

"So... Monday," Will said with one of those annoying smirks on his face.

"Yes. Give it a rest until Monday. That is four days away. Do you think you can cope?" Before he could answer, I changed the subject. "Ok, have you guys fixed the maze in the game? It was kind of... glitchy."

Will held up his phone. "Yeah, you can download it later. The maze walls don't wobble."

"Does it still completely kick you out of the app when you get to the end of the level?"

The two looked at each other.

"I think that's important too, you know. If you are going to try to charge for this thing." The devil was in the details. Well, not so much the details. But basic functionality. "And while I'm thinking about it, you should do something about your roots." The four inches of red that sprouted from his head and ended in deep black was amusing, if nothing else. "A little shoe polish would fix that up."

Will's eyes narrowed. "No. So much no." He sat up straighter. "Look lively, Watson. You have a visitor."

My dad stepped out of his cruiser, tugging on his uniform jacket, and headed in the front door.

Pretending like I hadn't seen him probably wasn't an option, nor was pulling out a book and pretending to study. I knew he only rode my ass because of what had happened to my brother. But it was still depressing to deal with at least four times a week.

"Hi, Mr. Officer Watson," Michael said cheerfully, saving me the burden of first contact. Now I remembered why I was friends with him.

Tucking his thumbs into his belt my father shifted his weight from his heels to the balls of his feet and smirked. "I had a feeling I would find you here."

Probably after he'd checked the library first. He could have just done a normal thing like call or text to ask where I was, but then he'd ruin the element of surprise. "So, you found me. What can I do for ya?"

He shrugged. "I was on lunch and just wanted to say hi." And check on me to make sure I wasn't getting up to something I shouldn't be. Even though I never did. The frustration was constant.

"Well, hi, Dad." I gave a small wave.

Will waved at my father as well. "My roots aren't four inches long, are they?" he asked, tugging on his hair.

My dad squinted. "I don't know. Maybe six when you pull the curls straight."

Will slumped, folding his arms over his chest in utter defeat. "I just haven't had the time to bleach it and dye it," he mumbled.

Dad patted him on the shoulder. "It's ok. A buzz cut will fix that right up."

Why did every social interaction that happened with me or around me have to be weird?

Dad turned to me, seemingly content with the conclusion of the discussion of hair care. "There's some stuff in the fridge that you can heat up for dinner. I'll be home at the usual time." 'Stuff' was secret code for casserole. It was one of the few things he knew how to make, and we had a silent pact never to talk about casserole or quiche in public.

"Barring catastrophe," I supplied. Same as usual. Everything was always the same as usual. That's why it was usual, and that's why it was the same.

Saturday, and whatever weirdness it brought to me, couldn't come soon enough.

##

I tried to download the new version of the game, but my Internet connection was too slow. I would have to do it at school tomorrow. Lousy Internet was just a fact of life in my household. Dad refused to pay the extra money for the faster connection, and so I just coped.

The connection was fast enough to load cat videos, if you were patient enough, however. I spread my books on the coffee table, tried to concentrate on AP history and whatever shenanigans were happening in the Habsburg Empire, but I was fresh out of ability to care. It only took fifteen minutes of trying before I was staring at cats falling off of things. A lot of things.

I scrolled through several pages of animals doing other funny stuff. The details were unimportant. Someday I was going to have a bulldog. Not one of the over-bred American ones that snorted because they were struggling to breathe, but a German one, built like a brick house but still flopping around on short little flipper feet. I just thought they were the coolest, funniest things.

The human race's near universal interest in animal videos could somehow be used to bring about world peace. Ok. Probably not. War and strife seemed inevitable, if my history book was correct about the tragically nonsensical history of Eastern Europe. Still, the lion who kept intentionally getting himself stuck in the tire gave me hope for the world.

Somehow, that video led to one of the police helping a family of ducks across the road, then a duck beating up a guy for a sandwich, nutshot included, and then a video with a thumbnail of a giant duck, like the kind a storybook giant would use in his ocean of a tub.

My hand lingered above the laptop's touchpad, but then I clicked in inevitable curiosity.

After far too long of a loading period, a feel-good news report about an anonymous tip leading to the return of the four-story duck before the river festival got underway. I grinned, quite pleased with myself, that I knew something that other people didn't. It wasn't important. Not nuclear codes or the plot to the next big superhero movie. But it was enough.

Picking up my phone, I texted Sherlock.

Bored with homework. Watched the duck video. Got any other cases you want to brag about?

Sherlock: You must be at the height of boredom.

I have been looking at animal videos for two hours.

Sherlock: Good lord. We must save you from yourself.

Tigers are really into catnip

Sherlock: I will be there in fifteen minutes.

I looked at the time on my phone. It was nearly eight. Which didn't seem late--to an actual normal human being, who didn't have an enforced and assigned bedtime.

I was going to text Sherlock back with all the reasons this was a bad idea. Some of them might actually be true. But the 'no visitors after eight' rule was probably meant for Will and Michael, because without it, they would probably just take up residence in our front room and *never* leave.

There was, of course, the often-used and seldom believed 'working on a project' excuse. This time it would be an actual legitimate reason to have someone over for a thing that did not involve video games.

Looking around the living room, I realized that my father and I somehow lived like bachelors. My own papers were strewn across the coffee table, three old glasses and a mug with a spoon in it sat on the lamp table, and the television was covered in a layer of dust that didn't bother me until now.

In disgust with myself and my own living habits, I took the edge of my shirt and wiped the top, then the screen itself, then dumped the mug and glasses into the sink

Pushing in the kitchen chairs, I got rid of the old food containers, the frozen pizza box, and whatever the hell was growing in the forty-four ounce soda bottle on top of the refrigerator. Giving the counter a quick wipe, I noticed the floor. It's amazing what you don't notice when you are looking at these things day in and day out. I swept the floor so fast I broke into a sweat. There was a knock at the back door, just outside the kitchen and the dustpan was nowhere in sight. With a racing heart, I opened the basement door and swept the crumbs and twist ties and banana stickers right down the steps, determined to deal with it later.

Tossing the broom down the steps as well, I crossed the kitchen and opened the back door just as a second series of knocks shook it. I wondered self-consciously if I was as...dewy as I felt. "How did you know to use the back door?"

Sherlock unbuttoned her black peacoat as she stepped over the threshold. "There is mail still in the box next to the front entrance. If you used that one, you would have taken it inside when you came home from school. Also, the exterior light is on in the back, but not the front."

I looked around, inspecting the place, somehow feeling very vulnerable. Backing up to give her some room, I stepped on an onion skin that had missed during the earlier speed cleaning. The garbage can being on the other side of the room, I shoved it into my pocket, not even daring to think of how it looked. Sherlock had no doubt, by this time, deduced that I was a slob. She'd seen my locker.

An awkward laugh later, I waved even though she was standing, satchel still crossing her chest and coat still on. "So, uh. Welcome to casa de Watson."

Sherlock looked around, more in an inspective manner than anything else. "Do you speak Spanish?"

"No."

"Please don't try to, ever again."

Blushing a little, I groaned. "How did you figure out where I lived, anyway?"

"There are an insignificant number of people with the surname of Watson living in the area serviced by District School Bus Seventeen. It was a web search followed by a simple process of elimination."

Privacy was a myth, I realized. "That's impressive."

Sherlock removed her coat, tucking it under her arm. "It's hardly impressive."

I closed the back door finally, before all the hot air escaped. "Well, if you don't know the trick, it's impressive."

"It's not a trick."

"What I mean... oh god. I just shouldn't even talk, should I? I end up saying everything wrong." I had absolutely no idea what was so intimidating about being around Sherlock Holmes, but somehow I managed to make a mess of my words regularly when she was involved.

The other girl's attention focused back on me. "It's alright. But it's not trick. I've explained the nature of my observations several times to you already. It shouldn't seem mysterious. Deductive reasoning is simply the application of what is known about the world to a specific case."

I headed to the cupboard for glasses. "So what you're saying is that I don't know anything about the world," I teased. "Something to drink?"

"Water is fine. No. You see the world. But you do not observe. You do not remember the details. You… all of you… let them fade away."

Closing the cupboard door, I turned around with the two nicest glasses we had. "I don't have anything bottled."

"I didn't expect you to."

Should I have been insulted? I didn't know. "I mean… are you sure you want water? It's kind of dodgy here. Hit or miss on whether it will taste like metal, or just… weirdness." I swore it tasted like river water, sometimes. And I would know; I swallowed enough of it when I almost drowned that one time.

Sherlock shrugged. "I've had worse."

"Only if you've been to Mexico," I muttered. I, in fact, knew nothing about Mexico, other than the water was supposed to make you sick there. And something about drug cartels and they did something with skulls once a year. That was the full expanse of my knowledge.

"Oh, I've been."

I handed over the glass of water. I supposed I ought to have put ice in it or something, but, well, it wasn't like Sherlock had given a lot of notice "So, what're we going to do, exactly?" An awkward dry laugh bubbled out as I tucked a few loose strands of wiry hair behind my ear. "We're not going to actually do homework or something, are we?"

Sherlock took the water and walked into the living room, sitting herself down on the arm of the sofa that was the least worn. Now, with Sherlock sitting on it, all proper and straight-backed, I could see how unclean the tan fabric was. It had most likely never been cleaned in the twenty years it had been in the house, now that I thought about it.

##

Sherlock...liked talking about herself. I should have known that would be one of her favorite topics. And to be honest, if you had as many skills and achievements under your belt as she apparently had under hers (violin, world travel, solving mysteries, a few minor scientific discoveries, and a thorough knowledge of bee culture) your favorite topic might be yourself as well.

Sitting on the uncomfortable living room sofa, we talked. Well, Sherlock talked. It seemed like she already knew everything worth knowing about me, and there wasn't much more that I was feeling especially excited about sharing. My brother's arrest was public record, not to mention the subject of town gossip. And then there was my mother... well, it was a story best not broached. Honestly, listening to Sherlock be an immodest braggart (and possibly an embellisher of tales) was far more fun than going on about my own shamefully dysfunctional and disjointed family. But it did make me wonder. If she actually was that good at her fact finding and armchair consulting, if she could tell me where certain absent members of my family were. And if they were ok.

At the moment, Sherlock was going on about her most recent project, which happened to be a prelude to her next experiment. "So, I have a few of those old 1940s-style fans that I found in the crawlspace in the attic -- oh, that's where my room is. But it's a big attic. There're a few spaces I don't take up. Anyway, I replaced the cords because those things were fire hazards. I made sure they were grounded and such, but they don't draw attention. Mrs. Hudson thinks they're purely for aesthetic purposes... or something. Who knows what runs around in that woman's batty mind? Anyway, she hasn't *said* anything about the fans. But I really only turn them on -- and I need to keep them on low for this to work -- when I am setting up the bellows."

I pulled a hand out of a bag of cheddar-flavored potato chips and held up a bright orange-covered finger. "Wait, the bellows?"

"Yes, bellows, a tool for..."

"Shut up. I know what a bellows is. I'm not stupid. But why do you need a bellows? In your bedroom? What are you doing? Smelting iron? Should I expect you to be starting your own line of historically accurate broadswords or something?" Anything was possible at this point.

"Smelting is not all you can -- never mind. You don't make broadswords out of iron. Well, you do. But you can purchase it with less impurities and move on from there. But if you're going to do that, you ought to just buy a lump of steel... really. I'm far too lazy to smelt my own metals..." Sherlock rolled her eyes.

I handed the bag of sour cream and cheddar flavored potato chips to Sherlock. She paused for a moment, seeming to try to negotiate the bag, then took a tissue out of the faux book that covered the box on the lamp table, and used that to grab the chips.

Somehow the behavior did not surprise me. "I can get you a napkin. Or latex gloves."

"I just don't like touching them. I don't want--never mind. I don't like touching them."

Laughing at her seriousness, I watched her eat them. She did genuinely seem to enjoy them. Well, inasmuch as Sherlock enjoyed anything that did not involve mystery, crime, and piles of dead bodies. "Whatever floats your boat."

Sherlock crossed her legs in front of her. "You think I'm pretentious. Brought up in the bowels of The Hills, and, therefore, so far out of touch with reality due to entitlement that I can't handle touching a potato chip."

I made a face. "I'm not saying that, but who doesn't touch potato chips?"

The other girl looked away at the vacuum hiding in the corner near the door to the bathroom. "I just don't touch potato chips. Alright? Anyhow, I'm using the bellows to conduct an experiment regarding the length of time various brands of cigarettes take to burn, the ash they leave behind, and their general odor. I don't smoke them myself; there's quite a limit to the number of cigarettes a human being can smoke in a single setting without becoming ill."

That sounded absurd. "You smoke."

Sherlock nodded absently. "For science."

For science. Of course, I sensed she was going to have to go into the litany of bad-to- terrible things that could happen to a smoker, especially one who had started at an early age. "And the fans strategically placed throughout the attic?"

Sherlock shrugged. "I have to circulate and push the air out of the attic. Otherwise, Mrs. Hudson will think that I am smoking in my bedroom."

Because... she technically wasn't, now? I didn't entirely understand the semantics of the situation. "And we wouldn't want that."

The other girl frowned, grabbing the bag of chips off of the sofa between us. "Her ire is far more trouble than it is worth, ultimately."

I bit my cheek. This really was far more information about Sherlock than I'd had up to this point. The fact that there were actually people in her life, and she was not some autonomous creature that had hatched from an egg fully-grown and deducing all over the place. "Mrs. Hudson is who, exactly?"

With a sigh, Sherlock explained. "Nanny, housekeeper, cook, jailer, nag and constant source of most of the pain involved in my existence."

I laughed so hard I collapsed against the stained back of the sofa. "You are a junior in high school and still have a nanny." At least I was allowed to be on my own. Mostly, in circumstances that did not involve more than one night of my father being away.

"Like, does she let you use the stove and stuff by yourself?" I giggled, trying not to let it turn back into an official laugh.

"She's the housekeeper. She does the cooking. Why would I need to use the stove?" Sherlock asked, in that arrogant tone of hers that spoke of her privileged upbringing on the hill. "Really." Shifting, she folded her arms over her chest and looked at me with a twisting lip and a narrowed eye.

At this point I was beginning to get used to the glare that denoted I'd said something stupid again. If it weren't so frequent, and so annoying, it might have been actually endearing.

Sherlock gave up on the 'stupid' glare and switched to her usual disaffected self, shoulders moving against the back of the sofa. "Well, she's more of a jailer than a nanny, truth be told. And does her best to prevent me from having anything vaguely resembling fun."

"I get the idea that your form of fun involves fire and dangerous chemicals and other things that could destroy or burn the house down."

"Yes? Your point?"

I laughed again, this time with my belly, shaking the potato chip bag. It was all crumbs now. "I can't even leave my shoes out of place, and I have an actual bedtime, and you're attempting to blow your own house up. I suspect your Mrs. Hudson is far more permissible and understanding than you think."

"Perhaps. Perhaps. But still, I would prefer if she weren't in every single aspect of my business."

"Apparently, you don't understand how adults work. I have it under good authority that even when you turn eighteen, they insinuate themselves into your life. Like septicemia, really. You don't want it, but it finds a way in."

"You really do make the most delightful analogies."

I blushed. I wanted to say thanks, or something. It would have been polite, but I didn't entirely trust my own voice. I sensed Sherlock didn't issue praise very often. I bit my cheeks until I knew I would not embarrass myself. "So... what're you doing here, exactly? I mean, not that I don't appreciate it, but me saying I'm bored usually isn't enough to get someone to drop what they're doing and come all the way down here from...well, wherever it is you live." Up in the hills, that was for certain. How far back in the hinterlands remained to be seen. The further into the hills, the older the money. And I had a feeling Sherlock lived as far up as one could get.

Sherlock waved a hand at me. "Oh, I was already out and about. I had Toby drop me off when we got close." Her smile was brief and tight. "I felt we should get to know each other better. If we are to work on this project in an efficient manner."

Yes, I thought with intense skepticism. It was entirely about the project. "Well, anyways, thanks for saving me from my own boredom. And it was nice getting to know you better."

Sherlock Holmes folded her hands in front of her, index fingers steepled and pressed to her lips. "Oh, the feeling is mutual."

Something twisted in my stomach. "I haven't said much of anything about myself."

"That's exactly it. It is in what you did not say." That sounded foreboding. The deduction thing was awesome when she was talking about other people. "While you are a difficult task to read, you are not impossible. Your father's restrictions, the absent mother, with only a smattering of family pictures in odd places, the rather amusing police report involving your brother's drunken escapades."

"Oh, you say they're 'escapades' now, like it's all some adorable joke. But he could have killed someone, like himself, for instance. Then it wouldn't be an amusing anecdote, it would be a terrible tragedy." I folded my arms over my chest, face scrunching in painful annoyance. I had no idea where my brother was, and I hadn't heard from him since my last birthday, but to hear Sherlock tell it, it was youthful shenanigans, instead of something that could have left me an only child. "And we don't talk about my mom, ok?"

Sherlock rubbed her lower lip with her index finger. "Interesting."

"What?" I didn't want to be interesting.

"Oh, nothing." She brushed it off.

My eyes narrowed in frustration. This wasn't some amusing crime story, like the ones Sherlock had been plying me with since lunchtime yesterday.. This was real life. Actually, it was my own real life, and I didn't like people...guessing. Assuming. Knowing things I didn't tell them. Or whatever little psychic tricks Sherlock played. "Look, some things aren't open for discussion, ok?" I didn't want to talk about mom. Not yet. But I did want to know where she was. Why she left? What kid didn't?

Sherlock smiled again, paying attention to something in the far distance that only she could see. "And that's what I like about you, Watson. Your foolish notion that your integrity is based upon your secrecy. While I think that's a boring line of thought, I respect how much it embodies your entire being."

"I don't even know what that means." I tucked my leg under me, trying to get comfortable on the beat-up couch. "So you said I passed some kind of muster. What does that mean, exactly?" I was curious. "Do I get a prize or something? Maybe a tiara to run around school in?"

"I am merely here to save my lab partner from perpetual boredom. That is all."

"Right." While it sounded plausible, it didn't quite fit what had been going on here. And, while I honestly had no idea what was happening, I was sure it was not a meet and greet. For some reason, this knowledge gave me the resolve to turn the situation around.

"So, you know Marybeth's older sister." She'd indicated so earlier, but even without powers of deduction, I knew an avoidance tactic when I saw one. "She went to Willowford when you did?"

Sherlock smirked. "Nice catch. There is hope for you yet, Watson."

It was probably meant to be a compliment, in Sherlock's own weird way. "So? Spill."

"I knew her. She wasn't nearly as bad as most of the other girls. Maybe sweet, even. Sincere, if nothing else. And I helped her with a problem as well."

"Problem?" Don't just leave it there, I wanted to beg.

"Oddly, all she wanted was advice. I'm glad she values my opinion so much, given the obvious age difference and all the erroneous thinking that obviously goes with that. Anyhow, she received a job offer that sounded a bit suspicious. One of those 'too good to be true' sort of situations, but with odd requirements. I poked around, as I do, and on the surface it seemed normal enough. And perhaps her future employers were simply a bit on the eccentric side."

Sherlock tugged at her collar, straightening it. This late in the day it was starting to wilt and curl inward. "So I told Violet to take the position, with reservations. And if anything were to go awry, she was welcome to contact me for a follow-up. It has been a month, so far, and I have not heard anything from her. So I doubt the job itself was as strange as it appeared to be. Or the money alone helped her overcome some of the more prominent eccentricities of the family. Money is a truly powerful motivator, Watson. Remember that." And she said it in that special tone that left me sitting there, wondering if I should be taking notes, due to a potential quiz later on these things.

And that was it. Silence. Not one that we slipped into easily like old friends, but more like uncomfortably folding the space between us and stuffing it into a too-small envelope. The air seemed to be bursting with things for either of us to say, but there was nothing coming out. The clock in the kitchen ticked loudly enough that it was audible in the living room. That was the type of silence we were hanging onto.

I broke the silence by scrunching up the used bag of chips and winced at the tearing in the quiet. "Lemme get rid of this." When I got to the doorway to the kitchen, I turned around. "So, why didn't Marybeth end up at Willowford? She's smarter than half of us put together." Marybeth was one of those people you could never copy homework from because it was far too correct. The teacher would know. Or if you did, you had to strategically mess up answers to throw them off the scent. Best part of Marybeth? She let you copy it anyway.

"They don't accept trans students," Sherlock said offhandedly.

I shoved the bag into the too-full garbage can, scrunching it down just a bit. "Well, then screw them. They don't know what they're missing. She's going to be the Foxhollow alumnus who goes to the moon or something, and they'll be sorry. Also: they're assholes."

I tied up the garbage bag. "I'm uh, going to take this out." It would save a conversation with my dad if the trash weren't overflowing when he got home. I yanked it out of the can and tied it up tightly, then headed for the kitchen door. "I'll be right back."

Walking to the outside bin, I felt the pre-winter chill run down my neck. It was soothing, cutting into the sweating I had suddenly bust out into. Over Sherlock Holmes.

"Joanna Watson, you can do this," I muttered to myself. "You cannot be weird around a girl who may or may not be a friend." Positive self-talk worked, so I'd read.

Opening the door and coming back inside, I saw Sherlock looking into my refrigerator.

"Are you hungry?" I'd be accused of being a bad host if I didn't at least offer to make something, even if it was late.

"No. Just looking."

"Just looking?" I didn't know what that meant. "Is that like snooping?"

Sherlock smiled tightly. "The contents of one's refrigerator can be a very informative insight into one's personality."

Reaching in front of Sherlock suspiciously, I grabbed hold of the top of the door and pulled it from her tight grasp, shutting it. "That's….rude. I think. Or something." I had no idea what refrigerator observation and infiltration counted as.

"I have found it very educational. Your father likes to make casseroles?"

There was half of one still left in there. I leaned against the refrigerator to prevent Sherlock from getting another look. "It doesn't matter. People need to eat." And also, neither of us really knew how to make anything that didn't involve putting everything in a pan and baking it, or adding everything into a pot and dishing it out with a spoon. We were the experts at the single bowl meal.

"I suppose that proper cooking would have been something you would have learned, had your mother not left so abruptly. You were very young then, weren't you? You would have to have been. If you hadn't learned anything at all from her about cooking. Oh, don't look at me like that. I am not subscribing to traditional gender roles, I am merely pointing out that neither you nor your father can do much in the way of cooking, but you have a host of cooking and baking pans in the cabinet next to the sink."

"Anything else of mine you've been through in the thirty seconds I've been outside?"

"Your medicine cabinet has also been rather illuminating."

I threw my hands up in the air. "There is something seriously wrong with you."

Sherlock immediately retreated to the living room. I knew I had said the wrong thing. I could have smacked myself, really. Usually, I wasn't this hideously bad with people. I just couldn't read her. "Look. I just mean... that's weird, ok? And probably kind of rude? I've not known you that long."

The girl grabbed her bag from where it had been resting against the sofa. "I don't understand you, Watson." Good. It was mutual. "I don't. You listen to me and talk to me like--like..." Her chin touched her chest and she closed her eyes. "And then it's like that." She gestured toward the kitchen.

As Sherlock slung the strap of the leather bag across her chest, I dug for the right words. "I wasn't expecting it, ok? I don't know what you're thinking, or how your brain works."

Reaching for her coat, Sherlock stopped mid-motion. "I keep *telling* you how my brain works."

"By strangling me and explaining how you know stuff about my mom taking off by looking at the casserole in the refrigerator? That isn't how things work." I did it again. "No, what I mean is, that isn't how friendship works." To the best of my knowledge.

"Do you think this is a friendship?"

I couldn't tell by the tone if it was an actual question, or a mocking of what I was talking about. "I'm *trying* to be your friend."

Sherlock folded her black coat over her arm. "The question is, *why* are you trying?"

"I'm starting to wonder myself," I muttered. But I wasn't letting it go there. "Because I think you're weird, and interesting, and everyone needs a friend. So why are you so damned hell-bent on *not* having a friend?"

Sherlock's shoulders slumped the barest bit. "I'm very bad at it."

"I can give you lessons. Step one: don't go through people's stuff like you're investigating them. I know you can tell a lot about me by just looking at me, but it's better to ask, ok?" I ran a hand through my hair, trying to keep from breaking out into another sweat. "Talk to me. Ask me questions. Don't strangle me in public. Try not to get me into trouble."

Sherlock seemed genuinely perplexed. "But you ask people things and they lie. Or they don't tell you anything."

I grabbed hold of the coat in her arms and pulled it free, putting it back over the arm of the sofa. "People need their secrets, Holmes."

She flopped back onto the sofa, more at ease than I'd seen her before. "People are difficult." Slouching further down the back of the cushion, her head lolled against the edge. "But it's nice to have someone to talk to, again."

"Again?" I asked before I could think about if the question counted as prying or not.

Sherlock got this uncomfortable look about her -- wriggling shoulders and a scrunched nose of discomfort. "I used to have a--oh, it doesn't matter. It's been a long time." She stared off into the distance. "I'm over it." The last was almost a whisper.

I was guessing she really wasn't. But we were on unsteady ground so I didn't press.

Against my father's repeated wishes, I sat on the coffee table. What he didn't know wouldn't hurt him. "Well, now there's me."

Her face and shoulders set and she nodded firmly in acceptance. "Do not investigate potential friends. It is rude."

Smiling, I leaned forward a bit, possibly invading my new friend's personal space. "And maybe don't tell them their life story when you meet them. Let them tell you. Even if you already know that their mom is a dentist and they once were bitten on the butt by a fish in a skinny dipping accident. Then you'll have the hang of the friend thing."

With the barest hint of a smile, Sherlock nodded. "That's tricky. How do you know if someone's going to be a friend, if you do not investigate them first?"

I nudged her leg. "Seriously? You're going to get into semantics with me? We'll never make you popular, if you keep that up."

Sherlock's nose shot into the air and she looked down with an air of snobbery at me. "Popular," she repeated with disdain.

Waving my hands in front of my face, I called off the comment and attempted to retract it. Too bad the real world did not act like the Internet where you could just delete a stupid post and hope no one noticed. "Ok. Maybe not popular. I was popular once and it sucked."

Sherlock smirked. "Once." Two fingers tapped against the sofa cushion.

"It didn't last long. For about fifteen minutes after I came through with a couple of goals in a playoff game last year. I was hot stuff until basketball season started. Fame is fleeting. Infamy is forever." I was friendly with a lot of people. But after that game, I suddenly had people coming out of the woodwork who wanted to talk to me. It had been disorienting.

"Wise words, Watson."

"I've learned some of life's lessons along the way."

Sherlock smirked, but sat up. I was suddenly interesting to her. "Do tell."

"Let's just say… they like you when you're on top, and when you're not, they kind of don't have a use for you any more." I sighed, staring at my knee. Beneath my stained jeans was a pink-and-red scar that was well-healed, but still said a lot about my situation in life. "I mean, I'm friends with the people I'm friends with. But other people don't talk to me anymore. And I thought we were friends. But I guess it was conditional, based on my performance."

"Most people aren't friends. Your two Tweedles, they are proper friends. People who let you copy homework in a crunch are friends. Other people may be friendly. But that is not a friend."

That actually made me smile. "Yeah. You've put it into words. What I've been thinking. Maybe you know more about friendship than you think. Marybeth--top notch in homework copying. If you copy hers--instant right answers. If she copies yours, she corrects all the wrong answers. Manesha--we hate the same people which is a solid basis for a friendship. The Tweedles are fun and interesting and they make me feel far less freakish sometimes."

"I am an observer of humanity. It is seldom wise for the observer to become part of the experiment."

I rolled my eyes. "So you're saying life is the world's longest experiment. And it's fine, as long as you are watching and taking notes. But god forbid you actually be the rat in the maze." I chuckled. "Taking notes can be fun. But so can getting cheese."

"I find your analogies fascinating." Sherlock's pocket buzzed. She pulled the phone out and read something, her eyes scanning a multitude of lines in record time, then she put the phone away. "Watson, should I choose to participate in the experiment and enter the maze, would you at all be interested in assisting me in fighting the minotaur at the center?"

I held my hands up defensively. "I said cheese. I said nothing about bull-dudes who rip you limb from limb. That was not in the promotional material."

Sherlock grinned. "How do you feel about blackmail?"

"Are we being blackmailed, or are we the blackmailers?"

Sherlock slapped my leg firmly. "Neither! But by the end, who knows? We could be engaged in both."

My head fell into my hands. "I'm going to regret saying yes, aren't I?"

Sherlock got to her feet, this time with a bounce and a much fresher attitude of engagement, bordering on delight. "Probably. However, you'll regret it even more if you say no."

A pitiful groan escaped before I could swallow it back. "Better to regret what you have done, instead of what you have not?"

The other girl's chest puffed up. "Excellent!"

I had a sneaking suspicion that my perfect track record for never getting into trouble was about to end.

Chapter 7

Blackmail. That is what I'd signed myself up for. That singular word hung out in space, suspended by its own possibility. Apparently we were neither to be perpetrating blackmail, nor to be on the receiving end of said blackmail. That left one possibility. I hoped.

"So you're investigating a case of blackmail."

"And a prize to the lady in the front row!" That familiar half-smile tugged at Sherlock's cheek and her eyes lit up. "It's wonderful, really. Magical." She let out some sort of cheerful grunt and clenched her hands in tight fists until they trembled. "This is like the Fourth of July. Fireworks, unicorns, rainbows. And those multi-colored dolphins you see on posters."

"Sounds... important?"

"You could say that. Ohhhhh, Watson!" She slapped both of my shoulders which made the right one ache where I'd been clipped in the same maneuver that had destroyed my knee "This is the best thing. Better than a body, and better than the two left legs turned up at the railroad tracks. Ahh!"

Better than a dead body. This blackmail thing had to be good. "Why's this more special than two left legs?" Even I had to admit that was pretty interesting.

Sherlock clenched her fists together again, as if trying to hold back an excitement that was threatening to burst out into some explosion of emotion that might end up being bigger than fireworks and unicorns. "This is the finest blackmailer in this portion of the country. Perhaps the entire one. Maybe the world. And he is blackmailing someone locally!"

"Why don't you just call the police?" My dad was a cop. I knew this was sort of their area? Crime and stuff?

"I just said he was the finest blackmailer. He's never been caught. No one has enough to implicate him, much less pin him to something. And if they ever get close, he simply blackmails them. Local constabulary, police, prosecutors, you name it. Blackmailed. He has something on everyone, and pays a high price for the right damning information. It's as genius as it is heinous."

Did people say 'heinous' these days? "More heinous than two left legs? That sounds like serious business."

Sherlock started pacing the living room. "Our blackmailer. He has something on anyone of any importance. Anyone of any money or standing. And they pay him to keep it quiet. Because no one will go to the police. Because what he has is so damning publicly or politically or legally that they don't dare. And if they do, they are ruined, and the police find themselves in a tangled web of blackmail they have no hope of undoing. Even the FBI has been caught in this."

I sat back down on the coffee table. Sherlock's fast strides, back and forth, were making me dizzy. "And you know all of this because?"

She waved me off. "I'm a fan. Also, I talk to people."

"Sounds like some well-connected people if you know dark secrets." It sounded like the plot to a television show -- one I'd probably watch.

"My family is boring. But they're involved in... things."

That was ambiguous. I was clearly about to get in over my head. I reached out for my glass and drank the remaining water in silence. It tasted especially weird at room temperature, and when I was trying to drink it slowly, as I allowed my mind to catch up. "So, someone in your family turned you on to this?"

"Oh no. My family's boring. I told you that. The point is, I know who this man is. I know what he's capable of, and the victim contacted *me* for help." She clapped twice, grinning in delight. "Word of mouth, Watson. Nothing can beat it."

"Ok, so who is she, and why is she being blackmailed?" I stared down into my empty glass, wondering how far this thing could possibly go.

Clasping her hands behind her back, Sherlock went back to pacing the small space in front of the non-functioning fireplace, her figure reflecting on the television mounted to the wall above it. "Right. So. The party in question is an aide at Senator Walton's local office. She's being blackmailed for an amount of money that she feels is exorbitant. She did not say in the email what material was being used as blackmail against her."

"And where do I come in?"

Sherlock's head turned so quickly I thought it might pop off. She looked startled that I'd ask such a thing. "You're my lab partner."

I resisted the urge to make a smart-assed remark. "Um. Right. Lab partner. So, what exactly are we doing? If the FBI can't get near this guy, and everyone is afraid of what he'll reveal, how are two high school students going to beat him?"

The handle on the back door turned slowly and my dad lumbered through, and a moment later I heard the door close.

"We're negotiating on behalf of the blackmailee, Watson," she said in a quiet, rushed tone as keys hit the table in the next room.

Negotiating? That brought up a thousand more questions I wanted to ask. But not now. "Hi, Dad," I muttered as he entered the living room.

He put both hands on his hips, right above his belt, about to say something until he glanced at the newcomer, no doubt expecting to see one or both of the boys in the ill-lit far corner of the room, trying to hide behind the fake plant that rested there. "Hello, what have we here?" he said. It was a question, a statement, and an exclamation.

I winced. "Dad, what did we say about the Lando Calrissian impressions?"

"It was an honest question, this time."

Sherlock glanced in my direction.

"Pop culture references. I know. Lost on you. We'll fix that later." I gestured to our visitor. "Dad, this is Sherlock. She's new at school and we're working on the biology thing…"

My dad shifted on his feet. "With none of your books out."

"We were discussing methodology," Sherlock offered in a cool tone, crossing the living room with a hand outstretched. "Joanna has also been catching me up on some essential knowledge of the school and its happenings. I have found it to be quite informative. Did you know that senior privileges were removed due to the appearance of a large catfish in the courtyard on homecoming night?"

Hand still extended, my father finally shook it. He looked clouded over. But then, Sherlock did that to people. And it was the first time she'd ever said my first name. I was used to being called 'Watson' by my teammates and by just about everyone else in school for that matter. Some things simply ended up sticking. Sometimes my full first name sounded weird in my own ears. Hearing it come from Sherlock's face was a whole different kind of strange.

After shaking firmly, Harold Watson looked the girl over one more time. "Let me guess. You play basketball?" I keep trying to get Joanna into winter sports…"

Immediately my hand slipped over my eyes. "Dad-- no."

"She thinks she's too short. But I bet you can slam dunk without even trying." He had that quirky smile again, evident in the way his moustache twitched. The way that made me want to die just a little bit more inside at the Lando Calrissian thing. Why did he have to be that way? Could he be… not like that? Maybe a normal dad with a normal moustache? That was all I wanted out of life at that moment.

Sherlock chuckled politely. "No. I'm afraid not. I'm not very good at team sports."

I could imagine not. "I'm completely too short for basketball. Also, I lack upper body strength. Someone got me into lower-body oriented sports at a young age." I scowled at my father in the hopes he would take the hint and stop… being so very him.

"Oh, I don't know about that. What you lack in hight, you have in speed. I bet you could weave through that forest of tall girls and whoosh." He bounced on his feet and made a free-throw gesture. "Nothing but net."

A tight smile tucked Sherlock's lips together. "I believe Joanna has chosen her physical activities wisely. I look forward to seeing her on the rugby field in the spring."

I was impressed with her social decorum. It was the antithesis of everything Sherlock was as a person, I suspected, but everyone had their secret talents. Sherlock could be polite, and I could do that balance the fork on a penny thing, which I felt was equally impressive.

"So, do your parents know you're here so late?" He looked at the clock on the wall. "Eleven fifteen, on a school night?" Wow. Could you be more obvious?

Sherlock pulled the phone out of her pocket with nimble fingers and pressed the unlock button. "I suppose it is a bit late. I can go, Joanna. We'll look at those slides tomorrow, and then I think I should be appropriately caught up?"

Such a smooth fibber. I could admire that. "Oh, yeah. Totally caught up. Just remember that we need to have this done by Monday, so we might need to really hustle this weekend."

Grabbing her coat and bag, Sherlock headed to the door. "It was nice to meet you, sir. I'm sure we'll be seeing more of each other in the near future."

Dad followed her to the door. "Where are you parked? I can walk you to your car; it's a little dark on this street." It wasn't. There were a full three street lights along this stretch. Either Dad was on a fishing expedition or he was being the gentleman-cop. Either way, I didn't like it.

"Oh, just out front. Joanna can walk with me." Was Sherlock really giving me an out from heart-wrenching awkwardness? It was possible that she wasn't as socially tone deaf as I had previously thought.

I grabbed my rugby hoodie off the chair in the kitchen and threw it on, knowing it wouldn't be enough against the quickly dropping temperature. The fact that I was not wearing shoes was secondary at that point. "I can totally walk you out." Before my dad could comment on my lack of shoes, I opened the door and dashed out, holding it politely for Sherlock.

"Thank you," I whispered as Sherlock crossed over the threshold.

"You can owe me one later."

Why did half the things coming out of Sherlock's face sound ominous?

The alley sloped downward and met up with seven short steps that led to the sidewalk. We always used the back because it was better than the seventeen steps that led to the creaking covered front porch and a door that stuck badly in the winter. It was far easier to bring things like groceries straight into the back, to the kitchen. Sometimes it felt a bit like the servants' entrance, though. Especially since we only opened the front door when we had actual visitors, like who rang the doorbell and stuff.

An SUV was stopped in the middle of the one-way street taking up all the remaining space between the cars parked on either side. The motor was running and steamy air mixed with exhaust caught in the headlights and made something like the mood of a thriller movie. See, I really did need to be wearing shoes right now.

Stopping on the sidewalk, Sherlock waved once. "That's Toby. He'll only give me a minute. I'll send you something about the situation in question. Proper attire for consultation with a client, location, time, other important information."

"There is a dress code for this thing?"

"There is a dress code for everything, Watson."

"Oh. Ok. Um… how did Toby know to pick you up right now?"

She stepped off the curb, between two closely-parked cars and then turned back and grinned. "I can't give away all of my secrets." Crossing into the smoke like some noir detective, she got into the car and it drove away, the tires and suspension bouncing on the yellow bricks of the old and uneven street.

I watched until the vehicle got to the corner and turned down another one-way street that led to the main drag. Letting out a misty sigh, I headed back up the steps, avoiding touching the freezing cold railing made of old painted pipe. The incline to the back door was a little steep, and the cement slabs a little cracked. Maybe it was a metaphor for my life, the budding writer in me thought. At least since my mother had taken off and my brother had gotten busted for DUI and had also taken off to parts unknown.

It made the tiny back yard too big and the house too quiet, and my father a micromanager of all my free time.

Pushing the door open, I saw my father there, divested of his shoes and belt, uniform shirt unbuttoned to the old and greying t-shirt untucked from his trousers. "It's a little late to be having *friends* over," he reminded.

Stripping the hoodie off and tossing it over the chair again, I slid past him. "Time got away from us, and don't use that tone with me. She's the new girl and we're sharing locker space and we're lab partners." Perfectly valid reasons to be in each other's company after bedtime.

"I'm just saying," he began innocently, which was how all nagging started. "You've never had a friend that's a girl over."

"Uh, I've had half the soccer team over here at one point in time or another."

"That's not what I meaaaan." The last was drawn out and changed tones like a horn as a car blew by. My father was the human Doppler Effect. In so very many ways.

Sometimes, he really got on my nerves. I couldn't tell if I was in trouble for having someone over late, or if he felt like I had a secret. Both probably. "Right."

I ripped the hair tie out of my uncooperative hair and ran my hands over the sticking-up bits. Mom had… crazy hair. It always looked dried and frazzled and too blonde, like someone who spent too much time in salty ocean water. That's what I had, despite my father's half-black, half-Italian, super-thick and totally not crazy hair (except for that damned mustache that could go to hell and die). I hoped I only got the hair and freckles from her, because I could deal without the meth addiction.

Gathering up my hair into a loose bun, I patted down those pieces of weirdly straight hair that didn't want to stay down. "I don't know what you think it is like, but it isn't like that. She's the new kid. I'm getting her caught up on things. We were, in fact, being so studious, that we lost track of time."

He waved his hands in front of his face. "I'm just saying."

I scowled. "If I ever end up dating someone, I will inform you by press release."

He threw one arm over the back of the sofa casually. "It's alright. I was a late bloomer too. I'm just saying. You can tell me."

Face burning, I headed toward the stairs. "Good night."

"Don't be up past bedtime again tomorrow night."

"I won't be." I took the steps two at a time, hoping that this was not going to be a regular conversation.

Harold Watson yelled up after me. "Use protection every time!" He laughed to himself like he'd just told the most hilarious joke.

Sometimes I wanted to stab him in the forehead with a spork. Why a spork? I didn't know. Why his forehead? Still didn't know. But I had no actual evidence he didn't work for an evil Empire so the option would continue to remain open.

Chapter 8

I was dragging myself around, dead-tired the next morning. After Sherlock left, I'd been unable to fall asleep. I stared at the stucco bump on the ceiling, wondering if I liked this particular set of developments in my life. Things changed. My brother was gone, my mother... well, we didn't think about that. My soccer season had been shot to hell, and now I had a lockermate who was a bit mad.

Going to bed at ten meant less than eight hours of sleep, which was fine. Going to bed after eleven was less than seven. Going to bed and lying awake until two in the morning, staring at the creepy shadows on your puckered stucco ceiling meant you were running on four hours' sleep, which was too little for me. It meant that I was either old or out of shape.

Well, I knew I was in worse shape than usual by the fit of my clothes. I'd taken to running again, but not every day of the week, and I hadn't even worked up to my former distance or time. And on days like today, I couldn't even fathom getting up early enough to run and go back to my old routine. Lately I got up about fifteen minutes before the bus came. Showering had become optional.

By the time I hit the cafeteria, the boys were already sitting, and I was ready for my nap. This was, of course, after having dozed for the half-hour trip up the winding roads to school. The bus took the longest way possible, and in my need for sleep, I had cared far less than usual.

Sliding into the booth with a long, drawn-out sigh, I tried to concentrate on what they were talking about. The game. The app we'd been working on for over a year. It was taking far longer than it ought. But we were also learning how to program. Well, they were learning how to program. I was learning how to break things. I knew just enough programming to get me into trouble. And that was as far as my interest went.

My mind drifted off somewhere around discussing why the worms in the fifth level kept killing the aliens too soon. It was a programming error for sure, but no one knew where. It went from that to Sherlock in a flash, and Michael and Will were gone from my mind even though they were being loud and obnoxious right in front of me.

Sherlock had said very plainly that she did not play team sports. I wondered what she did to stay in shape. And she was quite fit. Not in one of those annoyingly naturally thin people sort of ways. Which she was; one look at her jutting hip bones was enough to tell that tale. But she had toned calves under those well-cut trousers (not that I was staring) and her thin arms were wiry in a way that denoted some sort of muscles under that nearly translucent skin.

It was probably some sort of expensive rich person activity (which I had absolutely no knowledge of, truth be told) like horseback riding or extreme hiking or rock climbing. Not like the rock climbing wall we had here at school. Climbing real actual rocks in exotic places like Wyoming.

I had never been out of the state, much less the country, so my sense of geography west of the Mississippi River was a bit dodgy. Wyoming was 'over there,' and it probably had rocks in it. Rocks you could climb.

Anyway, she was more fit than I was, with my jogging three days a week and recently acquired muffin top. It made me self-conscious, more than I already was.

"Watsonnnnnn," Michael whined, pulling me out of my thoughts. "Waaaaaatson." Fingers snapped in front of my face and I blinked a few times, pushing his hand away from my eyes. "Daydreaming about New Girl? It's ok. Will does too," he said with mock sympathy.

I focused my eyes and glanced at both of them, but I was too tired to even scowl. "I was wondering if there were rocks you could climb in Wyoming."

"That's..." Will's face screwed up. "Weird."

"I didn't get much sleep last night. That's the stuff you think about when you are sleep-deprived. I have it in good authority, because I am living it right now."

"Oooh. What were you up all night doing?"

If Will was capable of subtlety, I would have been insulted. But he wasn't. "I was doing my homework."

Michael leaned in, practically crossing over the entire table to get in my face about something. He was lucky he was a friend. Because I needed my personal space. "Theresa said that New Girl was at your house till late."

"Theresa Weinstein is a peeping tom." But she wasn't wrong. "We were doing homework. Blood typing. All that."

Will wiggled his eyebrows. "Homework. Sexy."

I flicked him in the middle of his forehead with my finger.

"Ow, I was just asking."

I flicked him again. "You were implying. This is why you will never have sex with anything that isn't inflatable or a herd animal."

A slow clap started behind me, and I turned with trepidation. Sherlock was standing there, fancy bag on her shoulder, applauding loudly. "Bravo. You do have a way with words. I'm sure the insults fly faster when your inhibitions are lowered from sleep deficiency, such as now."

I glanced at Will, who was frowning in actual hurt. "Yeah. That's totally what it was." I wasn't normally that mean. Sarcastic, yes. Outright nasty? No. "Yeah. Totally what it was. Inhibitions. Deficiency. What she said."

"Whatever," Michael and Will said in unison.

"Think whatever you want," I said, not bothering to defend myself. It wasn't worth the effort. And while I hadn't been up late with Sherlock, I had sure as hell been up late thinking about her, and I would be damned if I revealed that information to another living being.

Speaking of whom: Sherlock bounced on her feet. She was wearing boots today, instead of her usual oxfords. "Mr. Stamford. I see you are still enjoying the fruits of my labors."

I glanced in his direction. He was squirting ketchup onto each individual potato chip in his possession before eating it.

"Uh-huh," he confirmed with a full mouth.

I snatched up the king-sized bag. "Salt and vinegar? For breakfast? Eww."

He snatched them back. "Don't judge me."

"We do," Sherlock announced with a sage calmness. "We do."

Michael's face curled. "What the hell? You don't even know me."

"Yeah!" Will chimed in, coming to his best friend's defense. "And you," he pointed his finger at me, "are the one who keeps hanging out with Princess Psycho-pants, here." He gestured to Sherlock. "Maybe you're into that auto-erotic asphyxiation stuff."

Oh, great. Everyone knew about Sherlock strangling me in the commons area. My life was complete. I opened my mouth to protest, but Sherlock stepped in.

"It's only auto-erotic when one derives sexual pleasure from depriving one's own self of air. In this case, it would have been erotic asphyxiation."

"Great. Thank you," I mumbled. Everybody in my life was fully prepared to help me to death.

"But mostly I was proving a point to Watson about how to strangle and drown someone at the same time. It was an educational moment."

Will opened his mouth, but closed it. He thought for a moment, then opened it again. "It's still hinky."

I rubbed a hand over my face. "Hinky? Who tried to pick up his cousin at his grandmother's funeral?"

"She has a point," Michael said, rolling up the bag of potato chips.

"How was I supposed to know she was my cousin? We never see that side of the family."

Sherlock smiled to herself, as if she suddenly knew every dark part of Will's soul. Will wasn't evil. Just oblivious. "Statistically, the odds of someone our age being at the funeral of an old woman who is *not* a member of the family is very low."

He threw his hands up in the air. "Thank you, Einstein, for pointing that out. I know that *now*. Geeze. She had a nose job and didn't even *look* related, ok?"

Sherlock opened her mouth to pursue the matter further, but the bell rang, saving Will from one of Sherlock's lengthy soliloquies on deductive reasoning.

The boys slid out of the booth, and Sherlock checked her phone for the time, then the oversized clock on the cafeteria wall, then her own watch, and hummed to herself about something. "I suppose this is where we go our separate ways, then. Good morning."

The boys had fled without even saying goodbye.

##

Biology was less awkward than it had been the last few days. Sherlock had even acknowledged my presence when I came into the room. It was exciting to be a real person in her sight again.

As we were pulling out our books and notebooks, I remembered something. "You said you'd email me about the 'consultation' thing?" It sounded so stuffy and professional.

She pulled out her wooden pen. The only one she ever seemed to use. Sherlock tapped the pen repeatedly on the surface of the black lab table, thinking. "I've given it consideration. Instead of giving you dress requirements, I am simply going to provide clothes that meet the parameters that are required. Namely, because you look to be roughly sixteen years old."

"That might be because I am, in all actuality, sixteen years old."

She smirked. "Therein lies the problem." She tapped the pen a few more times. "I need you to look at least four years older. And I doubt that is going to happen with the attire that currently hangs in your closet."

"Oh crap, when did you find time to go through my clothes?" I hadn't been taking the trash out for that long, had I?

A broad smile stretched across the other girl's face. "Merely a deduction based on information in the household already within my reach."

I pinched the bridge of my nose, wondering why this was as normal of a conversation as I'd had yet with Sherlock. "So, you know, I don't have any grownup clothes because of the contents of my fridge?"

Sherlock held up a finger "And because you called them 'grownup clothes.'"

"Fantastic," I grumbled, hating that I was so easy to read. I leaned back on the stool, folding my arms across my chest. "I just want to know how exactly you plan--"

"Ms. Holmes, Ms. Watson. The class has started," Mrs. Hall bellowed. Everyone else's paper-rumpling and whispering ceased as the new focus of attention in the room was brought into view. "I'm sure what you are discussing cannot possibly be more important than this class."

Sherlock's eyes narrowed, accepting the challenge. "I wouldn't be too sure of that."

Mrs. Hall's lips pressed together in a thin line of hate, but she didn't say anything. They locked into a staring contest until someone in the front row mercifully coughed.

Oh god, Sherlock had been saved by one of the Veronicas. It was a horrifying thought.

"This class moves far too slowly for it to require my full attention. And anything Watson gets behind on, she can learn from me in a much more efficient manner," Sherlock explained with confidence "I think that given a weekend of intense study, we could wrap up this course in a matter of days."

Mrs. Hall folded her arms over her chest. "Oh, really. You may be new here, but we don't accept rudeness. And I doubt it would be just a weekend. Or you would have tested out of this course when you started. Or you would have finished your high school education online. And even if you think that you can coast through this course, there are other people who need to pay attention. Your lab partner for starters."

My head slunk and I tried to hide behind my backpack, which was still sitting on the table. "Oh god," I whispered into it. They were doing this, weren't they? This was going to turn out like the first day when Sherlock had basically called a class unimportant crap, did a mic drop, and sauntered out of astronomy in victory. Only this time I was being dragged into it and I was going to go down with the Titanic.

"Actually, I would have much prefered online education or self-study, but some detestable human being in my family has it in their head that I need to be properly 'socialized.'" The last word stank with disdain. Oh, this had officially turned into a thing.

Mrs. Hall nodded, then pulled a yellow sheet out of the messy stacks of paper on her desk and took out a pen. "You are welcome to explain this to the vice principal. I'm sure he'll be extremely interested in your views on the educational system."

I froze, my teeth clenched tightly together.

"And perhaps your friend would like to go with you." She started pulling out another sheet.

Oh god, my perfect record. Twelve years of never being in trouble. "No, ma'am. I do not share my lab partner's views on the public education system. I love public education. I love biology. God, country, biology and school pep rallies. That's me." Statement made, I buried my head as deeply into the soft bit of my backpack as I could.

Sherlock took the paper in triumph and blew out the door, letting it slam in her wake. Everyone started looking around, meaning conveyed in facial expressions. No one dared say a word. It wasn't the best choice when Hall was on the warpath.

Mrs. Hall looked around, and slowly the students sat forward, eyes trained on her, and the projector that was going to make them endure another PowerPoint presentation. "Right. Pass forward last night's homework, and we can get started without any further disruptions." Of course, she was staring at me when she said this, as if Sherlock and I shared some sort of hive mind.

I smiled hopefully and opened my folder...to a completely blank worksheet.

This was a nightmare I had often. At least twice a week. I suddenly liked the ones where I arrived at school naked and had to take a final for a class I had never been to, simultaneously. My heart pounded in my chest.

"Ms. Watson, is there a problem?"

I looked around in panic. "Uh, um.... actually I have a problem with the educational system too and I would like to go to the vice principal's office to discuss it with him?"

My life had turned into a series of bad decisions.

##

My partner in crime looked up from the bench outside of the vice principal's office cheerfully, practically bouncing on the hard wooden seat. "I'm glad you're here to join me. You can help me explain the deficiencies in an educational system that still clings to 19th-century ideals of lecture followed by parroting by students, and demands total obedience from those same developing minds."

I sat down next to her with my own yellow sheet in hand, and let out a huff. "I forgot to do my homework last night because someone who shall not be named was distracting me."

"And going to the principal's office is less severe than not handing in a homework assignment?" One of those knowing smiles crept across her lips.

I could have slapped it right off her face. "I panicked."

Sherlock gave me a quick double-pat on the leg. "Oh, Watson, you have so much potential. And you are so very adorable. Like a bichon puppy. But you can learn."

"I'm not your damned puppy. What am I supposed to learn? How to go from 'potential scholarship student' to delinquent. Oh, great, I can pay for college and medical school bills by selling Adderall and Xanax on the black market."

Sherlock thought it over. "That would be quite profitable, really. If the scholarship thing doesn't work out. The current pricing for those drugs on the black market would certainly work in your favor. There is also a black market for albuterol inhalers, if you can fake asthma with your PCP. Odd but true."

"Oh, just shut up. You may not care about getting into trouble, but I do. And now here I am. I don't even know what the inside of the vice principal's office looks like."

The heavy wooden door opened and the man in charge stood at the threshold. "Holmes and Watson?"

Sherlock grinned and slapped my leg again. "Good news! You're about to find out!"

Chapter 9

The inside of the vice principal's office turned out to be a magical place filled with gumdrops and sugar plums.

Well, okay. It wasn't anything quite as dramatic as that. But it was nice. Unexpectedly so. It wasn't lit by the usual harsh fluorescent lights that destroyed eyesight and souls throughout the rest of the school. There was a torch lamp in one corner,and a small table lamp on the edge of the L-shaped desk in the middle of the room. The dark black desk matched the bookshelves, all dark and filled to the bursting. Some contained binder after binder filled with procedures and school records. Other shelves were bowing with books on higher education and administration.

And even snappier still, photos of his family and knickknacks from travels abroad sat in front of some of the books, taking up what little room was left. The desk had a large plush throw rug that sat under the two visitor chairs, which were a well-cushioned dark leather. I wasn't sure what statement he was trying to make with the calming atmosphere, but I was suspicious of it being a trap.

The vice principal sat in a large, leather-backed chair that made him look like the crown prince of the high school. He clicked away with his mouse for several moments, seeming to forget we were even in the room.

He stared at the computer screen. Probably looking at school records. My teeth clenched. This was it. The big one. I sunk into the chair and waited.

And waited. It dragged on forever. Mr Gregson was the newest, youngest and, conveniently, the most attractive of the school administrators. And he looked back and forth, slowly, from the screen to the yellow passes that he had collected and set side by side on his desk when we had entered.

I glanced at Sherlock, who actually had the audacity to have pulled out her book of North American poisons and was engrossed in a page on hemlock. Couldn't she fake being contrite?

Before the knot in my stomach could twist into full-blown nausea, Mr. Gregson looked up, his hands folded in front of him.

"Sherlock Holmes." That was all he said.

Fortunately, she had the decency to look up from her book, even if she didn't close it. "Yes?"

He nodded, thinking over the nature of her response. "Do you find your education here to be lacking?"

She put the bookmark back in her book, closing it, then placing it in her lap. Meeting his posture, she folded her hands and placed them on top of her book. "That is a question with many answers."

"You have been here for less than a week and you have already made quite a reputation for yourself."

Sherlock spread her hands in front of her. "You have my previous records. You know why I am here. Therefore, I don't see much point in the discussion. Expel me, give me detention. Whatever it is you do here. The woman is tedious, her lessons banal and ill-conceived, and of very little use to just about everyone in the room."

The man nodded. "I see. I understand you have some problems with astronomy as well. I suppose the question I should ask is what is your issue with the sciences? What can we do to solve the challenges you are facing in this new environment?" He folded his hands in front of him and leaned forward.

I bit my lips. I hadn't known Sherlock long, but I had a feeling she wasn't going to respond well to this sort of treatment.

And sure enough... Sherlock jumped on the answer like an attacking bear. "Less boring and juvenile material would be a starter. Blood typing? A research paper on plasma? Done on my own. In my sleep. There is nothing new here. Nothing beyond the elementary."

Mr. Gregson's smile tightened and became an act of professionalism and courtesy more than his actual demeanor. "I get the impression that there is nothing new to challenge you. Is that the reason you go looking for trouble?" And the VP was a psychologist as well in his spare time. "Maybe not here, and not at Willowford? Honestly, we want to keep you here. We want you to finish. But you do need to abide by the rules of this institution. Respecting teachers, no matter how wrong you feel them to be, would be a good start."

Sherlock sighed. "This is tedious. There's nothing new here. I'm bored with you, I'm bored with education and I am bored with life. Please send notice of my expulsion to the address on my record, so we don't need to continue with these trivialities." She grabbed her bag and prepared to stand.

The vice principal pointed a finger at her. "Not so fast. I think we also need to discuss the strangling incident." He looked at me. I had been forgotten to this point and I was kind of hoping I'd escape the worst of this.

Elbows already on the armrest, I dropped my head into my hands. "It was just a misunderstanding. She wanted to show me something, and she showed me. No harm, no foul."

"That's not exactly what I heard from a teacher. She said your face was red, and it looked like you were going to pass out. We do not play the strangulation game in this school, Ms. Watson."

Yes, yes, there had been an assembly about it last year when Rachel Troyan ended up passing out and had to be taken to the hospital by ambulance. I knew all too well what was allowed and what wasn't. "Yeah, I know. It wasn't like that. I, uh, told Sherlock I could get out of her hold, and so she tried it. But it turned out I couldn't. Haveta keep working on those self-defense moves. Being a slight girl and all." I made a fist and twisted a little, showing off my 'skills.' I kept my face stone-cold, actually proud of myself for keeping up a lie for nearly a minute. "Simple misunderstanding. Poor planning. Whatever. She and I are still cool."

He looked me over skeptically. "Cool enough to end up in my office?"

I chuckled. "Funny story about that. Um... I realized that I didn't have my homework and I panicked. I got all 'fight the system,' and that's how I ended up here."

"You panicked." He looked over the top of his papers at me.

Why did no one believe this could be a thing? "I've never not had my homework done before! Since kindergarten!" Too true. And there had been enough household and emotional turmoil in my grade school years that no one would have faulted me for never turning in a homework assignment until at least fourth grade. But no matter what was going on, who was in jail, who had run off, and how many times my heart had broken, I did my homework. Because that was the one constant my grandmother had told me, just before she died. Work. Even taxes could be avoided, she said with a sparkling eye. But hard work couldn't be avoided. It was good for the soul, and kept you out of jail. Mostly. So I always handed in my work. Even if half the answers were wrong.

His stone cold face was all I needed to see to know that he thought that my excuse was the single stupidest thing he'd heard in all of his two years as a disciplinarian.

I sighed, slumping further into the chair, hiding my eyes. "I panicked and I said I had a problem with the class, and I left because you should always go for the bigger mark on your permanent record than missing a homework assignment and go all out and end up in the principal's office because it is better to regret something you have done than something you haven't done." It all came gushing out, and I realized I had never done anything I might regret. Simply because I would regret it later.

I felt another anonymous essay coming on about living in the moment or some other crap that could be published in next month's school literary rag. Maybe writing it out would help me understand it. Because I knew a lot of people who had done a lot of things that were regret inducing, and I wasn't sure they were better for it.

After an anxiety-inducing silence, I winced. "It seemed like a good idea at the time?"

He shook his head, reading over my list of crimes again. "It says here you were having '*too much fun*' with your lab partner," he looked to Sherlock with a nod of acknowledgement. "Before becoming insubordinate."

That word bothered me. I wasn't insubordinate. I just texted during class. I did my homework, and I took notes, and I answered questions. I was taking an AP science class! I was not insubordinate. "That's such a harsh word. It's not the marines here." But I saw I wasn't winning any favors with my new-found outrage at the system. I let out an uncomfortable chuckle. "And really, can one have too much fun?" I wasn't insubordinate. I hated that woman as of thirty seconds ago.

"Yes, Ms. Watson. One can."

"I just mean, she's a little harsh, ok? Sherlock's right. It's all videos and PowerPoint presentations, and never anything that makes any sense. I wish she'd just teach us. Without all the...media. Or just hand out the slide show notes and we could be done faster. And I'm not insubordinate. I panicked. It's completely different," I said in a final attempt at self defense.

He scribbled some things down in red pen on a yellow legal pad hidden from our view. "I will take that into consideration. Now we need to think of how you both can make amends."

This guy was good. I was expecting strict 19th-century disciplinarian. Kind of like my dad. But this whole reparations thing was throwing me off track.

"So, um, what do we have to do?" I was the first delve into this new territory. Sherlock seemed to be contemplative at the moment, her mind already mulling over possibilities. I was glad someone was a few steps ahead in this instance, because it was certainly not me. These were uncharted waters for me.

My mind was spinning and unfocused. Detention. Or worse. Saturday school. Or worse-worse, expulsion. All because I panicked over homework. I wish I were in my seat, regretting something I hadn't done, right now.

Smiling, he rose. "I will let you two figure it out. Five minutes, please."

Then he left us there. Just stepped right out of the office. Leaving us to contemplate our own fate. To punish ourselves. "I hope you can think of something clever, because my brain went off-line somewhere around discovering I hadn't done my homework."

"I don't know," Sherlock contemplated. "You did a fine job with the strangling story. Just enough information to be true, just enough false information that we didn't get into too much more trouble. You are a talented liar."

Oh well, I was glad something came naturally to me! "That isn't what I mean! How in the world are we supposed to make amends? I don't even know how to do that. What do I say? Maybe I can wipe down all the tables in the cafeteria for a week or keep score at swim meets or..."

Waving a hand, Sherlock cut me off. "Don't go overboard. I think an apology to the class and to the instructor would be fine in this circumstance."

"Apology?" I did a doubletake. It sounded too innocent.

The other girl rolled her eyes. "Yes, Watson, even I am capable of an apology."

"And that is all it would take?" Call me skeptical but…

She relaxed into the seat, proud of her solution to the problem at hand. "Most likely. It isn't as if we broke into the library and stole computers or something."

"Why do you sound like you are speaking from experience?"

She shrugged, giving nothing away.

I rubbed the top of my scalp quickly, as if that would somehow make my brain work faster. The truth of it was, I had nothing else to go on. This plan was so simple it just might work. "Ok. We go with that. We offer to apologize to the teacher and the class tomorrow." I looked at my watch. "Yeah, it has to be tomorrow. Class is over in a few minutes."

Sherlock chuckled. "Ah, I am glad to be around someone who sees the sense in most circumstances. Beg forgiveness, kiss a few asses. This will all go away."

"What about my permanent record?"

With that, Sherlock started outright laughing. "Permanent record? Do you actually believe in those things? Of course you do--you've been keeping your own spotless since kindergarten. It's so adorable. And so naive."

"I am trying to get into medical school," I hissed with clenched teeth. "I don't have all the money in the world. In fact, I don't have any of it. I need a clean record, flawless grades and the exactly correct number of extracurricular activities that say I am a well-rounded individual so that I can get into a good pre-med program and get every scholarship I can possibly drag out of the system. You, on the other hand, can walk into Ivy League school with less than perfect grades, and for the right amount of money, they will let you wander their hallowed halls. I care about my record, Holmes. I care about it a whole lot."

Sherlock shook her head. "You misunderstand me." Her voice was a little kinder this time around. "Everything drops off the record eventually. I can assure you, they do not have your grade school records anywhere in this building. That time you urinated in the classroom is well hidden away. Dead and forgotten."

Unconsciously, I blushed. But I wasn't following. "But that record exists. At my grade school."

"It has fallen away. It is in storage and no one cares. When you apply to undergraduate programs, they will only ask for high school transcripts, not junior high. When you apply for medical, they will only ask for college transcripts and not high school. 'Permanent' is actually ephemeral and everything drops off the map eventually. And if I tell him it was my idea, he'll likely 'forget' to update your record for all to see."

"You don't have to take the blame." I considered myself an honorable person.

"Oh, what's another dark mark on my 'record'?"

My eyes narrowed. "Why did no one tell me about this?"

"Because they use the lie of the permanent record to hold over students' heads in order to force good behavior from them by creating a paranoia in the already complicit students that their future is in peril for thirteen years."

"Ok, that's just sick."

The door cracked open. "Have you two given some thought as to how you would like to make amends?"

Glancing over to Sherlock, I tried to use telepathy, or at least use my eyes to tell Sherlock that since it was her plan, she got to be the one to carry it out. Of course, the whole 'telling with the eyes' thing didn't work because Sherlock never looked my way. Finally, I spoke up. "Uh, Holmes--uh, Sherlock-- and I have decided that maybe it is best if we apologized to everyone in class for being a distraction and apologize to Ms. Hall, and learn to keep our opinions of her teaching methods to ourselves." A breath gushed out of me as I finished my statement, heart pounding in my chest. Was this what he was looking for?

Mr. Gregson looked unphased. My heart kicked up another notch.

I winced, searching for something else that maybe he would like to hear better. "Um, but we would be open to other suggestions for ways to make amends?"

He glanced at the two papers on his desk, hands on his hips as he thought it over. "That will be a good enough start."

So there'd be more? Like what? Standing on a street corner with sandwich boards declaring that we'd spoken out of turn in class. "Ok. We'll do that first thing tomorrow? I mean--not first thing. But first thing when that class starts?" I smiled tightly through clenched teeth.

He nodded with a somewhat affectionate smile that reached all the way to his eyes. And his low hairline. "Alright. Fine. Get out of my office. And take those sheets of paper with you. Ms. Stein will write you a pass to your next class."

Trying to hide my heavy breathing and sweaty palms, I stood, grabbing my backpack. Reaching forward, I snatched the sheet of paper off the desk. He wasn't even filing it? "Thanks," I muttered. "I'll be good."

Sherlock rolled her eyes and grabbed her own paper. "Watson, you're fine. Just say you're sorry, and it's all right."

I held my breath crossing out of the room and into the main part of the administrative offices. I had survived, and this was not going on my permanent record.

Sherlock got halfway out the door and turned back. "You'll have to excuse her. She is new to adolescent delinquency. I'll be sure to break her into a life of crime slowly."

But then she leaned in further, and I could hear the vice principal's voice, but not the words.

I couldn't tell if Sherlock was joking and I really didn't want to hang around for anything else to happen. Mortified, I walked up to the front desk.

Without even needing to be asked, Ms. Stein took out a pad of hall passes and started writing out the date and time. "What did you two get into? That's probably a record for a new student getting into trouble that quickly."

I fidgeted with the straps of my backpack, readjusting them on my shoulders. "We might have been talking in Ms. Hall's class."

Instead of scolding further, the woman just nodded, signing the pass. "It's happened before, and it'll happen again," she said ominously, like some oracle who was only to be consulted in times of grave danger and upheaval.

I let out the most awkward of chuckles, two little sounds that were almost a squeak.

Sherlock also received her pass. "Right. We are clear to go then."

Once we were out the door, I stopped. "What did he say to you?"

She shrugged, reading over the pass and then looking at the time on her watch, then on the clock on the wall. "It wasn't anything important, really. He knows about my reputation, this could be a chance to start over, blah blah blah. It doesn't matter. I will continue on as I have been."

"Consequences be damned?" That wasn't really my thing. Consequences were usually foremost on my mind.

"Not entirely. I don't want to get stuck in a meat locker for several hours again. But when it's important, I will go about things my way, whether it rubs them wrong or not. I am my own person. I'm not another cog to be stamped out and placed into a functioning machine to keep turning and turning until I am broken and useless and require replacement. I am, as it were, my own man."

I also looked down at my watch. "Well, only forty minutes till lunch. I suppose you can explain this consultation thing to me then. And why I need a new outfit for it. And when we're going to get the time and money to shop for it."

Sherlock shook her head, as if I were being intentionally dense. "We'll go to the shops directly after school. And I already said I would be paying for it. So please, none of your dull poor-child complexes. I'm paying for it simply so we can be on our way faster, and really, it's better than setting money on fire."

"And you know this because you've burned money." Of course she had. That's what rich kids did, right?

"Yes. Hundreds burn quite differently than fives, but almost nearly identical to the ones. I'm sure that knowledge will come in use someday."

This was probably like that cigarette thing. Some contribution to science and detection that only Sherlock could decipher the meaning of. So I tried to swallow my horror at the thought of actually burning and wasting money like that.

"Go on. Say it. It's a brash waste of money."

"Do you know how many tacos you can buy with a one-hundred dollar bill?"

"A hundred?"

"Ninety-one. There's tax on those things, you know?"

Sherlock almost doubled over in laughter. Her foot stomped against the hard white-and-grey tiles in the hallways as she tried to swallow down her amusement.

The office door opened and Vice Principal Gregson tucked his head out. "Class, ladies. Now, please."

We glanced at each other quickly, then went our separate ways, trying to appear properly chastised.

Chapter 10

That same SUV that had been in front of my house just last night was waiting for us at the front door of the entrance of the school. Sherlock grabbed the side door to open it for me, then paused. "Don't talk to Toby. He doesn't like it. Maybe avoid eye contact too. He turns into a bloodhound when he thinks I'm about to get up to mischief."

"Happens a lot?" I asked with sarcasm.

"Enough that he usually knows where to track me down." She yanked the door open and I got in. "And also, remember, seat belts save lives," she said in a twittering Mary Poppins-like voice before slamming the heavy door behind me.

She crossed the car again, and got in the other side, slamming the door behind her with equal firmness, then put her seat belt on. "Click it or ticket," she reiterated until I also put my seatbelt on. Maybe she and my father had more in common than I thought.

"To the mall, Jeeves," Sherlock ordered, one arm raised and pointing ahead, as if she were going into battle.

I hugged my backpack to my chest, sinking a few inches lower in the chair, as much as the seat belt would allow for. "Because that wasn't condescending at all."

"That's alright. Toby handcuffed me to the steering wheel once. We're ok, aren't we, Toby?"

The man looked at us in the rear view mirror, two hundred pounds, blond and buzz cut, his grey eyes looking into our souls, in a creepy Medusa sort of way. He didn't say a word to either of us.

Sherlock patted him on the shoulder with a stiff hand. "See? Completely fine. Like family, practically."

That seemed unlikely. Odds were 'Jeeves' didn't just kill Sherlock outright because that would mean an end to his paycheck, not because he was such a well-tempered soul. Of course, if I hung out with Sherlock any longer, I had a good feeling that I might end up wanting to kill her, or at least do her harm. Possibly permanent body damage. But somehow I would resist the urge, for now, at least. It depended on how close we got to getting in trouble again. Today had been a violent, hair-turning scare.

I looked out the window; the last remnants of autumn foliage clung to the trees, browning and crumbling even on the branches. A few jerks with long driveways had already decorated in excess for Christmas. I sighed.

"Yes, I know." Sherlock said in quiet agreement. "Soon Christmas will begin in August and the moon will be the only place we can go to escape from it."

I didn't ask how she knew what I was thinking. With her brains it must have been an easy thing to figure out. "How long are we spending at the mall? I thought you said we were talking to that lady today."

"Not very long. I can sort you out quickly. I already have something in mind."

I glanced at her, not turning my head. "I want to remind you that I am a fully autonomous human being and I am not a paper doll you can just dress up to suit a whim."

Sherlock smiled sweetly. "Now why would I think anything like that?

I looked her way fully this time, then turned back to looking at the ugly leaves and over-achieving front lawns. "Because I have a sneaking suspicion that you think of everyone that way? As--as puzzle pieces and obstacles and--I don't know. Not people with hopes and dreams. Vehicles for your own amusement? Or in my case, a dress-up doll."

My seatmate scoffed. "Everyone has hopes and dreams, Watson. It's called motivation. And everyone with motivation has motive for whatever unholy thing they think up to do to another person. A rule you should learn right now."

The quiet. No, just a regular silence. The kind that was thick and dense like humidity and just as sticky. But it didn't break with the onset of a sudden rainstorm of talking. It just went on as we made our way from the rural location of the school to busy suburban boroughs, and then to the highway that let off right at the new mall for which it had been built. The whole layout of the metro area was strange and made no sense.

I wanted to say something about the distance. There were at least ten strip malls between here and the bright and shiny new mall. One was two miles from school, and downhill all the way. I had walked it before. But Sherlock was obviously the brains of this operation. Common sense and politeness kept me from asking too much about my potential new gig.

Toby pulled around to the side of the mall with entrances to the most expensive shops. It didn't surprise me, but it did annoy me. "Can't we just go into normal stores?" I asked as the SUV pulled to a stop in front of the entrance of a store I had never even been in before. Just the displays out front of gracefully leaning mannequins who looked like they had escaped the Jazz Age were about all I needed to tell me this wasn't a place for me.

"I'm not really sure I'm wanted here."

Sherlock pushed the double doors open with an impatient sigh. "They like money. They will accept it from the poor and huddled masses."

"Great. Thanks."

"And it isn't even like it's real money," she said, producing a black plastic card from seemingly nowhere, holding it on display between two fingers.

I squinted. "Please, tell me you don't actually believe that. 'Cause we would have real issues we'd need to hash out otherwise." I looked around, lost, at the expanse of the store, overwhelmed with the size and design. Not your average J. C. Penney, everything was painted a cream color with white trim. The lighting fixtures were brass and even the floor was fancy. There were inlaid patterns on the floor in dark green and grey, with sections covered in high-pile carpet.

Sherlock nudged me, breaking me out of my gawking. "Of course, it's real. Ultimately, as real as ones and zeroes can be. But it is not real insofar as I am not paying for it. Well, the card is in my name. But someone else pays the bill."

"Do you think this someone else would have a problem with you spending it on clothes? For someone other than yourself? Because I have a problem with it, and I'm the person benefitting from this trip." I tried to pretend that I wasn't at the mall because she found my wardrobe to be insufficient for whatever mess we were about to get ourselves into.

Sherlock slipped the card away with the speed of practiced sleight of hand, and I had no idea where she had put it. I admired her proficiency. She looked around, trying to see what I'd been gawking at, but apparently she didn't understand why I was so darned impressed.

"The shortest distance between points A and B is a straight line."

"I'm so glad geometry is not above you."

"Hush. I'm explaining. Point A is gaining the confidence of our client. Point B is acquiring the information she needs to deal with her blackmailer on even footing. That straight line is my credit card to make you stop looking like a street urchin. You are so annoying sometimes."

"Annoying? With things like common sense? And I do *not* look like a street urchin." I in no way resembled a 19th-century homeless child.

Sherlock pointed off to the right and headed in that direction, past fancy dresses and pant-suits for women. "You are a series of random components that amount to an entire persona that will not instill confidence in our client." She stopped walking, looking me over, top to bottom, stopping at my hair and squinting. "Random components."

"I look like everyone else at school." I waved a hand at the cashmere turtlenecks behind me. "This is not like everyone else at school."

"My point exactly."

Why exactly was I out here with her again? Oh, right. She was good at solving mysteries, and I had one of my own she might be interested in.

A saleswoman in a silk shirt and pearl necklace had homed in on us during our 'discussion,' and was approaching rapidly. I wanted to bolt. Sherlock put a hand on my arm. Not restraining me, but something about her hand there made me keep from running for the nearest exist. "Hello," Sherlock said, engaging in the first volley. "I'm Ms. Holmes. I spoke to someone earlier?"

Oh. My. God.

"Yes. I did get that message. We have everything pulled. Do you want us to bring it out now?"

I thought I wanted to kill her ten seconds ago. Now it was straight up bloodlust.

"No. We will be visiting the salon first."

The woman nodded and backed away.

Why was murder even a crime? "Sherlock, this isn't just a change of clothes, is it?"

"Well, I'm not doing this again the next time we have a case that requires we both look like mature adults. I'm being efficient." She started walking again, not bothering to see if I followed.

I loved her assumption that there would be more of these fun outings. And that my entire wardrobe sucked. "Salon?" I asked, rushing to keep up.

"I would have gone to a more personal boutique but you're…" her eyes narrowed. "Husky. And I am only dealing with your hair once. Watson, when was your last haircut anyhow?"

She reached out to touch my hair and I slapped her hand away. I frowned, letting her know she'd come back with a bloody stump if she tried to touch my hair again. "My hair does whatever the hell it wants. I keep it up in a ponytail most of the time. My hair doesn't matter."

"My point exactly. Now. Let me handle this." We walked into a salon that happened to be inside the department store. Everything was white. Extremely, extremely white. Sherlock went straight to the counter. "Holmes. Appointment for Watson. Cut and color."

I wanted to say something about how I had not signed up for this, but I was so beyond fighting. I wanted to tell her where she could shove her cut and color, but we were already here and she had already spoken for me. She'd never be doing that again either.

I was led to a chair where a woman untied my ponytail and threw the band away. In front of me while I watched. In the front of the salon, Sherlock was sitting with ankles crossed, book of poisonous plants spread on her lap. So when the women began combing out my frazzled hair and tugging on it, there was really no one to complain to. I'd live. But I wouldn't like it.

A cut and a dye later (no highlights, thank god), and I was presented to Sherlock as if I were a prized showdog. And trust me, she looked me over as such.

She inspected the front, then walked around to the back , and circled back in front of me.

"Well?" I asked, annoyed. My damned hair was gone. Gone. In place of my shoulder-length cut, which fit into a ponytail for sports and running, I now had a pixie cut. With bangs. And they'd put so much crap in it, and straightened it that it actually sat down, the way a pixie style was supposed to. I doubt it would ever be a repeat experience, but for now it looked nice. Far too different. But if it were someone else's head, it would be cute.

"Much better."

"They dyed my hair the same color it actually is."

"One shade darker. Brings out natural highlights."

"Sure." Apparently she was also a hair expert.

She turned to the woman who had cut my hair. "Makeup?"

Of course, there would be makeup, I thought with seething anger. Why was I even surprised? More importantly, why was I so insufficient that I needed to be completely remade before we saw this client person?

"Felicia should be ready for her."

Sherlock put a hand on both of my shoulders and turned me around. "Go on, hurry up. We haven't got all day." She gently shoved me in the general direction of the back of the salon. "And learn something while you're back there."

Great. Awesome.

Past the blindingly white hair stations was a doorway that led to somewhere both dark and bright. Going inside, I could see the black walls and ceiling and the dark purple carpet. There were bright lights everywhere. Two chairs, and multiple mirrors. I could see the hair cut from every angle at once, and I didn't even recognize myself.

I hated how nice it looked, really. Was there nothing at all that she didn't know at least something about?

Felicia was one of those effortless women with a messy blonde bun with wisps of low-lights falling down at strategic angles and places. She wore little makeup herself, but was studying my face with scrutiny that was usually reserved for Holmes. I clenched my jaw tightly, trying not to speak my mind as I sat down in her chair, and I was ordered to lean back.. Before I knew what was happening, my eyebrows were being abused with wax, tweezers, and a pair of extremely pointy tiny scissors.

Some pore-closing toner thing and a cold compress later, she began rattling off product names. Something, something spray foundation. Little trick, do this with the powder, something my natural boyish face, and bronzer on my jaw and neck.

Again, it seemed like an awful lot of work for nothing at all to happen. My lips were lined with something that appeared to be the same color they actually were, and I could not yet determine the purpose of the matte lipstick that went on top of this. Felicia was still talking about dabbing the color on my eyelids, instead of swiping, as if I had ever actually used a brush to apply eyeshadow before. The confusing part was the diligence with which she was tapping the crease of my lid, and blending it, when the colors were so close to my own skin tone. I thought makeup was supposed to make you look like those women in the magazines. Plump, fuchsia lips, long, exaggerated eyelashes, dark and mysterious eyelids and sharp color just under the cheek line. That was how one wore makeup. Or so confirmed the girls in my classes most of the time. Those were some girls with some serious eyelashes.

So when Felicia put some clear thing on my eyelashes, ordering me to blink twice, I wondered exactly what the hell Sherlock thought would be going on here.

Two coats of actual mascara later, and I was given permission to look in the mirror.

I still looked like me. No blush streaks trying to imagine cheekbones where none had existed before. My skin tone was even but didn't look fake. Felicia pointed with the back end of a brush at the contouring she had done with bronzer around my nose and forehead and jawline. "Just remember to use it everywhere you'd normally get sun."

But my eyes had lost their usual tired look. The eyebrow thing had been weird; she had trimmed them and waxed, giving them a shape, but then she had still filled them in. And the mascara, despite secret invisible formulas and two coats of the other stuff, didn't look magazine-cover dramatic. I had eyelashes. That hadn't really mattered before. But I supposed it was nice that they were visible now. Petite and understated

"I'm done?" I asked, looking myself over suspiciously.

Felicia smiled to herself, satisfied. "Yes. If you're doing it right, on the average day you should just look like the best version of yourself."

The best version of me? I didn't know who or what that was.

Sherlock didn't wait for me to be presented. She simply wandered back this time, as if she owned the place. Might be a consistent habit of hers that I would just have to get used to.

Looking me over, she nodded. "Excellent. Now, we have to rid you of those clothes and possibly burn them."

I rolled my eyes at this new turn for the dramatic. "What about you? No hair change-over? No expensive makeup?"

She had that look of utter bewilderment again. "Why would I need makeup?"

"I don't know. Why do I need makeup?"

"Because you obviously need makeup, Watson." She walked toward the front of the salon, and I noticed a door leading to spa facilities. Somehow, I doubted Sherlock was the mud mask type.

"Why do I need makeup then?" I asked, using long strides to keep up. "Am I too ugly to go off on consulting adventures with you?" It seemed like my footing was always just a few inches from quicksand, and I would lean just a little too wrong in either direction and be swallowed under.

Paying, Sherlock shook her head. "My distaste for your entire wardrobe aside, your previous… look was not going to tell a story that would elicit the type of confidence that we require from our client in order to provide the best services."

"So spray can foundation is part of some service-level agreement."

"You need to look like you are in your early twenties and competent. The end."

And that was it. All discussion about my appearance, and its inadequate nature, and Sherlock Holmes overstepping her bounds ground to a halt as soon as she signed the credit receipt and took an over-sized bag from the woman at the counter. I didn't know why she bothered. I wouldn't know what to do with half of whatever she had bought. Maybe I should tell her to use it on herself, or to shove it where the sun didn't shine.

But dammit, I was so anxious to get onto the actual client part of this exercise.

She handed me the bag. "Don't worry. Felicia included copious amounts of instruction." Sherlock smiled tightly.

"I'm not above hitting a girl," I muttered as I turned around and headed for the salon door and back into the department store proper.

Before I could look for the exit to this mad place, Sherlock was on my heels. "Good. That's just the sort of person I need for this mission. Someone who doesn't mind hitting a man in glasses. Or, a girl, as it were."

"You were the girl I was referring to." I lifted the heavy bag up. "I'm going to pay you back for this." In a hundred years. "I'm not beholden to anyone." I was not going to be in her debt. Even if this whole 'new me' thing was not something I had requested for myself.

Shaking her head, Sherlock looked at the ceiling. "This is all a write-off. The client is paying for it."

"Oh. My. God." I couldn't fathom it.

She pointed to the counter where the woman from before was waiting. "Now, Watson. The attire of a college graduate."

"I'm not wearing a suit."

"Melodrama to the last."

She stepped up to the counter with the confidence of someone who had been here many times before. "Are we ready for Ms. Watson's fitting?"

If a tailor was involved, I was running away. As fast as my gimp leg would take me. God, I wanted to meet this client. Hell, I had my own mystery for Sherlock, if she were interested. But she drove me a little crazy sometimes.

The woman in the cashmere sweater folded her hands in front of her. "First dressing room. Everything is sorted by attire type."

"Good. Watson, come."

I'd been distracted by the crisp white shirts on racks embedded into dark wooden panels along the walls. By the time I looked over, she was already headed in a direction I assumed to lead toward the dressing rooms. "Is this the part where I am shoved into stuffy rich people clothes?"

"What?" She stopped.

"I don't want to be tossed into stuffy rich people clothes."

"The question was rhetorical. I heard you the first time. Are my clothes stuffy rich-people clothes?"

I bit my cheek. "Is this a trick question?"

"Tell me what you think of my clothing. Look. Really look. Don't just look. Observe."

Shrugging, I made a face. "I have no idea! It's black on white on black. You wear a variation on this same outfit every day."

Sherlock nodded. "Very good, Watson. You can't tell. Do you want to know why you can't tell? Because I work hard to keep it that way. And the best way to do that is to buy simple, classic clothes from an upscale environment. It ensures longevity of wear, and that the individual pieces will be mixable and matchable for quite some time. I avoid fad fashion. I stick to pieces that are anonymous in nature. It makes them more versatile for reconnaissance and undercover work."

She sniffed. "Anyhow, you can't wear black. It will make you look sickly."

"I have dark skin."

At the dressing room, she grabbed the handle of the door. "One can still look sickly with pigmentation. I wear black. Therefore you cannot wear black too." Opening the room, she practically shoved me inside. "Try the dark jeans with the blue top first, please."

Inside, I looked at the hooks full of layers of clothing. Nothing was brightly colored at all. Granted most of my clothes revolved around grey track suits and hoodies, but I expected to at least see something on the rainbow. All of the colors were muted. The sapphire blue square cut top was the brightest thing in the lot. Maroon, mauve, dark purple, two completely different dark greens. If her gimmick was black, what was mine supposed to be?

But I took the jeans and shirt off the rack. Skinny jeans? Really? I had thighs like a linebacker and I had a muffin top the size of a whole loaf of bread.

I slid them on, trying not to worry too much about the details. Maybe if they didn't fit, and Sherlock were wrong about something--anything--I'd have at least some small modicum of satisfaction.

But I didn't. When I pulled them up the bastards actually fit. They didn't hang down hopelessly over my heels the way most jeans did, and there was actually enough room at the top. Sliding into the shirt she recommended, I looked myself over. I felt uncomfortable. My neck was cold without all the hair to keep it warm, and the slit-neck of the tunic shirt exposed way too much collarbone for my liking.

"Well?" Sherlock asked on the other side of the door.

"Ok, you win. It looks nice. But it doesn't feel like me."

"Come out and let me see. And you're not you. You're Joanne Hannalore Watson, recent college graduate and assistant to one Sherlock Holmes, independent crime consultant. If you felt like yourself I would be worried. It's just dressup, Watson. Playing the part."

"You cut my hair."

"It was in the way."

And Sherlock Holmes was not one to let things get in the way. Even a bit of hair. The fact that it was on someone else's head was of absolutely no consequence.

"Now, let me see. And try these boots on. It's four-thirty, and we have things to do."

I opened the dressing room door, and did the slow spin without being asked. I knew she would want the full view.

"Perfection. That will do for today. The other items we'll have sent along anyway. There will be plenty more occasions to run around looking like competent adults." She thrust a pair of short grey slip-on boots at my chest. "Put these on. I need to see the finished product." She shoved me back into the tiny room and toward the bench. "Hurry. Things to do."

I sat and put them on, glad that I didn't have to bother with zippers or buckles. They were a soft suede dyed light grey, and had a nice tread on the bottom. Fashion and practicality. I hated that Sherlock was so good at this. Maybe if the fact-consultant (or whatever--she needed a better title) thing didn't work out, she could be a professional shopper.

And I, on the other hand, had no backup plan other than medical school and maybe a bit of writing on the side, so I'd really better not mess all of this up.

Standing up, I admired the complete effect in the mirror. It wasn't me. But maybe it could be in a few years. Confident, educated, a comfortable sort of stylish. Long lashes and lip gloss over a very light lip stain and just enough blush to give the illusion of cheekbones. I looked like someone who actually spent time on my appearance, instead of someone who was always just done being sweaty or about to get sweaty, between early morning runs, gym classes that required showing the boys that I could play hardball too, and sports practices after school.

All those showers did nothing for my hair but dry it out and accentuate the frizz. I touched the incredibly short dark hairs on top of my head. Maybe that'd be better for the frequent hair washing. I wasn't sure about the makeup bit. Basically, I wore lip gloss and that was about as far as I went with the whole thing. It was a combination of a lack of ambition, a lack of caring, and a lack of know-how.

I turned around and stared at my butt. I wanted to lose the weight I had put on. I constantly didn't feel like myself with the change in shape. But the jeans were very kind to my bottom. I almost flung the door open, prepared to tell Sherlock she wasn't such an asshole after all, but I thought better when a shadow much bigger than a slight yet tall girl crossed in front of the door.

"Now they are sending children to do work that cannot be achieved by scores of men?" The deep voice had an audible sneer in it, despite the obviously amused tone.

Hangers moved around on metal racks. "Shopping? Teenagers do it every day."

"We know that isn't why you are here."

I bit my lower lip. It looked like our 'case' had begun early.

Chapter 11

"Did you not hear? I am getting out more. It pleases certain parties. In case you have not heard, I have been classified as both a hermit and misanthrope."

Misanthrope, yes. Hermit? I didn't quite know about that one.

"Don't be coy. I know your reputation. Very big for so early in your career. The Gloria Scott? Touching. If a bit showy."

"I've been told I have a flair for the dramatic and would be quite good on the stage. Instead I make good with ships and giant rubber ducks. But then, I didn't sign that one when I delivered it. Charles Augustus, I presume?"

The shadow shifted left, then right, then moved away from the door. Slowly, I turned the handle and cracked the door as quietly as possible. When I got enough space to see out, there wasn't all that much to see. My view was taken up entirely by a mass of shoulder-to-ankle fur. The coat was enormous. Not just in length, but in girth. and poking out of the rigid collar of the coat was a balding head with the classic combover that fooled exactly no one.

"Would it be anyone else?"

"Truly? I expected minions. I'm glad to see there are still men in this world willing to invest themselves in the finer details."

Banter. They were bantering.

"I do like to get my fingers… dirty. As it were. Now and again." The mere mention of dirt had him reflexively wiping his fingers on the length of his scarf. Germophobic blackmailers. This is what we needed. "Does she think I will release the blackmail material to a child?"

Sherlock chuckled. "Oh, no. That is not at all what I have been employed to do. I am merely here in an… advisory capacity."

"Good. Then we understand each other."

Sherlock said nothing.

"Because I can destroy everything--well, what little-- you have left." The grin was evident in his tone. I didn't need to be looking at him to see it.

With all the patience I could manage, I closed the door as slowly as humanly possible and turned to my bag. From the front pouch, I grabbed the mace and turned back to the door, throwing it open, holding the bottle in front of me. Sherlock paused in leafing through a row of off-white silk shirts, and the hulking man turned around, holding a bowler hat in one gloved hand, and a small pistol in the other.

"I wouldn't, Miss Watson," the man said with a stern quietness.

An old woman looking through complicated wrap-around blouses looked up from the rack on the other side of the section. Augustus simply smiled at her with flabby lips and ruddy cheeks. Somehow this appeased the woman with the over-curled hair, and she continued on, moving away from the dressing rooms. Couldn't people even be properly nosey anymore?

And didn't they have cameras here? Couldn't they see the man pointing a gun at teenagers?

"He's standing in the blindspot, Watson," Sherlock answered the question I hadn't even voiced. "His hat is hiding it from the other camera. Besides, you have the mace can pointing the wrong way."

I looked at it. Sure enough I wasn't going to hit anything except the back of my own hand with the pepper spray. Scowling, I tried to defend myself. "Well... I haven't exactly needed to use it before."

The man's fleshy cheeks pulled back into a creepy, knowing smile. "Your effort is commendable. However, I'm afraid you've brought... even less than a knife. To a gunfight." He put the hat back on his head, and the gun disappeared somewhere into the furry folds of his coat. He nodded to Sherlock. "You can buy all the clothes you like, Ms. Holmes. Your client won't get out of this unscathed, if she, or you, choose to play by any other rules than my own."

Holding her head up high, Sherlock sniffed. "I'm an advisor. Perhaps negotiator. I know you will deliver on all of your promises. I know your work. There is no need to threaten two teenagers with a gun. That's like bringing a gun to... well... a department store." She tilted her head. "Though I do like the mother of pearl inlay. That is a level of quality and detail you just don't see anymore."

He flashed a quick smile that reverted back to dark seriousness in less than a second. Looking from Sherlock to me, then to Sherlock again, he dramatically closed his coat and stepped past us in long strides, faster than I'd thought a man like him could go.

I grabbed the sleeve of Sherlock's coat and tugged on it. "What the hell was that?"

Sherlock watched him leave through the doors we had come in earlier. Satisfied that he was gone, she gave me her attention. "That... is a mystery." She bit her lips, as if that could somehow hide the grin threatening to break free. "He's heard of me. He knows I'm on the case." She grabbed both of my hands and squeezed them hard, shaking them back and forth. "This could be the big one." Dropping my hands, she stepped back and looked over the outfit with the shoes. "Oh, that's lovely. Just right. Almost. Zip up the cardigan about half way. That'll do it."

"He just pulled a gun on us, and you're worried about my zipper."

Sherlock shrugged it off. "Well, he's gone now. There's nothing we can do about the gun thing. We can, however, make sure your clothes are done up properly."

I sighed. "I keep getting myself in deeper and deeper. Eventually I am going to be at the bottom of an ocean trench unable to see even a glimmer of daylight."

Sherlock punched my arm lightly. "The turn of the phrase. I knew there was a reason I liked you. But oh, Watson. My dear Watson. You are already in so far over your head it's just a matter of time before you cannot see the daylight any longer..."

"Awesome. Just awesome."

"I believe in full disclosure at all times, Watson." Sherlock's grin was cat-like and mischievous, and oh-so-pleased with herself at the same time. "This is much better than homework, though, you have to admit."

Chapter 12

We walked out of the mall with just a few bags. My own clothes were stuffed in my backpack. The outfit I had tried on was still on my person, and paid for. The other outfits Sherlock had purchased with that black credit card at the same time, and they were put into huge paper bags with the store's logo tastefully emblazoned at the top. It made me kind of sick to my stomach every time I thought about it, so I just tried not to. It was difficult when Sherlock was talking to one of the clerks about having the things delivered to my house. I didn't even know how I was going to explain the sudden influx of expensive 'grownup' clothes to my father. Maybe I'd just let Sherlock do it. She'd gotten me into this deeper than I wanted; maybe she could get me out of just a bit of it.

Toby, of course, was right outside when we walked out. I had no idea how he knew, but he did.

Getting into the vehicle, I squinted in the blinding setting of the sun. Once inside, I looked at the clock on my phone. "Do you mean all of that only took two hours?" It had felt like forever. I'd never had a haircut go that fast, even if the dying had taken a while. I had also never had a situation with a man with a gun. That could make the perception of time screwy.

Sherlock opened the door on the other side of the car and got in. "Time flies when you're having fun?"

I stashed the bags beside me on the floor. "I'm not sure I approve of your definition of fun."

Toby adjusted the mirror silently and looked at both of us, then put the car into reverse.

Sherlock leaned in with a sincere and excited smile on her face, then whispered, "I think the whole thing was brilliant. Because, if you think about it... why bother with us? Unless we pose some real and actual obstacle to his plans."

She rubbed her hands together, then rested them in a prayer posture under her chin, closing her eyes and thinking.

I let out a long breath that I tried to not make sound like a sigh, even though it kind of was. Sherlock brought that out in me. I tried to respond as quietly as possible, even though Toby could probably hear most of what we were going on about. "Are we even an obstacle? We haven't even met with the lady yet. We have a name and a time, that's it."

"And he knows who I am. And my family. That is positively thrilling. Toby, Senator Walton's office."

Without waiting for an explanation, or even a please, he turned out of the mall parking lot and toward the highway.

"Yeah. Sure. Ok." I took to looking out the window. That man. The blackmailer. He had pulled a gun on us. In a shopping mall and that seemed to worry exactly no one. My life seemed to make less and less sense the longer I hung out with this girl.

When I looked over again, Sherlock seemed to be lost in thought. Eventually, though, I had to break the silence. "I think your plan is crazy. Still... thank you for the clothes?"

Sherlock turned to me slowly, eyes wide with startlement. "Um, well, you're welcome. Anything for the case, you know," she added, recovering quickly. I wondered if people thanked her often, or ever. "You're a... modern classic, if I had to pin you, Watson. Yes, that outfit would do you in several eras. But as we are stuck in this one, it will do even more nicely. You should attempt to dress in a ... less jock-like fashion. It suits you."

"Ha, then what am I supposed to run around being a jock in?"

"We'll get you into full operating order, Watson. Once this matter is dealt with, we can introduce the school to the new you, and Murray and Stanford can spend some time rethinking their incredibly dull lives."

##

The senator's office was really not impressive. It was a small building that might have formerly been a bank. Well-trimmed bushes out front, dark green despite the cold, a white gravel parking lot, and an an eery white-washed exterior with a wooden hand-painted plaque denoting that it was Senator Walton's office in this district.

I was even less impressed when we opened the front door and a small brass bell above the door rang, informing the people in the back, down a narrow hallway, that someone had arrived. Not exactly what I had expected when it came to the high-flying world of national politics.

The secretary's desk was empty, and so was the other desk beside it. It must have been an early day. If it wasn't, I wanted to work for the government, where people got to knock off before five.

On the wall were two photos of the senator in question. The first was faded with age. Walton was a young man in that photo, stuffed into a light blue suit, shaking the hand of someone I only vaguely recognized as Gerald Ford. Or it might have been Jimmy Carter. I got the two between Nixon and Reagan mixed up.

In the second photo, he was much older, fatter and balder, this time in a dark suit with a deep red tie, shaking hands with the current president. The man must have been in office longer than god. Or at least Strom Thurmond. Since 'god' was probably not an elected position.

While I was trying to figure out the photos, Sherlock was also looking the place over. From the fake wood paneling on the walls to the mud smudges on the floor. She picked up a snow globe on the secretary's desk and rubbed her fingers against the bottom, then stared at the dust she'd pulled up. Putting it back down, she looked around the pencil well, then walked just past the desk, grabbing hold of the desk drawer handle as she did so, and slid it about quarter of the way open. Looking behind her at the contents, she slid it back into place with her hip when one of the back office doors opened and a man in his early forties wearing a wrinkled corduroy jacket came out holding a huge portfolio against his chest.

Behind him was a woman in an equally rumpled jacket, a scarf in a bright autumnal orange tied in an intricate knot down the front. "That is just the information he'll be looking for, so I don't see any reason to wait. Go ahead and e-mail me with the specifics, and I will make sure they get to the senator before that bill comes up for a vote." She smiled that effortless smile of someone masking the truth about how they felt about anything at all. She could have been incredibly enthusiastic about the visit, or could have wanted to dump the man out the door as soon as humanly possible. We'd never know.

Sherlock leaned against the drawer she'd just opened, crossing her ankles, and then her arms over her chest, as if she'd been put in some huge imposition for having to wait even a minute for the senator's aide.

The man walked past her with barely a glance. And past me too, for that matter. And I was standing in the middle of the waiting area. I was hard to miss. He left in a tiny diesel-powered Fiesta that had been in style years before I was born.

That's it. We were up.

The woman's practiced composure faltered as soon as the man was gone. She leaned against the wall, exhaustion taking over. "Sherlock Holmes?"

Sherlock nodded. "Ms. Blackwell?"

The woman tucked her dark brown hair behind an ear and sighed. "Yes. Uh--Eva. It's been a long day."

"So I have gathered."

Untying her scarf, the woman looked me over. "She can wait out here."

I raised a hand, looking down sheepishly. We had done all this work on my 'image' to make me look like a student in my later college years, and it had all been for naught. "Sure, I can--"

Sherlock smiled tightly, holding a hand out for me to say no more. "No. Whatever you say to me can be said in front of my trusted associate, the soon-to-be Doctor Watson."

My gesture of acquiescence turned quickly into a wave. Soon-to-be was more than just a bit of a fib. I wasn't even accepted to a pre-med program. I hoped I looked that much older, that she could pull off this particular lie.

The woman nodded, too exhausted from the day and the situation to question Sherlock's judgement. "Ok. The conference room…" She gestured behind her, down the hall. "it's probably the best place to talk."

We followed her down the narrow hallway to a decent-sized conference room. Glass table, speakerphone in the middle. Refrigerator in the corner, under a big screen TV with a webcam mounted on top. The woman walked to the fridge and pulled out four bottles of water. She gave one to Sherlock and another to me, then put the other two on the table in front of herself, and pulled a plush leather chair with a high back away from the table, and slid into it like a deflating lawn Santa. "Today has been--has been hell." She gulped down the first bottle, then cracked open the second and only took a single sip.

Sherlock pulled her chair out and sat down, crossing her legs and steepling her hands in front of her again.

Feeling left out, somehow, I rushed to sit. I almost tucked the chair under the table in a wholly respectable manner, but Sherlock hadn't pulled her chair in toward the table. In fact, she had taken a more aloof stance and had left her chair pushed away from the table. I went for something halfway in between.

Silence filled up the space, the way silence does, and I broke it with the creak of my chair and the snap of the plastic safety ring on the bottle of water. I'd have smiled self-consciously, but this Jo Watson was about to be a doctor. Doctors weren't self-conscious.

"Well, now that we're all comfortable." Sherlock's foot twitched. "Let's begin. You were contacted by Augustus. He said he would expose something devastating to your future, and asked for a sum."

Ms. Eva Blackwell nodded. "Yes. I have no idea what it could be. But two million?" She rubbed her forehead. "Who has two million just...lying around?"

"If you have it in assets, I suggest you cash them out and pay the man. No one has ever gotten the better of him."

"No one?"

Sherlock pulled her pen out of her coat pocket--the wooden one she liked so much. She had no paper in front of her, however. She simply twisted the nib in and out, giving her hands something to do. "No one. In fact, I have already met with the man tonight. He's prepared to turn his singular talents upon my own household if I do not stay out of the matter."

Eva's head fell into her hands, her lips pressed together as she tried to maintain her composure. "So you're not going to look into this. You're not at least going to tell me what I am paying two million dollars for."

"So you do have the money."

"I never said that! I just can't imagine what is worth that much. I'm--nobody."

Sherlock tapped her bottom lip with the pen. "You are absolutely certain. No one lives a life without sin, Ms. Blackwell. Everyone has skeletons in their closet." She point the pen at the bedraggled woman. "You do work for a politician."

"I'm an aide. I answer letters. I listen to people complain or make suggestions. I try to hash things out with local utility companies for people. That's what I do."

Sherlock nodded. "Yes. Thank you. Can you recall at any point when something big did cross your desk? Even by accident?"

The woman thought about it, massaging her temples. Some of her mascara crusted and ended up on her cheeks. "Not a thing. Not in the years I've been here."

"And before that?" I asked, feeling the need to insert myself somehow into the conversation.

The woman shrugged with a breath that came out as a tiny, bitter laugh. "This and that. Committees, charities, host this party, organize that fundraiser."

I frowned. I knew very little of politics or how society at these levels worked. This was educational, but I wished I had something meaningful to contribute, besides just being there.

Eva continued. "That's been my last twenty years. I was hired here because I'm good at fundraising."

Sherlock nodded. "You got this position because of connections. Your husband was, and is, the primary breadwinner. You don't need this job."

"No. I don't...need it. Necessarily. Which is what makes this all so confusing." She finished off the second bottle of water and held onto it tightly, bright red nails digging into the plastic.

Leaning forward, Sherlock grinned, gripping the wooden pen tightly in her grasp. "Then tell me about your husband."

"I don't know." Her shoulders slumped and she closed her eyes. "He's a banker. He works at PBR. He does something with corporate loans. I don't really care, and he doesn't talk about it much, so I don't know the specifics. Could this really be about him?"

Sherlock gestured with the pen again. "Go back further. I want to know everything about him. Where did you meet? What was he like then? Any detail may be of the most vital importance."

I took a long drink from my water bottle as the woman thought it over. I didn't know why I was here, and couldn't even imagine a good excuse. But I kept my back straight and my chin forward, the way a confident adult would do. Or at least I imagined they would do. Apparently my entire image of what an adult looked like was based on my father, which was probably some other can of worms.

But I hadn't even pointed the pepper spray in the right direction earlier. Making me look older hadn't actually made me older. Or wiser. I was just just going along as a passenger on Sherlock's joy ride. My history homework wasn't going to get done, and I'd had a gun pointed in my general direction by a blackmailer.

The woman looked back and forth at the table, as if her own reflection in the glass held some answers. "I don't know. We met in college. He was a business major and I was into history. We both had the same PE class, though. That's how we met. We both liked hiking and cycling, so those were most of our dates. He's been working with the same company for nearly twenty-five years."

Sherlock nodded. "No children. Dogs, I see. Coarse hair at your knee. He interacts with them often?"

She blinked and shook her head, taken aback. "That's what he does when he's not at work. Goes hiking with the dogs, or takes them to the park. But what does that have to do with...?"

"I'll be the one to decide what information is useful, or not," Sherlock said, interrupting her. Twisting the pen again, she continued with her questioning. "And what is his routine like? Varied? Consistent?"

"I don't know. I don't get involved in his day. He doesn't get involved in mine. He leaves for the park-and-ride spot at the same time every morning. Then he takes the bus into town because parking is a nightmare."

"And if you are behind the bus, you might as well be on the bus," I supplied. There was nothing worse than being behind the bus, really.

Somehow that put the woman at ease. "He says the same thing. And it's true. The traffic in downtown is mad at the beginning and end of the day, so he gets the bus near The Crow's Nest and takes it the rest of the way into town."

I knew The Crow's Nest. It was a seafood restaurant about three blocks from my house, across the street and right on the river. "He drove that far into town?" Into the crappy neighborhood? I wanted to ask, but kept my peace.

"He knows the owner, so he parks in the rear of their lot, next to the actual park-and-ride. And then he doesn't have to worry about something happening to his car all day."

I perked up. "Grey Mercedes? Silver trim?"

The woman nodded. "That's Jim's car."

"I just assumed it was the owner's car. But it's there really early."

Sherlock's head snapped in my direction. I supposed I was stealing the wind from her sails a bit. It felt nice. She waited for further elaboration from me.

"I pass it every day on the bus." I struggled not to say 'school bus,' but it seemed to have done the trick. "It hasn't really changed pattern at all, always parks in the same spot, always there at the end of the day."

Sherlock nodded. "Excellent, excellent. We can look into the matter further, and at least determine if the scandal is worth the price being charged. We may be able to talk him down a bit. But even if it is something as mundane as an affair (and those are a dime a dozen), I don't think you'll get out of paying him at least something that hurts your pocketbooks." She stared off into the distance for a moment. "It must be at least a tinge more complicated than this. Simple things like infidelity are far above his paygrade. Well, if you can say that about someone who pays themselves."

I shook my head, trying to comprehend the ease with which Sherlock ruled out various possibilities, and the detached manner in which she collected and processed information.

"Something more horrible than an affair?" Eva gasped for breath, her lips opening and closing like a fish. "What in the world could be worth two million dollars? I can't wrap my head around it. What would hurt my public image so much? Why not blackmail him, and go straight to the source?"

The one with the money, she meant.

Sherlock tipped the pen up with a bit of flourish. "And that is the question we seek to answer." She tapped the pen against her bottom lip again, thinking. "Nothing has changed with his habits--neither going in early or staying late. Has anything changed with his behavior at home, or his finances?"

Eva Blackwell shrugged. "Not at home. He takes the dogs to the park a little less, maybe. But it's winter. I really don't want to stand out there with them while they sniff every spot marked by another dog for an hour." She rubbed her forehead, trying to think. "The checking accounts have been the same. No lavish purchases, no suspicious receipts... Sorry. I have had too much time to think about this all day. Why blackmail me? Over something I know nothing about? Why not just go to him, if he is the source of the problem? If it's me, and I'm the problem, why am I not allowed to even know what sort of trouble I am in?"

Rubbing her thumb against the side of the wooden pen, Sherlock nodded, almost sympathetically. But not quite. Because this was Sherlock. "It is definitely something that will cause great embarrassment. That is how he works. Or destroy careers. Or lives." She looked up at the ceiling and nodded, thinking. "That's it, I think. Destroying marriages, public images, careers and lives are probably about all there is to wreck. Or at least to profit from. Unless you're a hitman. But he doesn't like dirty hands--" She cut herself off. "He's definitely not a hitman. If that makes you feel better. He's not killed anyone… well… that anyone else knows of."

Actually killed anyone? That we know of? That didn't reassure me, and I could tell our 'client' was not at all at ease. She opened her mouth to ask for some shred of hope, but Sherlock stood up abruptly, putting her pen away and buttoning her peacoat. "We will look into the matter further tomorrow. What is your deadline for procuring the money for Augustus?"

Eva Blackwell flushed, her lips moving but nothing coming out for a few seconds. "The sixteenth."

Sherlock nodded, working on the button closest to her chin. "I suggest you begin gathering up funds. Remember--I told you when you e-mailed that I would be a negotiator. I am not here to get you out of this, and I am certainly not equipped to topple an empire built on dirty deeds. I'm not sure anyone is, really."

Chapter 13

On the way out the door, I asked why Blackwell was being targeted, if she wasn't the source of the blackmail-able offense. Sure, Eva herself had asked, but maybe Sherlock would actually *tell* me.

Sherlock pulled her gloves on, stretching the soft leather as she moved her fingers around. "She gave none of the usual stressor indicators for lying. There is a certain amount of cold sweating and fidgeting one does even imperceptibly if one has done wrong and is now sorry for being caught, as opposed to the offense in question. But I do know why she was targeted. She has more to lose than her husband, probably. She's not just a clerk. That second desk out front is not for general office business, or another staffer--it is for her own secretary. That much was evident when I rifled through the drawer."

"You are like... dangerous-smart. Just so you know." I was smart. I qualified for every Advanced Placement class the school offered. Sherlock was like a razor blade. She thought faster and concluded faster than I could process a situation and ask a question. I knew when I had met my better.

"Careful, Watson. You will inflate my ego."

I zipped the sweater all the way to my chin. "More than it already is? I'm afraid you'll explode like an overfilled balloon if I go much further."

"A risk I am not willing to take. Only tell me how extraordinary I am in small increments."

The SUV was at the bottom of the driveway, parked on the street, a respectable distance from the office. "So, what did you tell Toby about why we went to the senator's office?"

Sherlock looked at the time on her phone. "He doesn't ask."

"Is he like your bodyguard?" I waved politely as we walked down the sloped drive to the vehicle.

Sherlock glanced over to the car. "Toby? No. He's more of a driver-cum-Jiminy Cricket. He used to try to keep both of us on the straight and narrow. Now he just tries to keep me from ending up in jail."

"Both of us?"

Sherlock's eyes locked with mine, wide and a little glassy. She swallowed, like her stomach was churning. "Nothing. Nevermind. What I mean is--he has given up on most of those things and just tries to keep me in school and not expelled." She chuckled. "I suppose as far as drivers go, he's done a poor job of it. But, well, it was just that once. It's not like expulsion happens every day."

I shoved my hands into the pockets of my jacket. "Seriously? Somehow I can't see you getting expelled only once. I have a feeling you got tossed out of preschool."

Sherlock grinned again, that mischievous thing that went all the way from her lips to her eyes, when so many of her smiles did not. "No, no. But I did get someone else held back a year. I got *him* to eat the paste."

"And he got held back for eating paste? Who didn't eat paste? I thought that's what the paste was there for."

"Oh, no. That wasn't what got him held back. It was when I asked for a sample of his excrement that he got in trouble."

"You did not."

"You can't prove I didn't."

I looked her over critically, hands on my hips. "You're messing with me, Sherlock Holmes. And I'm freezing. Let's just get in the car. Toby's been waiting long enough."

Sherlock didn't move. "But he gets paid to wait for us!"

With a sigh of disgust, I opened the rear passenger door. "I get this sense that manners are not in your wheelhouse. Helpful hint: even if people get paid to wait, it's not polite to make them wait forever." With a harrumph I slammed my butt into the seat and reached for the seat belt.

As if waiting out of spite, Sherlock took a whole minute to get herself into the car and ready to leave. "I'm so sorry you are forced to drive around someone with no common courtesy," I told the driver. He didn't give so much as a grunt of acknowledgment.

"My people are paid well for the indolence they endure from me."

I ran my hand through my short, soft hair, still adjusting to the lack of coverage on my forehead and neck. *Your people?* You have people?"

"I have people. Do you think my family would let me live on my own?"

She lived alone, except for 'her people'? That sounded particularly isolating and awful. Granted, I had been what was delicately termed a 'latch key kid' from the tender age of six, but that was different. It was out of necessity. "Why don't you live with them? If you have family."

She shrugged. "They're busy. They're in other places I don't care for." She leaned forward. "Back home," she told Toby, who pulled away as silently as ever. "And we don't talk. There was a thing once."

"What thing?" Usually only grownups got into grudge-matches that lasted for years and years. What kid held a grudge with family so hard that they didn't actually talk to their family anymore?

"I wouldn't have called it a 'thing' if I had wanted to talk about it."

And that was it. The rest of the ride was completely silent.

##

The sun set even before we got back toward our end of the metro area. By then all I had to look at was the lines in the center of the winding roads as we went past the railroad tracks and the river, where I lived and ever upward into whatever secret places rich people hid. There were also some craggy leafless trees that canopied overhead in some places, like creepy fingers lacing together over the road. I could see dusk through it, then moonlight.

After the moon slid behind the clouds, I just watched my own reflection and the white lines on the side of the road, until we turned up a particularly steep but narrow driveway.

"Home sweet stupid home," Sherlock announced with a sigh.

I opened the door, getting my first look at the place. The front was lit with those exterior architectural lights, showing a dark stone facade and green shutters on either side of the windows. The door was framed in white but painted red, and all the trees were old and tall evergreens, probably meant to hide the property from prying eyes.

I remembered to close the door, somewhere between gawking and noticing that the driveway continued to the side of the house and past, to something that looked like a smaller version of the tall Victorian monstrosity, with the same trim and paint. Only it held multiple garage doors, and some sort of living space on-top.

As soon as we stepped away from the car, Toby pulled away from us, toward the garage thing. We walked up the few shallow brick steps to the front door, and Sherlock pressed down on the thumb latch. "So, here it is. My house." There was something of trepidation in her voice, which seemed odd, considering she clearly had the upper-hand as far as housing went. We'd already explored the deficiencies of mine the night before.

Stepping into the foyer, I looked around at the dark wooden furniture and the iron chandelier hanging overhead. There was a dark, red rug right at the door, and I wiped my feet, pitying whoever it was that cleaned the slate tiles in the entranceway.

Down a short hall, I stepped into a wide living room. I wasn't even sure it was a living room. Maybe a sitting room? Enormous rich-person living space? Looking everything over, from the sofa and the chairs arranged around the enormous fireplace and dark wood mantel, carved in all kinds of scrolling shapes, complete with wooden pillars at the ends. I ventured that I could probably stand, hunched over, in the fireplace. Around the room were various centers of activity. An old-fashioned bureau with a wooden chair sat near a tall glass window, something that looked like a vintage bar set, complete with decanter and highball glasses sitting on a highly reflective silver tray.

There were chairs and plants in various corners of the room, pieces of art and sculpture filling up the space until the entire room was like some sort of nest. "Actual human beings live here? It isn't like a museum or something?"

Sherlock sighed. "Yes, actual human beings live in here, Watson. In fact, I am one of those human beings. Speaking of which..." She unbuttoned her coat. "Mrs. Hudson!" she bellowed through an oversized arched doorway. "I'm home! I have not been arrested, nor have I died in a gutter!" Sherlock tossed her coat onto a wooden chair and ditched her leather satchel next to it.

"That's nice, dear! No warrants out for your arrest then?" The voice was equally forceful, but with some British accent I couldn't place. I knew there were different ones; it was just they all sounded 'foreign' to me, instead of denoting some particular locale.

"Oh, and I brought someone home with me," Sherlock yelled back. "Watson will be staying for dinner."

I unbuttoned my own coat. "I am?" I whispered.

"Of course, you are." Sherlock waved a hand at me to hush. It all seemed so logical in Sherlock-Land. Drag someone home with you, feed them dinner. "Why wouldn't you? You're here. It's nearly dinner time. And we have food. Not eating would be a travesty."

"You brought someone home." The voice was closer this time, echoing off the walls. A moment later, a plump woman with white hair waddled into the room, her arthritis obviously getting the better of her. She dried her wet hands on the bottom of her apron, looking me over. "You've brought someone home." The first time she'd said it, there'd been disbelief. Now there was a question there, the subtext was quite evident. "Why?"

And it hung there. Just like that. Sherlock wanted to defend herself. Mrs. Hudson, once explained to be Sherlock's jailer, wanted to know.

I fidgeted, wondering if things could get any more awkward.

It probably wouldn't. So I decided to be a good goalie and dive for the save. "Sherlock's my lab partner. We're working on a project together."

The woman jabbed a chubby, swollen finger in Sherlock's face. "This had better not be one of your experiments."

Sherlock sighed and rolled her eyes. "I promised I would not do experiments on live test subjects without their written permission. And I have kept to that. And Missy Norstrop didn't need *that* much therapy."

Oh, there was a story here. It seemed like Sherlock was full of stories. Or potential stories. Stories it would be all too fun to hear about and maybe write about. Anonymously, of course. With the names and faces changed to protect the guilty. I could at least type up the story of the master blackmailer with the totally unnecessary and over-kill gun in an upscale department store.

The school literary magazine had not rejected any of my other real-life essay stories so far. And they hadn't really been anything exciting. They would sure eat this stuff up with a spoon.

"I would love to stay," I said as politely as possible. "If you can have me, otherwise, I can have my dad pick me up or something." I had manners and things.

The woman shook her head, then pushed up her round, wire-rimmed glasses that had just a hint of grease clouding them. "No. No. No... We can't let a house guest go! I will set an extra plate! I will make dessert!" She grinned. "It's been far too long since we have had someone around for dinner! A fresh tablecloth.." The woman hobbled away briskly, muttering to herself about things that needed to be done.

It almost began to sound like the 'Be Our Guest' number from *Beauty and the Beast*.

"Don't get many visitors then, I take it?"

Sherlock threw my jacket overtop of mine. "Don't be obtuse, Watson. Of course, we don't get many visitors, I am hardly the social type. A few people come for Mrs. Hudson once in awhile. And there is Wayne who brings the groceries and the gossip. Mrs. Hudson likes that. I can't say I blame her for that. The world thrives on gossip, really." She grabbed the banister of the short, tight stairwell in the room behind the huge receiving area.

I followed, mostly because I didn't want to get lost in a house like this. "You like gossip?" I headed up the steps, taking fast turns like a long-time pro.

"It has its uses. The secret gossip news network can spread information faster than a wild fire."

The stairwell got darker the higher it went. "It gets closer at the top. Sorry. Old servant's steps. Bypasses the second floor and goes straight to the attic."

Of course the house formerly had servants. And of course there were quarters for said servants. "What's up there now?"

Sherlock pulled a skeleton key out of her pocket. "Me." Unlocking the door, she turned the crystal knob that led to another final flight of steps, this one shorter than the rest. "I moved my room up here, well. Years ago. I needed more room in which to spread out."

Coming up the final few steps, I saw why. The room was crammed in every space with something--old mixed with new. A bed neatly made and tucked up against a sloped wall. A bay window with a chair, a small round table, and a dangling skeleton. Bookshelves covered nearly every wall. And in the center, an old, scratched-up dining room table crammed with modern lab equipment. Sherlock hadn't been kidding--the blood typing project was definitely well below her own means. "Wow!"

Sherlock kicked off her shoes in front of a cupboard. "It's just stuff, Watson. Currently, it suits my needs."

I walked around, giving myself the tour. There were other things I'd missed at first glance: the chipped and broken gargoyle being held up and straightened by a stack of books, a black-and-gold Pirates baseball cap hanging lazily off of one ear; antique medical equipment on the wall next to the skeleton; a strange assortment of new and old things; plaques on the walls made out to people other than Sherlock; tiny pewter cannons in front of books on bookshelves; new books on modern forensic techniques mixed with everything from histories of execution methods to a grave robber's handbook. The desk near one of the windows had a bellows rigged to stand upright on its own, rows of cigarettes and their respective ashes filed in small Mylar envelopes probably meant to preserve old baseball cards.

A rug sat under the table, complete with chemical stains, papers, portfolios and file folders everywhere, and a trunk at the foot of the bed with a scarf and a new pair of shoes sitting atop of it and to the left, probably where Sherlock sat to get dressed in the morning.

Out of curiosity, I knocked on one of the bookshelves. The sound it made was deep and muted, solid wood.

Unsurprising, of course. There'd be no hand-me-down Ikea furniture in here. I was curious as to the function of the displaced bright yellow beanbag in the corner near the potted plants that I was sure contained actual pot. "What's up with this?"

Sherlock sat down at the computer on the desk next to one of her experiments. "It's where I hide my contraband. She never thinks of looking in here."

"Contraband? Do I even want to know?"

"Probably not. It's all illegal, and you are the daughter of an officer of the law. I would suggest leaving things as they are, for now. Just don't try to sit on the chair. I think I found all the packets of poisonous spores. But you never know."

"Great. Awesome. Thank you. Good advice." Sherlock was mad. I had known that from our first conversation. And yet here we were, having a conversation about poisonous spores while I wore clothes worth more than my dad's last pay check. It all made perfect sense, if you took into account that my lab partner was utterly bonkers. And I had definitely stuck my toe into the pool of crazy before jumping right in. "What exactly are we doing here at your house? I mean--I know we're regrouping or working on the case or whatever. But can we get to that before I have to go? My dad is very seriously serious about curfew, just so you know."

Sherlock flopped onto her bed, then began tapping the pen against her lip again. "We need a strategy, Watson. We need a method of attack."

"And we're going to find that here." In this macabre, fixated bedroom of a future serial killer? I only even thought that because the only poster on Sherlock's wall graphically denoted the differences in various types of human skeletons.

"This is where I work, Watson. It's where I think. I am going to formulate a plan for how to effectively manage spying on Eva's husband tomorrow--a schedule, if you will--and you are going to sit there as quietly as possible."

"Glad to hear I am such an intricate and valuable part of the process." I frowned and looked for a chair with the least amount of stuff covering it, then plopped myself right onto the papers and folders.

Sherlock opened one eye and glanced in my direction. "I need someone who understands how to navigate the public transit system."

"You are pathetic," I muttered, pulling out my phone to check messages for the first time since I had stepped into Sherlock's car in front of the school. Nothing. Not a single text from my father, or from Michael and/or Will. Not even a message mocking me for spending so much time with 'New Girl.'

"I will show you how to use the stupid bus tomorrow. Because I plan on writing up this whole weird adventure and submitting it to the school literary journal. And I'm sure everyone will be pleased to know that there is yet another rich kid living up on the hill who has absolutely no idea how to navigate the real world. I ought to be charging you for this, honestly."

Sherlock said nothing, but conveyed through her usual dismissive hand gesture that it was of no importance to her. "Send me a bill if you like. Just hush."

With nothing better to do, I pulled one of the folders out from beneath my backside and began flipping through it. Open and shut, a suicide, really. Gunshot wound, so it was extra messy, and lacking enough material for an open-casket funeral.

Why did Sherlock have them, even? It wasn't solved or unsolved, really. The coroner had signed off on it, and that was good enough for me. There didn't even seem to be anything fishy about the situation. Just some poor fellow with issues and access to a gun.

What was it that Sherlock hoped to learn from these sorts of cases? I pulled another out from beneath me. It was accidental. Or appeared to be. Nothing as messy as a gun. The good old classic asphyxiation. They appeared to have choked to death on a Happy Meal toy. The college student had been dared to put as many into his mouth as humanly possible. It was a stupid way to die, even if it provided a decent laugh.

I pulled one off the floor, and it was also pretty open and shut, as far as my meager understanding of law enforcement went. If I read enough of them, I could probably write a book on ridiculous ways to die.

The others from the floor ranged from unfortunate deaths and dismemberments to robberies, car collisions and abductions. It ran the gamut of crimes that could probably be deemed 'interesting' by someone like Sherlock Holmes.

She probably studied them. Or tried to solve them. No telling, really. I glanced over at the bed. Sherlock was still in some sort of trance-like state, with her hands steepled and resting on her chest. As many questions as I had, I wouldn't be getting answers to them any time soon.

Bored, I started pushing things around on the table next to me. Under papers and some long, dried-out tobacco leaves was a ceramic bowl, filled with tiny miscellaneous things. A single pearl earring, no backguard. Two faded ticket stubs for a cartoon movie that had been in theaters at least five years ago. An old-looking pin for a fraternity that I vaguely recognized as being for the medical profession.

There was a bit of dust at the bottom, and two tiny ceramic frogs, one green, the other dark blue. I turned over the green one. 'Sherly' was scratched into the white bottom. The other had 'Sherry' in another childish script.

On the other side of the oversized room, Sherlock sat up suddenly, and I dropped the frogs back into the ceramic bowl with a high-pitched but forceful clang. "Sorry. Just looking."

Sherlock scowled. "Not at those things." She swallowed something painful and dangerously angry, her nose flaring. "Did you learn anything?"

I let out a slow breath, not entirely sure how to respond. "You like frogs?"

"No. I don't."

Who was Sherry? I was desperate to ask, but I had enough tact to know when to keep my mouth shut.

I shuffled some of the folders into something resembling order while I thought of what to say next. "Do you have any ideas?" That sounded fairly neutral.

"Plenty of ideas--but an extreme lack of data. What I have contrived is a method by which we shall acquire the data necessary to understand what our client is bargaining for. After that, I may be able to get the price lowered, depending on how magnanimous Augustus is feeling on any given day. Then we collect our fee, and we are on our way."

I sat up straight. "Fee?"

"Everyone has expenses, Watson. Even a freelance consultant."

"Is that..." Ethical? I wanted to ask. "Decided upon before or after you solve the case?"

Sherlock shrugged. "The fee is the same for everyone unless I choose to charge nothing at all, which I do when the client is sufficiently pathetic, or the case sufficiently interesting."

Folding my arms over my chest, I mulled it over. "How many times have you done this? How many cases have you had?"

Sherlock shrugged. "Since I have started leaving cards with clients, I've had an uptake in business from word of mouth."

She probably did know how many clients she'd had, down to the decimal point. But I suppose that would have taken away from the mystery of it all. "You do know how to make other people feel like they've done nothing with their lives thus far."

"Oh, don't be like that." She pulled off her vest and began unbuttoning her shirt. "We--I started when I was eight. You just have some catching up to do."

Before I could ask what in the world that meant, the door at the bottom of the steps creaked open. "Dinner's ready. I won't take no for an answer," Mrs. Hudson's voice boomed up the steps and echoed on the angled bedroom walls. "Wash up, two minutes."

Sherlock shrugged as she tossed the white shirt away, no care for partial nudity in the company of others. "I suppose my plan will have to wait until later. Mrs. Hudson is far too firm about dinner, and dislikes the idea of my consulting. Well, dislike is less harsh than her true feelings. Despises? Wishes I would give up on the whole thing and become a proper boring person who hosts parties and fundraisers like our dear Eva? Either way…" She headed for the steps wearing a crisp new shirt. "I would rather die."

My eyes narrowed. That was… an odd way to phrase it.

It seemed like I now needed to keep an eye out for a death wish on the part of my lab partner.

##

Ok. I have to admit to having a tremor of terror when we came downstairs and passed through an enormous dining room. At rough estimate, the table appeared to be able to seat forty-two. There was something really uncomfortable about the idea of sitting in a room like that, with deep red carpets and sideboards filled with crystal and silver.

Much to my relief, we settled in the kitchen. While still grandiose (there were two ovens and two ranges, in addition to an enormous industrial stainless steel refrigerator), and it was bigger than two of the rooms in my house combined. It was still smaller than that dining room, and therefore instantly felt smaller and cosier. It was also modern, stainless steel everything, light stone flooring and a round wooden table cast over near the bay window where the plants hung. The other rooms had been so dark and old and smelled too much like wood polish and wax. The kitchen was much better.

I sat down and thanked the woman. Sherlock continued to look quite imposed upon. I waited a moment, trying to be polite, but eventually I dug into the chicken and dumplings in a thick sauce. Something homey, and not entirely what I had been expecting. I'd been prepared for something unidentifiable and requiring more utensils than I could classify. I liked being mistaken for the better.

I was half done with my bowl before anyone said anything. Mrs. Hudson found her tongue. "How is your project going?" She had that overly sweet tone of voice that my father had when certain subjects came up. "Will we be seeing more of you, Ms. Watson?"

Oh god. I wanted to tell the woman no. There would be no grandchildren yet. "Things are going well. I think I am supposed to come over Saturday to work on part of it, at least. We're making some good headway, though."

We hadn't done so much as crack open a book, or discuss the division of labor.

"Oh good. It's nice to see Sherlock working with someone again. I hope she's been behaving herself. Being polite."

Sherlock blushed, just a little bit, then suddenly invested herself in her food.

"Oh yeah. A perfect lady. We've been having a good time working on it." I filled my mouth with two large dumplings before anyone asked me to elaborate.

"She's a bit of a wild child, this one." Mrs. Hudson smiled affectionately at Sherlock. Perhaps their relationship wasn't as adversarial as Sherlock had led me to believe. "Don't let her get you into any trouble. Especially trouble that could land either of you in jail."

Sherlock just rolled her eyes.

"I will try, ma'am."

The old woman sighed. "That's all I can hope for."

"Did her, uh--" I frowned, putting down my spoon. "The last person she worked with." Mrs. Hudson had said 'again' after all. "They're not around anymore? Did they move away or something?"

Sherlock's jaw clenched, and she looked away, turning her entire body from the table. The wrong question had been asked. That much was evident now.

The older woman shook her head sadly. "Much worse." And she let it hang there, not elaborating further.

I was having trouble imagining 'worse.' "Did you have to bail her out a bunch of times?"

"Something like that. Finish your peas." The woman pointed with her spoon at the neat stack on the side of my wide bowl.

So much for getting around eating the little veggies that just so happened to have the same texture as pill bugs. I stared at them, and wondered if there was a polite way to say that I had a complex about eating peas after an incident in my childhood that involved the actual consumption of a pill bug,

I was just about to say something about being allergic or something when Sherlock got up from her spot at the table, the heavy wooden chair scraping against the stone tiled floor. She left without pronouncement or permission, and headed to some unknown part of the house that I had not been acquainted with thus far.

"Is she ok?"

"Oh, we just don't talk about it. Even though it's been a few years now. It puts her in a mood every time it comes up. Give her a bit."

"What puts her in a mood?"

Standing, Mrs Hudson grabbed her own bowl, and then Sherlock's, taking them to the sink. "She'll tell you when she's ready, dear."

"Is this about the person she used to work on cases with?"

Turning from the sink, the old woman's eyes crinkled with a weary sadness. "It is. Just give it time. She doesn't like it when I talk about it with outsiders. I suppose you'll have to wait for her to loosen up."

"I don't think Sherlock has ever relaxed in her life."

Mrs. Hudson then took my bowl as well to the sink. "Well, she's taken to you quite thoroughly. I think you will do her some good." Turning on the tap, she didn't look back or speak to me again.

When I couldn't stand the awkwardness any further, I pushed my chair slowly from the table, and went in the direction Sherlock had headed off in, only with absolutely no idea where she'd gone after that.

The back of the house was, well… different. There were other rooms with closed doors, a long hall that was mostly ill-lit, and another large room that seemed to make no sense. The hallway did not branch off, or come back around to the front of the house again, so I simply followed it to the end.

There was a double set of glass doors that led to a room that was mostly glass. The windows were fogged over, but there were plants inside, tall trees with thick, waxy leaves. The incandescent bulbs along the sides created a shadowy, misty atmosphere. The amber lights that didn't seem to penetrate the middle of the room, leaving everything grey and brown. Metal furniture, including tables and chairs were scattered around the room.

A stiff, tree-like figure sat in one, elbow on the table, hand on hip and one leg locked under the chair, and the other slightly forward, looking like a painting of some sort of Byronic hero.

I slowly opened the door, but not silently. It seemed like the best way not to startle someone out of their thoughts. Walking up to another chair, I stood behind it, waiting for Sherlock to say something.

But Sherlock just continued to rub her two fingers against her thumb, as if flicking crumbs from them. She just carried on with the action and she stared forward blankly at trees and glass.

"Tonight," she said in a dull, hushed tone. "I will sleep over at your house. If I stay at home, Toby will drive me to school. This will not do, since we need to follow the husband. He gets the bus from a park-and-ride near your house. Staying at your home is the most efficient use of our time." Her tone was even and emotionless, and the words trotted out at such an even pace, I almost wasn't even sure it was Sherlock for a moment.

"My dad doesn't let me have people over on weeknights," I said in the same muted tone.

"He doesn't need to know."

"I will think of something," I promised. Quietly, I pulled out the metal chair and sat down, watching Sherlock. "So we follow him to work. Then what happens?"

Sherlock continued staring ahead, eyes slightly out of focus. "We will investigate his day. The hours he keeps. The people he visits with. His actual job title and responsibilities. An affair is unlikely. Or Augustus would have gone to the husband directly. I'm still unclear as to why, if this has to do with the husband, Augustus would go to the wife. That is not his usual style. He's a slippery one, Watson. And the best we can do is to mitigate the damage."

I nodded. "It's... weird, isn't it? All of this?" Having a gun on you. Skipping school with absolutely no discussion of the matter to spy on a man you'd never met. Sherlock led down some interesting paths, if nothing else. "I mean--never mind." My shoulders slumped. "I'm sorry about before. Whoever it was--whatever. We don't need to talk about it. But if you want to…" Saying I'd be there for Sherlock, to listen, was more than trite or banal. It was partially offensive. It didn't seem like we had known each other long enough for that yet.

Still twirling her fingers and staring off into the distance, Sherlock explained exactly how it was going to be. "We don't need to bring it up ever again. That would be sufficient." If she wanted to live in the happy land of denial, or a world where she'd put that person away, filed on some corner shelf only to be taken out and dusted off during more emotionally stable times. Maybe I'd get the real story someday.

I nodded, willing to play the game, since I was the one who had put my foot in it, earlier. "I need to text my dad and make sure it's ok for you to stay over tonight."

"Watson," she said quietly. "It's better to beg for forgiveness than to ask for permission."

Nodding, I pushed my finger back and forth against the glass table. "This room is a nice, uh… atrium? Plant room? Is it a good place for thinking?"

"It used to be," Sherlock whispered, slowly getting to her feet. "I'll shower here. Pack a bag. I shouldn't be more than twenty minutes."

"That's one hell of a short shower." My brother used to tell me about the timed showers when they were deployed in places that didn't have running water. But Sherlock seemed to be taking that one step further.

Sherlock smiled at the compliment. "I can be out in under four minutes, if necessary. And sometimes, it used to be."

Without waiting for my reaction, or for me to follow, Sherlock left.

Chapter 14

I was so glad that my room was relatively clean. It hadn't been vacuumed in ages, but there were no dirty clothes in piles since my dad had forced me to do laundry last weekend. The usual pile of sports equipment was in the corner, none of it put away from last season. Half of it was on a chair, the other half under it. I could lie and say it looked purposeful, in a pinch.

My desk contained an old hand-me-down laptop and stacks of papers and books. Some were fiction, some were articles or things that I'd found interesting regarding the human body. My current fixation was trauma surgery. Before that it had been physical abnormalities. When I looked over my own desk surface, I knew I had no right to judge Sherlock's room, or the skeleton in the corner of the bay window up there, yellowed and etched with an accession number, and gathering dust.

"This is my room. Not as cool as yours. But it's a place to sleep and keep stuff." I frowned. "I guess you can sleep here, and I will sleep on the sofa. But I'll still have to explain to my dad why I am down there." I put my hands on my hips, searching for an alternative. "Or you can sleep down there and I will still have to explain why you are here. I guess I can sleep on the floor in here…"

Sherlock rolled her eyes and took out a long night shirt and matching silk pants in a light grey. "Your bed is big enough for both of us, unless you flop around like a fish in the night. Then you have to explain nothing to anyone." Again she began stripping right in front of me. A shirt was one thing.

But when Sherlock went for the bra, I spun around awkwardly and started tidying up my bedside table.

"It's just nudity, Watson. We've all got the same basic parts."

Somehow I had expected someone who dressed as conservatively as Sherlock to have a slightly stuffier view of body politics.

"You may turn around. I am once again fully clothed."

Turning, I still couldn't bring myself to look at her, so I pulled back the blankets. I'd already changed--in the bathroom--about fifteen minutes prior. "I haveta sleep on this side so I can turn off the alarm."

Sherlock didn't seem to have an opinion on the matter. She pulled the wet bun out of the back of her hair and braided it with fast, deft hands, affixed it, then climbed into bed. She rolled over onto her side, hugging the edge of the bed.

"You can move closer to the middle if you want."

"No, no. This will do." Sherlock readjusted the pillow under her head and wiggled to get comfortable, then stopped, as if comfort had been achieved.

Wondering if that were actually the case, I shut off the light and sunk into my own pillow, exhausted. Shopping, and men with guns, and accidentally disrupting the emotional order of a household did that to people.

"Good night, Watson."

I smiled to myself, closing my eyes. "Good night, Holmes."

##

The morning had been a little awkward. At some point in the middle of the night, I had flipped around to face Sherlock's back, and we were now sharing a pillow.

I crept my head back to my own pillow as slowly and quietly as I dared, hoping not to wake Sherlock. I had a habit of waking a few minutes before the alarm, and that held true today. I was thankful. There was no telling what Sherlock would read into the situation.

"If you're awake, I suppose we could shut off the alarm. I don't particularly want to hear that sound."

"Crap," I muttered, rolling over toward the edge of the bed and grabbing for my phone. I turned off both the regular alarm and the emergency alarm. "What am I wearing?" I asked as I rolled out of bed, hopefully making it to the bathroom before my houseguest.

Sherlock shot up and got to the door before I could even contemplate putting my feet under me and getting up. "Similar to yesterday. The rest of the clothes won't be delivered until later today, so I had them bag up something and put it in with your old and retired clothes."

"Retired? I like my--"

"Retired. They're awful. And I need you to look like a college student, or recently graduated. Looking forward to medical school."

"I'm sixteen. No one is going to believe that."

"Our client believed it last night." Turning on her heels, she dashed off for the bathroom, ending that conversation.

A minute later she returned, face freshly washed and long hair combed out into a very adult-ish sort of wave. "We're going into the business district in broad daylight, so we'll have to wear makeup."

"Not my favorite thing." Of course, my whole life had slipped out of my comfort zone at some point this week. "I'm not even good at putting it on. The last time I wore makeup-- that wasn't last night, it was my grandmother's funeral."

She stared at me for a moment, wheels turning. "You wore a dead woman's makeup to her own funeral." I didn't want to know how she had surmised that from what I had said. "It wasn't like she was using it. Besides, they airbrushed the hell out of her till she looked like a wax figure in a museum. It wasn't like a little four-year-old Revlon was going to make a difference." I still kept the lipstick in the bottom of my top drawer. It smelled like her.

Sherlock's hand went to her stomach and she laughed, perhaps too loudly. "See, Watson, that's the spirit! Practicality above purpose of sentimentality and custom."

I finally stood up, pulling one of the blankets with me. My room was a touch on the cold side. "I'm sure there's a compliment in there somewhere." I frowned. "You know, I didn't feel weird about it until just now."

Sherlock grinned. "I like you so very much, Watson."

I wanted to ask exactly what the hell that meant, but by then Sherlock was going through her bag, getting clothes out, and then on and off with no respect for my (apparently) delicate sensibilities. I just hoped my dad didn't wake up during all these shenanigans. It was too early for reasonable explanations.

After she was dressed, Sherlock pulled a department store bag seemingly out of nowhere. "Wear the grey shoes again. The jeans worked, so here's a pair in another color. Slightly warmer sweater, though. You'll need it." She tossed the items onto the bed.

I picked up the pair of thick socks that had bounced off the clothing and had landed on a ripple in the blanket. "And what're these for?"

"I hate your socks," she said simply. "Also, I anticipated the shoes not being broken in properly, and I also saw you looking at the red marks on your toes. Deduction is a science. It's not a mystery. Now I have my own things to do," she answered smartly, getting out her own makeup container. It was a leather box that looked more like a theater kit than anything the girls around the high school carried. I had never really bothered with makeup. It sweated off in gym or rugby or running, so it seemed pointless to apply multiple times a day.

"Do I get to make any decisions for myself ever again?"

Sherlock shrugged, sitting at my desk with the box. "I'm sure at some point." She waved me off. "Shower, blow dry until slightly damp. If you dry it all the way, your hair will become crisp and unbearable with lack of moisture. Once damp, add the product as you were shown yesterday to add lift and hopefully it will not require further styling." She smeared a white line of goop under her eyelids and blended it to her cheek bones.

"For someone who doesn't care about the feminine aesthetics, you sure do know a lot about it."

"It's part of the art of disguise. Go. Before I have any other suggestions."

My shower took far too long. Longer than normal. I was lost in thought, and a hundred different kinds of worry. Somehow blackmail and a man with a gun had taken up the same amount of headspace for me as the worry I felt for putting on makeup and remembering all forty-two steps that

I had been shown yesterday toward being a brighter, shinier me.

I dumped out way too much shampoo. I wasn't used to having so little hair. I would have to wear scarves while jogging. That sounded particularly awful. But it would have to be done, now that I had no hair to cover my neck. Sweaty scarves turning frozen in the cold. That was pretty bad. As bad as the blackmailer and the makeup.

Priorities, Watson. Priorities. Some things were worse than others. Probably.

The water started to go cold, and I shut it off quickly, getting out and dried as fast as I could. Standing in front of the medicine cabinet mirror, I looked myself over. I did kind of have cheekbones and a jawline now. I supposed that was good. But Sherlock had a full head of long hair to hide behind. Obviously, she didn't understand that there were times when one needed a curtain between oneself and the world.

Trying to comb out the short hair, I realized how stupid it was--my usual comb tines were too far apart. I found my father's comb and went after it, pushing all the hair on top of my head forward, and then putting that expensive goop into it. I didn't see the difference with the goop or not, really. Hopefully someone else would, and make this transformation worth it.

Putting on the clothes I had been issued, I tromped back to the bedroom. Sherlock was still messing with makeup. I watched her for a minute -- huge white and dark smudges around her face in configurations I wasn't ready to understand. She had been working on this while I took my twenty-minute shower?

"Watson, don't stare. Some of us were not blessed with a feminine face."

171

I looked away, toward the bed, then grabbed the socks and shoes,clutching them to my chest as something to hide behind. "I think you look fine."

"Yes, thank you. But I don't."

"Learn how to take a compliment." I flopped down on the bed, and then started with the first sock.

I expected something snarky from Sherlock. We did have that sort of rapport, but she turned on the chair at my desk with slow intention and frowned at me. "Really?"

"Yeah. You look fine without makeup. It suits you."

Turning back around slowly, she began dabbing a new color onto her face. "Well, thank you," she muttered, almost to herself.

I looked at the makeup she had meticulously set out on my dresser. "I only vaguely remember where to start with this stuff. Foundation, right?"

"Moisturizer," she reminded me absently.

Great. Which one was that? I stared at the bottles, wondering which one to pick up first.

"Just give me a minute. I will help you. Before you irreparably destroy your face."

"Thanks?"

"I need that face to get me into a bank today. Uh... I meant..."

"I know what you mean." How did a human exist in the world without ever learning and utilizing tact? Maybe instead of trying to play detective with blackmailers asking for two million dollars, I should do a study in Sherlock. One seemed like it would be more educational (and safer) than the other.

When she was finally done, Sherlock got up and came over to the dresser. I blinked a few times. She looked... kind of like those TV hosts that reported on celebrity news, except her eye makeup wasn't quite that dark. "You look like ten years older."

"Fifteen if I'm lucky." She handed me a bottle with a pump. "Moisturizer. Or your skin will crack between the makeup and the dry air."

After that, it only took about five minutes to make me look older. One layer of blush, Two shades of powder, three shades of eyeshadow, three applications of mascara and a nearly invisible lip gloss and I was done. I looked at myself in the mirror hanging from my wall precariously. "I am not as done up as you." Honestly, it felt like I was wearing nothing comparatively.

"You need to look seven years older." That was all she said, then grabbed her coat off the chair where my sports equipment had collected.

That was really all the explanation I got. And perhaps all I really expected.

After that, we were out the door faster than I'd ever been in my life. There'd been no lingering. There hadn't even been breakfast.

We'd headed out to the alley and took the seven steps down to the sidewalk. I pointed up the street. "Down to Fifth, a right at Main, then quarter of a mile past the turn-on for the highway, which is always fun to cross on foot during the rush hour. Then we wait." I was close enough to the park-and-ride, but less close than I would like to be on a day like today. It was only November and way too early in the season for this.

With the cold wind hitting my face, despite the faux fur of the new puffy brown coat that obviously wasn't my usual sensibility, I wanted nothing more than something hot and caffeinated. I never had time in the morning for it, but

173

today was a special day. The day I skipped school and possibly ruined my academic career. I shoved my hands into the pockets of the foreign coat, and tried to make myself as small as possible against the wind.

""So," I muttered between clenched teeth as we walked down the old, rust-stained sidewalks. "This plan. Do I get to know it now?"

Sherlock tugged on her black leather gloves, pulling them up against the wind. The air wasn't particularly bitter, but the breeze coming off the hills was dry and cutting. "Nothing especially challenging at this juncture. We walk to the park-and-ride, and we ride."

I squinted sideways at Sherlock for half a block as we headed in the direction of the bus stop in question. "Seriously? This is what took an hour for you to come up with last night?"

A moan escaped Sherlock. "There are other steps in the plan. Don't be willfully dense." With that she picked up her pace.

I took a few quick steps to launch myself after her and her terribly long legs. "What are they?"

Securing the top button of her long black coat, she remained silent until she was done with it, adequately adjusted the back of the collar to cover her long neck. "When the time comes. For now, it is need-to-know."

I folded my arms over the chest of the puffy coat. "Let me guess, I don't need to know. Awesome."

A bright grin lit up Sherlock's entire face. "That would take away the fun of the surprise!"

"Somehow I suspect your idea of a fun surprise is vastly divergent from mine."

We made the walk in what I guessed to be a typical amount of time. Getting across the entrance ramp for the highway was a bit tricky, but we made it without being killed. I figured some river rat's luck would run out eventually, and there'd be a mess to clean up. Of course, if some kid like Sherlock found herself splattered all over the entrance ramp, there'd be a light at the intersection installed immediately. I wasn't being jaded. That's how these things worked.

We beat our client's husband to the bus stop, which left us milling around innocently, not really watching our target as he eventually walked over to the shelter.

I bounced on my feet a bit, trying to restore some warmth to my legs. Even I knew there needed to be a layer of air between trousers, especially jeans, and the skin, in order to hold heat. That whole 'skinny jean' thing may have looked appealing (even to me, now that I was wearing them) but it was less than practical. No matter how flattering the jeans looked.

I stared into the stream of my own breath for a bit, but that got old fast. "We've followed. Now what's the next step?"

"We get on whatever bus he gets on."

"Yeah, I guessed that part, MENSA."

Sherlock grinned. "You're funny when you're sarcastic."

My lip twisted. "Is that sarcasm?"

Sherlock held up a hand. "God's honest truth," she vowed.

Before I could come up with some sort of clever or memorable retort, a bus pulled into the parking area and over to the shelter. A handful of people got on, including the man we were following. We almost missed getting on the bus because we had waited too long. The driver was closing the door when we suddenly appeared with apologetic grins.

He let us on, but probably started to get annoyed with us again when I paid for both of us primarily in nickels.

Sherlock led us to the middle of the bus, all the better to keep an eye on our client's husband. He was in the seat just behind the ones intended for the elderly and handicapped. Well, at least he wasn't a total douchebag, whatever he was up to.

Sherlock observed for several minutes before commenting. "Self-important. Not enough that he would be the guy who sits in the reserved seating. But if he could get away with it, he would, in a heartbeat. Proud. Look at the coat. Not a speck of dust, or animal hair. Haircuts every three weeks." She bit her cheek and frowned, trying to figure something out. "Stubble. Didn't have time to shave properly? Shoddy electric razor? Doesn't fit the profile of someone climbing the corporate ladder through any means possible, including those that would mean dubious dealings." One gloved finger tapped her lips. "This has just gotten interesting."

"And it wasn't before?" I whispered. Two days ago she'd been doing jumping jacks at the prospect of going up against a prolific blackmailer, even if it was just in an advisory capacity. Hell, yesterday we'd had a gun pulled on us. And only now it was getting interesting?

I was letting go of the idea that Sherlock was utterly bonkers, and was latching onto the idea that Sherlock was either an alien, or was from a dimension slightly out of phase with our own. Well, at least, I had my next literary magazine piece. I was tired of writing about my semi-dramatic childhood. Trying to figure out which planet Sherlock came from would be far more fun. 'My Life with a High School Alien.'

The bus stopped again for the fifth time in five minutes, letting passengers on and off. Public transit was annoying.

My companion gave my leg a quick double-pat. "Oh, Watson. I have an entire tiered system of levels of interest, puzzle complexity and cases which are merely a notch on the bedpost, if you will. I try to avoid the latter, but in this case, it is now shaping up to contain all three elements. It's extraordinary." She clenched her gloved fingers together in such excitement they were trembling. "This is so much better than a missing giant duck."

"Except with the rubber duck there was a lot less chance of getting…" I whispered, "shot. You know that man had a gun on us yesterday. That isn't normal. Normal people are supposed to be terrified of that sort of thing." I winced. I hadn't been quite as terrified as I thought I ought to have been.

Sherlock held her hands in front of her, but her index fingers were pointed upward, resting on her lips. "It was an antique Derringer. Odds were probably about even that it would blow up in his hand, as to actually hitting either of us. It didn't look particularly well cared for. And it only had two shots. It wasn't like he was going to go on a killing spree. It isn't like he could have fired that gun and made it out of the shop. It's entirely to his disadvantage to kill or maim us in the ladies' dressing room section of a well-attended department store." She shrugged. "If he kills us, he has no one to play his little game with. It was all smoke and mirrors and intimidation tactics."

"Game? Seriously? This is a game to you?" Screw the separate plane of reality. Sherlock was back to being nuts in my mind.

"Not to me, Watson. To him. He is at the top of his art. He's blackmailed everyone from socialites to celebrities to ambassadors. He's bored."

"Right. Bored enough to play with school kids."

Sherlock tilted her head lower and closer to me, since this was not a conversation for prying ears. "He's going after the bottom feeders in a place where he is bound to be noticed. If I had not caught wind of the situation, I am ninety percent certain my brother would have, and then his game would have really reached new stakes."

Her brother? Well, everybody had to have family, I guess. He sounded somewhat important, I supposed. I wanted to ask her about him, or, at least, have a witty comeback, but I was fresh out. This 'game' thing was too weird for me to figure out the purpose of. Who cared if a teenager was involved? Did Sherlock's reputation really go that far? Having a bunch of business cards hardly made one a top professional in the field. "I guess I will have to defer to your superior judgement."

"Good idea, Watson. It means you are smart and have excellent taste."

Right.

Our target reached up and tugged on the yellow cord at the stop before the one where nearly everyone would get off. I slid out of the seat, Sherlock after me. We hurried down the steps off the bus and out into the street, which was full-up with early morning commuters trying to hide against the wind.

As soon as we were off, we scanned the crowd for the man. Unfortunately, he was of average height and build and whiteness level, so he looked a hell of a lot like everyone dashing across the streets, entering tall buildings with glass-encased lobbies and vanishing among the marble and steel.

Just when I was accepting defeat--that we'd lost the guy before we'd even discovered what he was up to, Sherlock pointed. "There." And sure enough as far as we could tell, it was our man, ducking into a public parking garage two full blocks from where he worked.

Heels clacking as we crossed the street, Sherlock still managed a fair clip, as far as speed went, even in the uncomfortable shoes. I was almost surprised I could keep up. We both slid near the entrance to the garage.

There was a ramp that twisted around the whole parking building, all the way to the roof. And from what I could see, no connecting buildings. "You take the ramp," I ordered, looking at Sherlock's fancy shoes. "I have the stairs."

Without waiting for permission or confirmation, I took off for the rested metal door on the ground floor of the garage and ran as hard as I could, up the chipped yellow-painted steps, feeling the burn above my knee. My current workout routine absolutely had to increase after this, if I was going to continue hanging out with Sherlock.

My lungs burned in the cold air, but I made it to the top in record time, with no sight of our client's husband.

"Damn," I huffed, looking around at the empty top level of the garage. Spending precious seconds catching my breath, I took off running down the ramp, toward Sherlock. Cars passed me, going up toward the empty spots, and a few of the drivers looked at me like I might be insane, but I didn't care. I watched each of their faces to be sure none were our man, and continued barreling downward.

I made it down two levels before I finally saw my friend. We were at opposite ends of a ramped level where we both came to a skidding halt on the oil-stained cement incline, both of us with our arms raised in a question neither of us had the breath to ask.

I walked the rest of the way down to Sherlock, who was not moving from her spot. My legs felt like they were on fire from the unexpected exertion, and my lungs would have prefered less biting weather, but the endorphin rush was great. I hadn't felt like that in ages.

By the pressed line of Sherlock's lips, and the flair of her nose, I could tell that Sherlock was not similarly high from the case. She just kept looking around her, trying to figure out where things had gone wrong.

Still trying to catch my breath when I made it to Sherlock, I put my hands on my knees and bent over for a few seconds to force the air into and out of my lungs. "We lost him? There's only one way in and out!"

Sherlock shook her head. "We lost him. How the hell did we lose... argggggg!" She reached down and took off a shoe, throwing it at the silver Lexis across from us, letting out another primordial sound mixed with a string of curses. When the shoe with the sharply pointed toe and thin modest heel hit the car, the alarm went off.

Chapter 15

The car alarm echoed in the winding cement structure. Sherlock paid it no mind, and howled again. "I'm never wearing shoes like this ever again. I don't care what the consequences are!"

I'm sure the shoes hadn't helped, but they couldn't have been solely to blame.

Rushing over to blaring the car, I snatched the shoe, wiping the small black mark off the bumper. I looked around quickly to see if anyone had noticed. There wasn't a soul around, and even I was smart enough to know to look for cameras in the usual places; there were none.

"Great," I breathed, handing Sherlock back her shoe. "Now we need to get out of here before someone asks why we're vandalizing cars." An old Buick passed us, and we smiled and I waved. "You didn't see him in any of the cars that went past?"

Sherlock slid her shoe back on, eyes narrowing and an evil look spreading across her face. "No, Watson. I never thought of that. Of course, I was looking at the interior of each vehicle. None were our man." The car alarm sounded in angry tones that almost met hers.

"Ok, ok. Calm down. We'll figure something out." I held out an awkward hand and almost gave her a pat on the shoulder, but I think we both knew it would be too weird. Instead, I settled for an insincere smile. "You're smarter than this guy, aren't you?"

The scowl I received in reply was priceless. "I'm smarter than most of you."

"And extremely modest too." I walked past Sherlock slowly, finally getting my wind back, and headed down the parking garage's ramp structure. I stared rudely inside every single car that passed by, a few people scowling when they looked back at me. The garage was filled with every type of car--the expensive ones, like the car Sherlock had assaulted with her shoe (the alarm was still sounding in the background, now several levels up), minivans with multiple car seats in the back, cheap sedans filled with the contents of the average student--textbooks and fast food wrappers, and the clunkers held together by layers of pollution and hope.

There'd even been a service van on the second floor that had looked especially pathetic in that area--a dragging tailpipe held up by wire ties, a dented and rusting exterior that had been white, but had long since gone grey with city grime. Even the logo of the business was very nearly entirely peeled off, and I almost felt bad for the neglected van, but that was because I anthropomorphized inanimate objects sometimes.

Sherlock caught up when I was nearly at the attendant station, which was busy with people taking tickets, or using their monthly pass to get in. We cut in front of a red Mini as the owner took a ticket, and slid out past the attendant, who intentionally seemed to pay no notice of us.

Once we were back out into the street, the real world seemed to suck in around us again--pedestrians rushing past in every direction, the stop and go of cars and the hiss of the hydraulic system on the buses. It all seemed very normal and city-like.

Sherlock seemed to have found her equilibrium as well. The twisted snarl was gone from her features, leaving only a look of intense concentration in her narrow eyes and clenched jaw. She looked up and down the street, watching people hurry across intersections and around us. "Well, Watson. He's giving a merry chase. My compliments to him on that." She started walking back in the direction of the bus stop, and I had no idea what was going on.

I took a few strides and fell into step with her. "Wait. Just a minute ago you were cursing up a blue streak about it."

"That was cursing my human fallibility, not the ingenuity of my opponent. This one is actually worthy of my time. Far more than a bunch of frat boys with a duck." Shaking her head, she walked faster toward the intersection where everyone was crossing from the bus stop.

"But I thought the duck thing was brilliant!"

"Simple minds, simple things," Sherlock muttered.

"Wow. Who has a driver's license? You might want to be nicer to the person who can drive, and who understands bus schedules."

We crossed against the flow of pedestrians just as the blinking man turned into a yellow hand, ordering walkers to stop. "I didn't mean it like that."

Once we were safe on the other side, I got in front of Sherlock, turning around and cutting her off as the traffic light changed and the cars sped past behind us. "No, no. Tell me how you did mean it. I can't wait to hear this one."

Sherlock had that deer in the headlights look… literally. I had seen it before: dodging deer on the roads was a local pastime in early fall. Wide eyes, pupils dilated, completely blinded by what was happening in front of her, and possibly not a single thought in her head. "Huh?"

"I want to hear what you did mean," I said slowly, enunciating each syllable, as if I were talking to a very small child. "Go on, explain it."

People pushed past us. We were taking up precious room in the middle of the sidewalk and the people coming in and out of the coffee shop one door down were even less friendly than everyone else about it. Several bumped purposely into Sherlock's shoulder, but she still hadn't snapped out of it.

Unable to watch any further, I pinched Sherlock's sleeve and dragged her against the building we were in front of, just to get us out of the way. My jaw jutted out in disgust as I waited for Sherlock to come back to reality. "Look," I whispered harshly. "You might be used to talking that way to your people, or whomever you talk to like that, but not to me. Or if you're going to treat me like the village idiot, you have to at least bother explaining why." I refused to mention the number of advanced placement classes I was taking, or my grade point average because I felt like I shouldn't have to justify myself or my intelligence. Sherlock shouldn't be treating anyone like that, in my most humble opinion.

"Eh?" Sherlock looked around us, focusing on actual things again. "Sorry. Brain was buffering." As she looked around, she continued to catch up on the last several minutes of time and space. "It's just something that slipped out. I didn't really mean it. The duck thing looks impressive to the casual observer but really it's not when you factor in all the details involved in the case..." She drifted off again.

If she was going to keep doing this buffering thing, it was going to get really annoying. I shut off online videos if they did this more than once. You shouldn't 'shut off' actual human beings, but maybe Sherlock needed a sobering face slap or ear twist, like on TV. "Procurement of...?" I prompted.

She stared off past me in the direction from which we had just come. "What was I saying?"

...And Sherlock was gone again. I sighed and waited until I figured out what Sherlock was paying so much attention to: a man. A panhandler, actually, lumbering his way from near the parking garage toward the intersection we'd come across.

He asked for something from a businesswoman in an obvious hurry, but she stopped and handed him whatever was in her pocket. His already hunched body bent a little lower and he said something to her as she continued on her route. The man had irregular, almost distorted features, but I couldn't make out much more than that. His coat was military, but it was old. It well predated the current fatigue style and camo patterns which had all gone 'digital' around the time my brother had joined the Marines.

The man crossed at the light, and others seemed to give him a wide berth. Not shocking, considering how dirty and world-worn he appeared to be. His gait was uneven, and his shoes had been taped over several times with worn duct tape. When he made it to the other side, I was ashamed to admit, I looked away. Some things were just too painful to deal with. But it only lasted a moment. Because the man was too fascinating not to gawk at. There was guilt in that as well; staring at the salt of the earth like he was a freak show oddity was probably just as bad.

He stopped someone else on the corner, muttering something to a man in a heavy work coat and enormous black boots. Again, the man stopped and gave the panhandler something. The panhandler bowed again, and with another comment, maybe of thanks, stepped out of the guy's way.

I saw his face now. The scarred right side had a drooping eye and a twisted lip. Possibly a souvenir of his military service. Now, I really wanted to look away. Because that's what people did, especially downtown. They looked away from the homeless, and from people with visible signs they weren't like everyone else. Scars, wheelchairs, trembling hands or a walking stick. I knew I was no better, though I wanted to be.

After he successfully got coins or dollar bills from a few other commuters, he came up to me and Sherlock. A panic jolted through me, but I kept it together, hoping it meant I could hold myself above everyone else for just a moment or two.

I forced eye contact with the man. I tried not to stare at the scarred side of his face. He had a smell about him of car grease, mixed with unwashed hair and a sour garbage water which did not inspire me to swallow my pride and slight repulsion.

He held out a hand to us. "The evil that men do lives after them; the good is oft interred with their bones," he said gruffly, his uneven stoop just a touch more pronounced.

"Julius Caesar," Sherlock muttered, edging forward.

"The burial scene," the homeless man replied, never raising his head. "You... you know it? It was my favorite."

Sherlock and I both shifted uneasily. The statement hung between us until Sherlock grabbed my arm and stepped past him, discreetly passing a folded fifty dollar bill to the man. "Get something warm to eat," she told him.

He bowed again in thanks. "Let all the number of the stars give light to thy fair way!" The man then continued down the block, still favoring his right side.

Sherlock watched him go, face scrunched in thought. "Antony and Cleopatra, act three, scene two," she whispered as the man turned the corner, out of sight and onto new territory.

The earlier tiff with Sherlock forgotten, I nudged the girl with my elbow. "That was a good thing you did."

Holding a hand out to where the man had disappeared, she shook her head. "That? That was nothing at all. It was just money."

We headed toward the coffee shop two doors down. The line was nearly out the door, but we joined the end of it. "Yeah, when you have a lot, it's just money. That was really something to him."

Sherlock unbuttoned her coat as we crossed the threshold. "It'll feed him for a few days. A week at best. I don't know. I don't care. But it won't do him any lasting good." The line moved forward and we shifted with it again. "Add it to another of today's failures. Let's hope we have more luck at the bank's corporate office later this morning than we did the parking garage, Watson." She rubbed her forehead with a gloved hand. "Or I just don't know what I will do with myself."

The sudden-setting melancholia caught me off guard. Her chin was tucked against her chest and hands shoved into her pockets in miserable silence as we moved forward in line, one person at a time. We said nothing as we enacted the sad parody of a queue for an amusement park ride. But still, this early in the morning, maybe caffeine was as good as a heart-pumping roller coaster ride.

It gave me some time to mull over what Sherlock had said. Maybe it did only help for now. Not long term. I didn't think about homelessness--it was more than I could handle. Homeless veterans had become an epidemic after wars in two theaters, and people with repeated tours coming home with problems that no one could understand, nor were they able to help. They became throw-away people. I wondered again if my brother was somewhere out there, among them. Maybe Sherlock would know.

Finally we got to the counter. The barista looked as tired as I felt. We ordered, which was the first time Sherlock had spoken in possibly ten minutes. Her voice was quiet and almost monotone. She paid for both of us, per her earlier agreement, then stepped aside to wait for our brews.

"I think you're right. The problem... is senseless. Maybe I wish I could do more?" For all of them, yes. For one person in particular, mostly.

Sherlock slid her wallet back into her leather bag. "Good." Taking her unadorned hot tea, she turned from the barista and glanced at me. "It means you're not a soulless asshole."

That was encouraging. I took my coffee and headed to the bar on the far wall, doctoring it with half-and-half and a handful of sugar packets. After a thorough stir and putting the lid back on, I walked to the tall bar table Sherlock was sitting at. "You know, you were able to do something decent today, and you did it. That makes you pretty ok."

Sherlock finally took off her gloves, placing them on the table next to her cup. "He used to be someone. Of consequence, I mean. Educated. Former military. Injured significantly, never healed properly. What makes an officer return from duty and...drift away on the wind? He had some life before what he is now. People who loved him."

I looked away, biting the inside of my cheeks, trying to hide a quivering lower lip.

She blew on her tea, staring out the window. "I think... I think, Watson... we're all just one bad day from being that poor wretch."

I smiled sadly. "Or just a long series of bad decisions," I muttered into the top of my cup, thinking back to the long slow descent my brother had made.

We were both subdued, each caught in some private memory of an even worse time. "You're the anonymous essayist who contributes to the school magazine, aren't you?"

Looking down at the table, I shrugged. "I didn't even know you knew about the school publications yet."

"I read them online before I even started. Best to know the lay of the land."

Rubbing my finger around the edge of the cup lid, I studiously ignored eye contact. "Yeah. It's a way to scream at the world. Without screaming at the world. My brother's like that guy. Lost in the wind somewhere. Mom, too. She pops up now and again, when she's looking for money. Sometimes I get a card for a holiday or something. According to the postmarks, she hangs around Florida, which is more than I know about my brother." My father had made the wrong call, kicking my brother out. But it was done, and could not be undone.

Sherlock held up her large paper cup of green tea in something like a toast. "We live in a dark and broken world, Watson. Maybe we can make it a little less broken where we can."

I raised my cup to that. "And at least figure out what our client is being blackmailed for."

Sherlock smiled at the mention of 'our' client. "In for a penny, in for a pound, eh, Watson?"

"Oh, shut up and drink your tea. This is just so I have something to write about for the magazine instead of maudlin accounts of my broken family life and how my grandfather was a professional clown."

"Interesting. Do tell." Sherlock leaned forward in rapt interest.

"He was a clown. And he was a professional at it. People paid him money to be a clown. That's the definition of a professional."

"Oh, don't be obtuse." She looked at her watch. "We can't reasonably attempt to storm his office until at least nine. So tell me a story, Watson. And make it a good one."

I took a long drink from my cup, trying to think of where to start. "I don't know. He died when I was two or three. My grandmother had photos of him dressed up. Bald cap, fluffy side hair, the whole bit. Used to scare the crap out of me every time I saw them on the wall. When I was older I found his trunk full of makeup and props and costumes. It basically ruined the circus and dress-up for me forever. Oh yeah, and he was called Harold, both in real life, and as a clown. Maybe there wasn't a difference between clown life and real life. Which is frightening, if you think about it. I have all these terrible visions of him being in bed with my grandmother, (if that's not bad enough) and then him honking a bicycle horn at her once they get going. And then I have to wash my mind out with bleach." I shuddered. "So, there you have it. My too-much-information story for the day."

Trying to hide a smile, Sherlock tapped the table with her fingertips. "No, no. It has been educational, as always, Watson." She set her mobile phone on the table, checking the time once again. "We still have about half an hour to kill. I suppose I should reciprocate." Her lips pressed into a fine line as she tried to decide on something personal, but probably not too personal, if I was reading her right. "Ah, the skeleton in my bay window."

"I thought it was pretty cool. Really nice reproduction. The age discoloration was a really nice touch. I bet it cost a fortune." I'd been looking into getting anatomically correct bones, or a complete skeleton for a while, and they were as expensive as hell.

Sherlock grinned, knowing she had me lured in. "It's not a reproduction."

"Wait, that's--"

"Yes."

"How?" It wasn't like you could just buy one. They were only sold to medical schools, anthropology departments, and other places with credentials for those sorts of things. "Please do not tell me you stole it, or that you acquired it through nefarious means."

Sherlock waved a hand. "No. No. Of course not. If you look at the skull, there is an accession number. It belonged to an anatomy department at a teaching hospital decades ago."

"Ok…" I wanted to see where this was going. "And it came into your possession how, exactly?"

"Well, you said yourself, it's quite aged. It's well over a hundred years old. Dating back to when bodies were in short supply. I'd wager, if you had looked carefully, you'd see the repaired fracture of the C3 and 2 vertebrae. Hangman's fracture. Our little friend may have been donated to the medical profession by the state, or he may have been a victim of body snatchers." She grinned. "Mother kept him in the library, posed with a book in his hand. She got it from her father, who was a doctor, who probably got it either from his father, or made it disappear from storage, or during a change of hands somewhere in the school's history. Why let a good skeleton go to waste? That's what I say."

Intellectually, I knew it was morbid. But I also had a desire to watch my own leg surgery. They did give me a copy of the recording made, after I had begged for weeks. So maybe I was a little macabre as well. The rest of me was excited the skeleton existed, and lived in my friend's eccentric and bohemian attic. "That is so cool."

"It's no clown-relative, but I am quite pleased that an ancestor of mine saw the benefit of liberating a whole human skeleton from an institution of higher learning and bringing it to some place where it would be more appreciated."

I laughed. It had almost come out loud and ugly, but I'd managed to cover my mouth in time. "God. Listen to us. We're kind of creepy. Clowns and century-and-a-half old anthropology experiments. We're two chainsaws and a jar of pig fetuses away from a horror film."

What made me laugh again, so hard and uncontrollably my face turned red, was that Sherlock had absolutely no idea what I was talking about. "Look, you catch me up on everything I have missed in the wide and wonderful world of detecting, and I will not waste your time and only give the CliffsNotes version of modern pop culture. It can be… educational."

"I doubt that. But you must admit. The skeleton story is much better than an escaped giant duck."

I finished off my now-cold coffee in a few gulps. "I don't know. I really liked the duck. I got my picture taken with it twice."

"Why does this not surprise me?"

I sat back in my chair, folding my arms over my chest. "Because I am sure that there is very little that surprises you, Holmes."

Chapter 16

We ended up passing the time until the 'respectable' hour of nine in the morning by ordering second drinks, this time with muffins. It was more than I was used to having, since granola bars were my go-to breakfast food. Of course, I'd been doing a hell of a lot running around today. I was sure I could spare the calories.

Sherlock explained a bit of the plan--the hardest part would be getting into the building. But the coffee cups would help. Maybe it would make us look older and more refined. Most of the instructions coming from Sherlock involved me simply doing as I was told, and going along with whatever Sherlock did. And while being a follower wasn't something I was entirely used to, I decided it would probably be best to let the only person with a plan take point on this one. It was technically Sherlock's show, but she also knew how to get exactly what she wanted.

Once we got in there, it ought to be relatively smooth sailing to the man's office. After that, Sherlock was entirely sure we'd have this portion of the case wrapped up by nightfall, and then we could decide what was a fair negotiating price for Ms. Blackwell to avoid public scandal.

I was happy at the chance to get home before curfew. I felt like I was too old for one, and all the rules governing what time friends were allowed to be over, and when homework was to be done. But I was a fan of taking the path of least resistance.

It didn't explain what I was doing here now, and not in school. But I wasn't sure missing out on this was an option anymore.

We took our time walking to the building that housed PRC Bank. Maybe Sherlock's nine o'clock invented appointment was not as stringently timed as she had made it out to be earlier. We casually waited at the crosswalks and moved no faster than any of the other late-morning commuters.

"Now, just follow my lead," she reiterated. "I'll do the talking, you do the nodding and obeying."

I squinted in the late morning light, partially out of sun blindness and partially to restrain myself from saying something rude to Sherlock. "Nodding and obeying," I parrotted smartly.

"Yes, exactly." Sherlock moved the strap of her bag over her head so it was no longer crossing her chest, and let it rest on her left shoulder.

"What exactly am I agreeing to, and what, exactly, are you going to have me do?"

Just outside the PRC building, Sherlock paused, a tight smile stretching with menace across her face. "If I told you, it would lack the spontaneity necessary to get the job done right." She pulled her black portfolio out of her bag, pulling a few of the neat and tidily stacked papers out just a bit, making everything look just barely messy and out of place.

"Oh god, I'm going to hate this," I moaned.

Sherlock took one of her perfectly twisted waves and ran a finger through it, loosening it and pulling it in front of her face, giving a slightly haggard look. "It depends on how good you are at improv." With that, Sherlock took off running up the steps and skipping the revolving door, heading straight for the handicapped entrance. Grabbing the shining handle, she tore the door open and crossed the lobby to the security desk, skidding to a stop.

I scrambled after her, undecided on the revolving doors or the handicapped door Sherlock had flown through. I paused a moment, looking at both of them before following Sherlock's lead, then crossing the lobby to where Sherlock was panting, hanging onto the counter like she was about to pass out.

"I have a--I have a nine o'clock appointment for the internship in accounting... I'm so late..."

"Who is your appointment with?" the guard asked, looking through his directory.

Sherlock never paused in her portrayal. She opened her portfolio and looked through a mess of papers,. "Mr.--uh... maybe Jones? No. Miss. She had a really long first name? Oh my god, I've messed it all up..."

The guard closed the directory. "Calm down, calm down. I think I know who you're talking about." He handed her a visitor's pass. "Ninth floor."

I turned to go with her, but was immediately stopped. "Not you."

Sherlock looked back, horrified. "She's my ride. Seizures and stuff. Jo, it's ok. I'll be fine."

The guard immediately tossed me a pass. "This never happened," he said, writing the second badge number into the visitor's log.

Once we were in the elevator, Sherlock hit the button for floor twenty-one, and leaned against the wall, finally relaxing. "One hard part down. There's always a Jones with a long first name somewhere. Statistical probability. People with common last names often try to give their children unique first names to help them stand out amongst all of the Joneses and Smiths in the world.

My heart was still racing. "What you told him back there? About seizures, is that true? 'Cause it's really something you should know about someone if you are going to go running around getting into trouble with them. It's only polite."

"Oh no. I just said that so he'd let you up. Epileptics are more prone to seizure during emotional upset or great stress. The security fellow doesn't want to be responsible for me if I should happen to have a seizure while on bank grounds. It was a gamble, but based on my deductions, a good gamble to make."

I slumped against the other wall of the elevator, my shoulder and cheek pressed against the mirrored wall. "You are going to give me a heart attack at some point."

"Well, everybody dies eventually."

"Let's not make it any time soon. My dad isn't done paying off my knee surgery."

The elevator bell chimed and the door slid open. "Cremation is seven hundred dollars. If you leave your body to science, they'll pay you. Or your next of kin. I, personally, wish to decompose in a body farm." She stepped off, one confident foot forward, and then the other.

I stood there for a moment, blindsided. I knew exactly what a body farm was. Letting your body decay in some bushes or in the back of a trunk under certain conditions for science.

Sherlock turned around. "Oh, come on, Watson. Before the door closes. If I can't be of any use on this earth in solving crimes while I am alive, I would like to assist in continuing to solve them after I am deceased."

Stepping off the elevator, I barely got clipped by the doors closing. "That's fine. Whatever butters your bread, or floats your boat, or whatever."

"That's two metaphors too many. One more and your prose will turn purple." She glanced around, then pointed at a sign for a stairwell. "There we are."

I didn't follow. "Wait. We took the elevator so we could take the stairs?"

Sherlock pushed the door open anyway. "There are cameras in this building, Watson. If there is cause to check said cameras, it is best for us if we do not take a direct route."

"Ugh. I hate it when you make sense."

Legs still burning from earlier in the morning, we hiked up five flights of steps to the floor our banker's office was on. Even Sherlock needed a break when we got to the floor in question, and both of us leaned against the wall until we had our breath back.

"I haven't had this hard of a workout in ages." My jogs had turned slow and casual since the knee surgery and I had never stepped them up further.

"Steps are good for you. Bleachers are better." Sherlock handed me her portfolio and her bag without explanation. She tucked her loose strands behind her ears and took off her coat, folding it neatly on the floor by the door. "Bag?" Taking it back, she reached inside and pulled out a pair of fashionable dark horn-rimmed glasses and slid them onto her face. She rolled up her sleeves, cuffing them just below the elbow and pushing her suit jacket's arms as well. Taking the files back from me, she again adjusted them so they were neater but still a bit disheveled. A working person's set of files. "Right. You are my intern. Ready?"

The knot in my stomach asked what could possibly go wrong. But I chose to ignore it and go along for the ride. The worst that could happen would be that I'd get arrested. I was still a minor. My father couldn't kick me out. Apparently, my mind had gone from scholarship qualifications to arrest record in less than a week. Sherlock Holmes was a terrible influence.

Before I could ask questions or explain how horrible of an idea it was, or run away, Sherlock pushed open the fire door and charged forward with her plan.

Sherlock slipped into character effortlessly. She was her usual self on the inside of the fire door... but she pushed it open and became someone else. Someone sophisticated, elegant, older, and much more feminine. Walking behind her, I couldn't help but notice the way her hips swayed as the slit in the back of the pencil skirt waved back and forth just below her knees. She put one foot directly in front of the other, the way those runway models did, and it made her shoes look even more intimidating.

I tried to keep things up on my end. My head held high, I put on the look of someone who was supposed to be there, and was in no way intruding or trespassing. Sherlock had said that all you had to do was walk around like you were supposed to be there. But this was a banking facility and not a school cafeteria. And the stakes were a little higher than a case of ketchup.

She looked around the corridor, quickly scanning the name plates as she marched with purpose past open and closed doors on both sides of the corridor, past men in boring black suits and women dressed very similar to her. I just pressed on, holding the few things Sherlock had given me to carry, like I, too was on a mission. The meter in my head that gauged just how arrested we could become monitored the situation closely. The needle bounced back and forth with each office we passed.

Turning down two more halls, we obviously had not come upon what Sherlock was looking for. She sighed and her eyes narrowed. Spinning around, she marched straight past me until we came back to an office with an open door and a heavy-set woman with cheerful desk decor inside.

Sherlock knocked and leaned past the threshold, waving a manilla folder. "Hi. Sorry to bother. I'm looking for Jim Blackwell? I have something for him to sign off on."

The woman turned in her chair and looked up at us, eyes devoid of anything other than burn-in from her computer monitor. Apparently, office jobs killed souls. "Oh, he hasn't been here since… I'd say April when they got rid of the Power and Light accounts? I can probably sign off on whatever you need."

Sherlock shook her head and handed the folder to me. "Oh, thanks. I'll have to have it typed up again. But then I'll bring it by. Just out of curiosity, do you know where Jim ended up? I'm just surprised. That's all."

The woman, Melissa, by the name plate on her desk, shrugged. "No, but I'm pretty sure he landed on his feet, though. I still see him around at the end of the day, getting on the bus to go home. If I see him again, I'll ask."

With a smile, Sherlock thanked the woman, and we left even quicker than we'd come. Shortly thereafter we were back in the stairwell and Sherlock was sliding back into her coat. "Informative, Watson."

"Yeah?" I handed the papers back to Sherlock. I would hold onto stuff for a case. But being her lackey in real life was degrading. "It's not a crime, him not working here anymore.

Or even a public shame worth blackmailing someone over. People get laid off all the time. There's no shame in that."

With a grin, Sherlock grabbed the handrail on the flight going upward. "That's exactly the thing, isn't it? Where is he now? He comes downtown every day. He gets off at the same stop, then disappears. Spends eight hours doing something, then goes back home again."

Groaning, I followed her, much less light on my feet than before. "Couldn't we have gone *down* for once? Instead of up?"

The bounce in Sherlock's step was just as smirky and snide as she was. "We want to make it difficult to track our movements. The fact that the floor was not key card entry only was nothing shy of a miracle. Let's not push our luck."

I had only just barely caught up by the time Sherlock had pushed open the door and marched down another hallway, toward the elevators. I dragged myself along, wondering just what sort of shape someone had to be in to keep up with Sherlock Holmes. Whatever kind of shape it was, I wasn't in it.

"If he doesn't work here anymore... where *does* he work?" I barely got the sentence out as I continued to lag two steps behind. "I mean, this is what she's being blackmailed over? They have money. Why are we negotiating a price? I think this whole thing is mad, and these shoes are a little tight on the pinky toes."

At the elevators, Sherlock hit the down button a little harder than necessary. "Nothing I can do about the toes. But you ask good questions, Watson, for someone who has been in the detecting business all of three minutes. That woman's been in that office at least since Blackwell got restructured out of the company. The light above the door dinged in a mechanical, old-fashioned sort of way as the car itself came to an audible and (hopefully) complete stop. "If you get laid off, why would you not tell your wife?"

We stepped inside, and the door slid shut, leaving me staring at our reflections in the brassy mirrored surfaces of the elevator walls. Even Sherlock's shoulders were slumped a bit. "Shouldn't she have known? Because she thinks he still works here."

I looked myself over and made a face, poking myself in the side. My thighs had always been large from playing running-oriented sports, but the largeness had shifted. Now there was a layer of fat between the muscle and the dark jeans.

"Oh, Watson, your legs are perfectly acceptable. Keep more closely to your exercise regime and all will be well." Still, she looked in the reflective surface at herself, head tilting back and forth. She fixed a few locks of hair that had fallen loose. Apparently, Sherlock wasn't above vanity. It warmed the cockles of my cold and bitter heart. "You know, a quick look at his financials would be helpful. Find out where his paycheck is being deposited from."

"And how do we find that out?" I asked as the doors slid open. "Just ask a banker?"

Sherlock stepped out with a long gait, pulling a phone from her pocket. Not a banker. But I have people."

"You have people? Why am I not comforted? Holmes, how does someone even get people?" I grumbled as we tossed our visitor passes on the front desk and pressed onward, not bothering to sign ourselves out of the building, or really make it known that our business was complete.

I wrapped my scarf around my neck again, preparing for the wall of cold air just a second before it hit us as we left. Outside we clacked down the granite steps and Sherlock headed toward a retaining wall made of the same material. She leaned against it and put the phone to her ear.

Shoving my hands in my pockets, I waited. There were privacy laws and things. You couldn't just ask for someone's financial information. It just wasn't done like that.

"Wally, hi. Oh, you know who it is. I'm calling in that favor."

And yet, that's exactly how Sherlock was doing it. At some point I would stop being surprised, but not yet. Sherlock was explaining what she needed and reminding this Wally character how much he owed her. There may have been a hint of how this person would have been in prison without her, instead of working for a major banking institution. Listening too closely made me feel like an accessory.

Sherlock nodded as the man on the other line spoke. "And the size of the deposits has not changed in a year. Bi-weekly. Money order deposit so the statement doesn't say who it's from. Who the hell doesn't have direct deposit these days? This stinks."

I was doing a hopping sort of shuffle type dance, back and forth trying to keep some warmth in my legs, when Sherlock spun around, pointing the phone at me like a weapon. "Alright, so his wife didn't notice anything with the bank account, nor did anyone else, because the size of his deposits made no noticeable shift. And he's depositing money orders, for huge sums." She started walking back toward the main flow of pedestrian traffic. "We have to find out who is creating those money orders. It doesn't matter where they are from. It matters who they are from."

"And how do we do that, exactly?"

Sherlock shook her phone in the air. "I haven't quite figured that bit out yet. But that's the fun of it! I could pose as IRS. I suppose. That could work."

"Because there is nothing illegal at all about pretending to be a government employee." I felt compelled to point these things out, as the child of a police officer. Especially if she was talking about doing something that moved from the murky middle and definitely into the illegal territory. "Seriously, Sherlock. There is *no* other way to get this information? Like digging through their trash or something?"

Sherlock tapped her lip with two fingers repeatedly, staring off into the distance. She almost collided with two pedestrians but I dodged in front and blocked, forcing the two men with crispy, over-styled hair and huge wool coats to move a bit to the left so we could get by.

"I suppose one of us could pose as a bank official. Then get a teller or banker to just access the deposited checks system and get the money order numbers and locations, and then we can track down who paid for them and where."

I helped the ever oblivious Sherlock around a college student with an enormous backpack. "You really aren't going to be happy until I end up in jail, are you? I get the very strong sense you're doing everything in your power to ruin my chances at maintaining a clean record so I can go to medical school." I crammed my hands farther into the pockets of the coat in frustration.

"I already told you. Permanent records don't exist."

"You are not hearing the words I am saying. All I want is to get out of this without a record I need to explain."

Sherlock sighed like I was the one being dense. "Juvenile records can be locked away or expunged, assuming there's a conviction. You worry too much, Watson. If you know the right people, anything can be made to go away."

"I don't know the right people," I said dully. "River rat, remember?"

This earned me a punch in the arm. "You know me! And I know people!"

My shoulders slumped. Knowing people who knew people didn't make me feel more secure. "Great. Sure. Cool."

Chapter 17

We ended up in a three-story corporate bookstore a few blocks from the bank's headquarters. I hated these places. They had a lot of books -- like libraries -- which were good, but their lights were bright and unfriendly. It was like some kind of book prison or something.

"What are we doing here?" I don't even know why I bothered asking. I wasn't going to like the answer.

Sherlock glanced around the space, spread the entire length of the building, with high, vaulted ceilings where the escalators reached up to the top floors. "Thinking."

"What're we thinking about? Can I help?"

Sherlock glanced at me, then walked straight to the Russian literature section. She held out a hand, letting the spines of the books brush against her fingertips. Her face was screwed up in frustration, or concentration. Maybe both. "I'm thinking. I'm thinking about this. About why a man goes to a job every day that he no longer has. I'm thinking about where his money comes from. I'm thinking about breaking into the IRS to figure out what his tax situation is like, but you like that idea even less than hacking into a bank. Therefore, I am thinking about this and I need you to leave me alone."

Closing my eyes, I counted to five. Because murder was bad. With a resigned sigh, I made my way to the coffee bar in the middle of the store. I would have asked if there was anything Sherlock wanted, but she'd already moved from Russian literature to the history section. Getting to the counter, I rattled off my order, noting that our lab partner and locker column-mates pact had gone well past normal boundaries ages ago.

I kept an eye on Sherlock until my coffee came. Wrapping my frozen fingers around it with a death-grip, I wandered toward the science fiction and graphic novel sections, wondering just what in the hell Sherlock was doing. Flopping into a big leather chair with a book I hadn't read yet, I set the coffee on the table beside me, taking out my own phone to check messages. Sherlock was a self-proclaimed detective, she could locate me when she was done wandering amongst the books.

MIchael had finally noticed I wasn't there. He'd sent texts asking if I were sick, and if he should pick up my homework. I didn't answer the first question, but said 'please do' to the second.

Will was slower on the uptake, and his messages had a much later timestamp. He had noticed that Sherlock was also not around, and was begging to know what we were doing, in between making a request for a box of barbecue sauce in addition to the ketchup and explaining that he had done some work on the game last night, and he might be able to get it to make new levels on its own, at least up to the final boss battle. The graphics were trash and the game itself had taken three not-programmers a year to get this far, so if he could get the puzzle part of the game to not need our help so much, he was a brilliant idiot and I would hug him later. We could have this game in the app store sometime before we graduated from college.

Thanking Will, I promised to take a look at his breakthrough later, with no justification of my absence. I had a feeling anything I said would be fuel to the fire of whatever story they had made up in their heads about me and Sherlock.

Just in case Sherlock wanted me, I set the phone face-up on the table next to my coffee and opened a thick compendium graphic novel, trying not to break the spine, so I wouldn't have to buy the stupid thing. I tended not to buy the books and I used bookstores as libraries sometimes. I took a big gulp of the still bitingly hot coffee and began speed reading through the book.

It was probably for the best that Sherlock was off somewhere having deep thinky-thoughts. It gave me time to catch up on green monster superheroes. I had a deep and meaningful connection with a promethean rage-monster, which might be far too telling.

Of course, Sherlock could be done with me altogether. That might have been what marching off into those rows of books had been about. If she never came back for me, I'd read the rest of this book, polish off the last of my coffee and go home on the bus. Nothing gained, nothing lost. And if she did happen to come back, well, it was best to stay in one place in order to be found. Like a plane crash victim. But hopefully no one would have to resort to cannibalism before the day was out.

##

About an hour later, I finally put down the four-hundred-page compendium I had flown through. I shook my coffee cup, which had gone cold, and a quick swig told me all the sugar had run to the bottom. Hardly ideal, but I'd had worse. Namely my father's coffee, which could kill a man at twenty paces.

"'Scuse me, can I reshelve this?" A young man, a few years older than me, asked, pointing at the huge book. He was wearing a green polo shirt, like all the other clerks that buzzed around the place.

I blushed and winced. "Sorry. I really got into it." And had finished the whole darned thing. I handed it to him.

He shrugged. "We're supposed to discourage reading and not buying. I don't care. I get paid the same either way." He half-smiled. "Hulk, huh? How do you feel about the X-Men?"

My mouth opened, and nothing came out. I stared at him for a moment, knowing there was no correct response. It was a trap. "Well, I haven't been keeping up with all of the X-titles lately…" That seemed judicial. Wars had been started over less.

"Oh." He glanced away. "Well, anyways."

Yup. I'd screwed that one up. Apparently, the 'walking on eggshells' answer was also the wrong one. I should have just admitted I thought Cyclops was a douchebag and see where the conversation had gone from there. "I mean--I'm just waiting for a friend."

He picked up my empty coffee cup too. "Your friend wouldn't happen to be the one touching all the books?"

I clenched my teeth tightly, wondering how much trouble Sherlock could have possibly gotten into in an hour. "She's not causing grief or anything, is she?"

The young man's face twisted in a pained expression. He was also searching for some delicate way to put something. "She's not causing trouble, exactly. But she's touching everything and muttering to herself? It's bothering a few people."

I grabbed my coat and stood up. "I'll take her out of here or something."

"It's not like that--I mean, I don't care. But management."

I tried to keep my tone as even as possible. "It's ok. I know how it is. Not in your control. I'll see what I can do about her. The world can be safe again for big box bookstores."

He smiled, then scurried away with the book. If I was reading it right, I had been about to obtain a phone number. I wasn't sure if it was the mention of Sherlock or the X-Men that had made that fall apart. Either way, I had no books, and I needed to fetch a wayward junior detective.

When I found her, two floors up, she was still touching the books with her right hand as she walked the aisles. I stopped just to her left. "Sherlock--um--apparently you're scaring management."

Sherlock continued down the aisle, past the end display, back into the next aisle, fingers running absently along religious texts. I caught up to her again. "Sherlock, it's almost lunchtime. We can get something to eat, and pick up where we left off."

As I passed by this time, I reached out and caught her sleeve, which stopped her dead in her tracks. She spun around, yanking her arm out of my grasp and holding it to her chest like it had somehow been injured. She glared at me, something angry and wounded in her cold blue eyes. "Don't touch me like that again."

"Like what?" I truly didn't understand.

Sherlock turned back, staring off into the distance again. "Don't touch me when I am thinking."

"Can we think someplace else? Your way of thinking is a little, um…" weird. "Intense. And folks aren't used to it."

That had sounded so diplomatic. I mentally gave myself a pat on the back.

"Fine. I was nearly done anyway. I will think somewhere away from the plebs."

"You did not just call people who shop in chain bookstores plebeians, did you?"

"No. The fools who work here," she elaborated.

We headed toward the escalator, past displays for books I would never read, much less buy. "Not everyone. I met a nice one down in the science fiction section."

"Then you should have gotten his number, Watson,'" she directed, not even bothering to look my way when she said it.

"How do you--look. Never mind. It doesn't matter." I hadn't even been clever enough to look for the name tag on his shirt.

A tight smile crossed Sherlock's thin lips. "I would have liked to have seen that, I think. I've never witnessed the actual initiation of flirtation, leading to the exchange of contact information."

You are so weird, I wanted to say. "First of all, I am not a flirtation science experiment. Second... never? Never got a phone number from anyone?"

Sherlock scowled, her nose crinkling in disgust. "Watson, I said I had never witnessed the transaction." She then left it at that.

##

We ate lunch at the single non-chain pizza place in the vicinity. It was a small storefront above a 'gold exchange' that smelled pleasantly of dough and oregano from all the way across the street. I nudged Sherlock and pointed, explaining we could get in before the lunch rush. This idea seemed attractive to her, who, for all her bluster, didn't seem to like the crowds that were inherent in the city.

The interior was warm and carried wafts of tomatoes, flour, and garlic from the kitchen. It was a comforting kind of homey smell that I always wished could be captured in pine tree shaped air fresheners, or, at least, one of those plug-in things.

LIke most mom-and-pop places downtown, it was of questionable cleanliness, but I didn't care. After a morning of consuming nothing but sugar and caffeine, I needed to get some real food (and grease) into my system. Possibly before my heart pounded straight out of my chest. And, really, the grey streaks of dirty mop water on the broken linoleum floor were part of the charm. If you thought about it.

Sherlock, for her part, was still thinking. Arms folded over her chest, jaw locked, she sat in the white formed booth with closed eyes, totally unapproachable until the girl behind the counter came out to take our order. Then she opened her eyes and smiled tightly, some perfunctory form of politeness at play.

I ordered a small square pizza drenched in olive oil and sauce. Sherlock contented herself with a cup of coffee. I tried to make a face that indicated that no, Sherlock should not have the coffee from a pizza shop, but either Sherlock didn't notice, or didn't care.

Coffee from places that did not regularly sell coffee tended to be burnt because it had sat all day, or it was made fresh, dripping into a burnt and disgusting pot. For all of her deductions and brains in subverting the security staff and back personnel, Sherlock seemed to have a lot of gaps in her education. Avoiding massive intestinal distress from a dodgy pizza shop was just one of those life skills I felt it would be necessary to impart upon my friend. Then I would move on to teaching her about Star Wars.

The coffee came with my enormous over-iced fountain drink. It couldn't have been good. It smelled a little… well-done, and had probably been hanging around for ages, possibly since yesterday.

"That may actually kill you," I told her, staring at the cup.

Sherlock ignored me. For someone with her obviously refined tastes, the questionability of the provenance of the coffee didn't seem to bother her. Apparently, she was perfectly alright with coffee capable of peeling paint. She simply dumped two packets of artificial sweetener (two different types, pink and blue) into the coffee, stirred it with a fork, and sipped at it as if it were just another flavor of coffee from the shop we'd spent time at earlier in the morning.

She stared off past me, the mug occasionally pausing too long at her lips, and I wondered what that brain of hers was mulling over. I felt reasonably smart. Or at least smart enough to get into medical school, if I kept working hard. My science classes were easier for me than other parts of my course load. But I still couldn't quite work out the way Sherlock's mind must have turned everything around inside of it, tearing it apart, and putting all the information back together again in some way that only made sense to her.

Then again, maybe it was better that way. What if Sherlock's mind put things together in some Frankenstein's monster of an order, and her deductions were just what she let loose on the world.

Don't ask, don't tell. That was my new official policy on the way brains worked. Neuroscience was definitely off my list of fields for specialization.

##

The food came, a seaming square of pie in a black, well-seasoned pan, gripped by a pair of pliers by a girl in a hideous uniform who looked exhausted already, even though the busy part of the day hadn't happened yet.

The girl set two plates in front of us, under the normal assumption that we would be sharing, and asked if we needed anything else. I shrugged, and she left.

I dished out one of the four slices for myself. The nice thing about the personal-sized pizza was that it was all crust. And the crust was the best part of the Sicilian pizza. Sliding the small spatula under another slice of pizza, I partially lifted it out. I wasn't in the mood for Sherlock to snap at me again, but it was polite to ask. "Want some?"

She ignored me entirely.

I ate my greasy food in silence, not trying to ruin her thinking again. Checking my phone, I saw that the Tweedles were practically melting from the need to find out where I was, and what I was doing. It would have been too much to ask that they just keep up the assumption that I was home sick. Hopefully my dad hadn't figured out I wasn't in school. I had never skipped before. But I wasn't ready for whatever hell that would bring down. I had exactly no leeway thanks to my brother.

Was it fair? No. It drove me nuts. I wasn't going to disappear into the night like my mother. And I wasn't going to wrap my motorcycle around a tree like my brother. The worst I could probably do is get suspended for Sherlock's antics. But considering how one of my classmates had just backed his F-150 into a gas station and took out the brick side of the building, and all the refrigerators, I should have been well in the clear of being the worst kid he ever met.

"Does your friend need anything? The waitress in the ugly uniform asked, breaking my thoughts about how I was going to get suspended and lose all chances at scholarships, even though I was hardly the most reckless of everyone around me.

She had dark skin and freckles like me, but hers were far more endearing. I found myself staring at her too long, and looked away and tried to fill the gap of silence that developed. I looked into Sherlock's cup. "I think she's good on half a cup for now. She's, uh, thinking. Probably best to just leave her in peace." I offered a depreciating smile, hoping it would cover over my creepy staring just a moment earlier. However, the waitress didn't even notice the gaffe, because all of her attention was on Sherlock. "I'm sure she'll tell you. And me. And everyone in this place when she's ready for more coffee. That's her. Silence or… dominance." Oh, that sounded wrong.

The polite customer service smile kicked in for the waitress. But then she did actually put one hand on the table and lean in toward me. The smile and the closeness were mixed signals so I didn't know what to do. "I'll, um, wait for her signal then? What about you? Another refill?"

I glanced around quickly and nodded. "Yeah. That'd be great. Hey… are you the only one working in the front during lunch time?"

She shook her head. "Jemma's in the back, slicing some stuff. Someone else is out helping with a delivery. Don't worry. You two won't get forgotten when the lunch rush starts."

I handed over my empty cup and our fingers brushed against each other. Possibly intentionally. "I'd hate for you to be running like a mad-person all day."

Beneath her visor, bearing the small company's logo, the girl blushed. "Um, thanks. I mean, it'd certainly be better tips if things worked out that way. But yeah... I would probably go nuts from all the rushing around." She looked out the window, at the office buildings surrounding us. "Believe it or not, business people can be kind of demanding."

A sputtering laugh escaped me, some of my own tension from the morning dissipating. "Yeah. I get that sense. We've been hanging out downtown only since this morning, and I already think they're all weird. It's just reaffirming my decision to go into medicine instead of business. Having your hand in someone's thorax sounds way more appealing than whatever it is they do in their tiny little offices all day."

"Oh," the waitress said, leaning further in toward me. "Trauma medicine? That sounds cool. Are you in medical school now?"

I blushed. Whatever Sherlock had done with the clothes and the hair and makeup had been super-effective. "No, not yet. Just trying to keep my grades up so I can get in."

The waitress put the glass on the tray. "I go to Central College. Where're you at?"

"Foxhollow?" I answered with a wince.

"The high school?"

"Yeahhhhhh." The word protracted then dropped off with a bit of shame at the very end.

"You look a lot older." She took a few steps back from both of us. "I'll just get the drink."

Second time today I was close to getting a phone number. Apparently my school was awful for my attractiveness to other human beings, but suddenly I was super cool in the real world. I ran my fingers through the short hair at the front of my head, marveling at the strange texture. It was so… smooth. Apparently, a makeover was a good thing, too. I would be dabbing my ends with pomade in the future if it meant other human beings noticed me as anything other than a jock, or "Mike and Will's friend."

Sherlock was still staring off into nothing, her hands wrapped around her mug. At least, Sherlock would not have editorial comments on where that conversation had gone horrifically wrong. Next time, Sherlock would tell me, lie. Pick a college or university and stick with it.

A few people in semi-casual business attire and bundled against the cold walked in, making the buzzer above the door sound. Someone different came from the back and out to the counter to take their order. The same woman came out with my drink a few minutes later. The other girl, whose name I still didn't know, wasn't even talking to me because she didn't want to get into jailbait territory.

Dejected, I put my attention back into my pizza. It was good. A lot of cheese, a lot of oil. I tried to forget that I possessed hips and vowed to run more than my usual lazy five miles tomorrow, and every morning henceforth. Especially if I was going to continue consuming carbohydrates at this same rate.

As I bit into the last piece, Sherlock was startled out of her thoughts. "You blew that one too, Watson."

"Nothing was going on."

"You could have had her number. Or given her your number. I need data, Watson. Phone number exchanges, live and in person." Sherlock gulped down the half-cup of cold coffee, setting it down a little too hard on the table.

"Holmes, I have a fantastic idea. How's about you get your own damned phone numbers. Since you seem to know everything in the world except for who Han Solo is." Out of spite, I shoved the remainder of the last piece of pizza into my face, not feeling at all lady-like at the moment. Not that I did at most other times, but that was a different story.

Sherlock ignored the comment. "Also, I don't like it when people make faces at me."

My head fell into my hands. "Your brain has a buffer built into it, doesn't it? You've been walking around like a zombie all morning since you 'started thinking,' and apparently, I'm not flirting loudly enough for you or something? Why don't you just get first-hand experience? Have you ever been on a date?"

Sniffing, Sherlock picked up her mug and swirled the last drop of coffee around the bottom, staring at it like it could tell the future. "No, I haven't. Well, there was that one time I became engaged. But that was for a case. So, I am sure it doesn't count."

Only she would see someone as 'a case' to begin with, then insist that a relationship with said person didn't count. She was a genius. I had no problem admitting that. And a mad hatter besides. "Well--whatever. Why do you think I know how it's done? Apparently there's flirting and complimenting each other and exchanging numbers or Twitter handles or whatever, and you see how it goes."

"I know that. Do you think I'm incompetent?" She was taking it personally. "I was engaged once, by the time I was done with that case, after all."

"Done with? So you just...threw them away when you were done? That is so... heartless."

"It was for a case! It doesn't count! I needed the inside layout of the dean's office, and the location of the safe. That's how I got what I needed. Everything worked out alright in the end. Well, except for the expulsion bit. That didn't go to plan. But even that had an upside. Otherwise, you'd be sitting in a dull class thinking dull thoughts about dull topics and planning to do dull things with dull people." She reached across the table and punched me with hardly any force at all.

Had she just insulted my entire existence? "This has worked out so fantastically for me. I got the privilege of meeting the Illustrious Sherlock Holmes."

"Exactly!"

Sarcasm was lost on some people. "Lucky me," I muttered. "I get to skip school with some girl who fancies herself to be a detective--or truth detector or something--with business cards and everything--and your fake fiancee gets a broken heart. That's wonderful."

Maybe Sherlock just didn't see the chaos she left in her wake.

"I don't fancy myself to be a detective. I am one. Or I will be. Just as soon as all of this insufferable schooling is over with. I am sure whatever-her-name-was is over it by now. It's been like... three weeks."

I blinked rapidly, trying to process the statement. "You have a very high cluelessness level for someone with your intelligence."

Sherlock frowned, dissatisfied with where this conversation was going. "Cluelessness about what? Relationships? Things that don't matter? I already said I am trying to gather data on the flirting and dating process. How I synthesize that data is completely irrelevant, only insofar as it pertains to cases."

I actually growled. "Those things matter. They may not matter to you. But they do matter in general, and they matter to other people. So if you want to... I don't know. Operate in this world? Be a for-real detective? You're going to have to at least consider other people's feelings." I looked at the time on my phone. I had three messages from the boys. "Are you done thinking now? Can we do something else? Anything else? Because I'm going to school tomorrow. Whether this thing is finished or not."

There was still no sign of understanding on Sherlock's face. "You're angry with me."

"You're very perceptive."

"Because I didn't take into account some girl's feelings?"

I blinked rapidly. "You really have no idea why I am angry with you."

Sherlock gave a long ponder. "I suspect it has something to do with the cleaning girl I was engaged to. But you're not exactly confirming that for me."

My head fell onto my arms and I groaned. "The fact that you do not see the problem is, in fact, the problem. That you would do that to someone--lead them on--you know what? Never mind. Just never mind." I slid out of the booth. "I'm going to the bathroom. When I get back, you'd better have a plan, or something, or I am taking the bus home." Not waiting for a response, I headed to for the restroom.

Before taking care of what I needed to, I checked my messages and texted the guys back that yes, I was off doing something stupid with Sherlock, no, it wasn't any of their business, and that I would mess around with the new version of our app before I got back to school.

Maybe I spent too long with my hands under the hot dryer, but they, and my feet and backside seemed to be destined to be perpetually cold with all this dashing around outside. It wasn't even Christmas yet, and the weather had already turned toward the severely disagreeable. At least when I was running in the dark before school, I just kept running, and never slowed down enough to get cold. Or worse yet--have the sweat freeze on my neck. There was no cure for that.

If I was going to continue hanging around with Sherlock Holmes, I really needed to pick up my pace and distance with the running thing, and be far more regular about it.

Making sure my hands were as dry as humanly possible before potentially going back out into the chilled weather, I came out of the restroom, and looked back toward the table we'd been sitting at. The empty pizza try was there, but Sherlock was gone.

In fact, I only barely caught sight of Sherlock marching up the sidewalk, away from the pizza place and back toward the building where our quarry hadn't worked since roughly around the time I had blown out my knee.

Anger flared, but it changed to sinking disappointment. I hesitated at the door. Maybe Sherlock had meant to leave me behind, after our latest tift.

No.

She didn't get to just leave Joanna Watson places.

With hot-headed determination, I pushed the door open and stormed out, sliding past two guys in enormous down coats, charging in the direction of my lockermate.

"Sherlock!" I called angrily, as the other girl crossed the busy intersection--against the light.

When I caught up, Sherlock Holmes was going to get a piece of my mind. It would be the equivalent of a strongly-worded letter. But with screaming and possible violence.

Chapter 18

The light turned red, and other than the two cars who ran the light, it was relatively safe to cross by the time I got there. But Sherlock crossed yet another street as two buses rushed past and I lost sight of her. As soon as the noontime traffic cleared enough that I could cross, I didn't bother waiting again for the light. Traffic and jaywalking laws were for other people when Sherlock Holmes was involved. Running across the three lane street, I almost got hit by some jerk in a new and shiny black Lincoln Town Car, but I managed to catch sight of her when she had to stop to let some lady coming out of a department store with a bag half-stuck in the revolving door get by.

"Sherlock!" I shouted, unsure if she couldn't hear among all the city noise or if she was just ignoring the sound of her name.

I dodged two people not paying attention to where they were going due to cell phone usage. It vaguely amused me to think that they might be texting with each other and not even know it (wouldn't that make a great short story? I'd file it away for later). I cut around them with a speed and accuracy I hadn't put into play since last spring. It felt good to let loose despite how dangerous dodging pedestrians and street traffic truly was. There was more danger of doing more than getting tackled and destroying my ACL. But being fueled by fury had a tendency to diminish one's capacity to care about such things.

At the next intersection, I almost lost Sherlock again. The light was turning yellow as I approached, and instead of being a good little pedestrian, I sped up, practically falling over the hood of a car that had started creeping through before the light had even turned green. A horn blasted and I shouted an obscenity, complete with relevant hand gesture, then continued after Sherlock. The further I ran, the more anger overtook me, propelling my tired, freezing legs just that much faster.

Sherlock opened the door to a PRC branch that wasn't near the corporate headquarters, and then went inside, so plan obviously in motion.

The idea of screaming more obscenities was tempting. Who did she think she was? That was the thought spinning in my head like a cranking, angry bike wheel.

The not-quite-midday light wasn't bright enough to reflect off the all-glass exterior of the building, but there was just enough light and reflection that I lost Sherlock once she went into the bank branch, which seemed to take up the entire first floor of the skyscraper's retail space.

Once inside, I scanned the sea of people, looking for her, past tellers to patrons in lines winding through the open spaces. Dammit.

"Can I help you?" A deep and authoritative voice asked from behind me, nearly making me jump.

I turned slowly and came face-to-chest with a man in a brown security uniform, and looked up slowly. "I'm looking for my friend. Tall girl--lady, dark shoulder-length hair?"

The security guard adjusted his belt. My eyes focused on the bright yellow stun gun on the side where normally a firearm would be. I really didn't want to get Tased into next Tuesday, but with the way things were headed, it wouldn't surprise me if a trip to the bank ended in me twitching on the floor. Hanging out with Sherlock made all things possible.

But the rent-a-cop looked me over again one more time before pointing to an early and fake Christmas Tree in the middle of the bank floor. "Other side, there. She's in the office with one of the bankers."

I thanked the man and stepped around it to see some chairs in a makeshift waiting area and a row of offices. I hated that I had no idea what new level of trouble I was now accessory to. I turned back to the security guard and waved a hand. "Thanks. She keeps forgetting my legs aren't as long as hers." Or I had been ditched. One of the two things had happened. I almost wanted to give the benefit of the doubt. Almost. But she really had to learn not to leave a Watson behind. That's how too many problems started.

The man gave me something that might have been a grunt and a smile. Or just a grunt. And was on his way, back to the front door to intimidate more arrivals.

Doing my best not to rush or seem too anxious, I crossed the open space, and made my way around the Christmas tree, which actually wasn't as randomly placed as it had first looked. It helped mark off a makeshift waiting area with a few chairs and a sign-in podium.

The doors to the offices were all open. The first one held an older lady with a huge pile of paperwork and a banker typing into the computer and offering the woman reassurances. The second was much the same--it looked like a student starting a new account. There were three more semi-public offices. Sherlock was in the second-to-last one with a man twice our age, who kept leering at her when she'd turn back to the paper in the portfolio she'd used in literature class last week. The pages still covered in notes about the closed-door mystery. The way the man in the light grey suit looked at Sherlock made *me* feel uncomfortable. I wondered if there

225

was a way to report a bank worker for leering at a teenager in what had to be a grossly inappropriate manner.

For a moment, I entertained the notion of barging in. But this was Sherlock's show. She had come up with the plan that I had not been privy to, so my best bet was to let this play out. I found a seat next to the tree and waited for Sherlock to finish, or to indicate that she needed to be rescued from Pervy McPerverson.

Arms folded over my chest, I waited. I couldn't hear, but I could certainly see the man paying my classmate far too much attention. I was angry and skeeved. It took me a few minutes to realize Holmes was leaning over the corner of the L-shaped desk intentionally, at regular intervals, and had now touched the man's arm twice.

The third time, she let it linger so long that *he* was uncomfortable, and spun around in his swivel chair to grab her some pamphlets. He took a card off the holder on his desk, scribbling something on the back, and shoving it all into a folder bearing the bank's logo and a picture of the branch in sunny weather, then handed it to her.

Had she just gotten Pervy McPerverson's number?

Maybe she was doing it to punish me. To teach me some lesson about how Sherlock could indeed flirt. That had to be it. There was no way she was interested in a guy like that, with his expensive haircut and overly-crisp shirt. His tailored suit and Bluetooth earpiece alone screamed 'douche' loud enough for everyone in the vicinity to hear.

Of course, maybe that was her type. Please don't let that be her type.

Sherlock pulled the card out of the folder, flipped the card to the hand-written side, and put his number into her phone, then held her hand out.

226

He handed over his own silver Blackberry. She opened the address book and typed something into the phone, pressing a few more buttons before handing the phone back to him.

For some reason I wanted to kill her even more now than when I'd been dumped at the pizza shop. And if anyone had ever met Sherlock Holmes, there probably wouldn't be a jury in the world that would convict me.

##

Sherlock left the banker's office, and made brief eye contact with me, both brows arching upward. Did she honestly think I wouldn't come? Tilting her head to the side, she made the most minute of gestures toward the doors, through the crowd, and past the security guard, who got a brief nod from me of thanks.

Once outside, I stopped directly in front of Sherlock, blocking her progress. "What the hell was that?"

"I was solving the problem of finding out where our friend's deposits were coming from."

"With *flirting*?" Thank god she wasn't actually interested in that douche. That was reassuring. Maybe.

Sherlock sighed. "Yes, Watson," she said in exasperation. "I was solving the problem via flirting. Because that's really all flirtation and human relationships are good for, in my line of work."

I scowled. "You don't have a line of work. You are a high school student. We flip hamburgers and if we are very lucky, we get to graduate to working at The Bagel Palace." I rubbed my forehead. I was still hooked on this mystery. "Ok. You've got me. What did I miss?"

"You know, if you continually sell yourself short, you're never going to get anywhere. You're well beyond bagels. Watson, I think quite highly of you."

She opened the folder and pulled out the business card once again. Flipping it to the back where a number was scrawled in smudged blue ink. "Terrance's cell number."

I was not impressed. "And you put yours into his phone. Does he know you're jailbait, Lolita?" I stepped out of the way of the little old woman who had obviously finished up with the reassuring banker, and was now leaving for the day.

The other girl gave me a look that I was becoming familiar with--the pursed lips and the cold stare down the nose. "Of course, I didn't put my phone number into his phone. I'm not that insane. I was reading the other names and numbers in his phone."

I loosened my scarf in frustration. "And this does us good...how?"

Sherlock's jaw jutted forward as she stared skyward, like some statue of the pained and crucified Christ, asking the lord for forgiveness for the ignorance of those around him. "Eidetic memory, Watson. Keep up."

"No, no. I think you having a photographic memory was somehow left out of the brochure when I signed up to be your sidekick. Or whatever I am to you."

"I thought you said you were my friend?"

Catching me off guard, Sherlock took the opportunity to step around me, but I was clever enough to get in front of her again.

I waved my hands in front of her face. "I thought we were friends, too. I said I was going to the bathroom, and then you could tell me about your thinky-thoughts that I've put up with you thinking about all day in every weird way possible. Touching books and staring off into space, and who the hell knows what you were doing."

Sherlock's shoulders slumped. "It's a long...thing."

I folded my arms over my chest. "I have all the time in the world."

"I've never had to explain my process to anyone before."

"This is different. If we're doing this, we are full partners in it. Otherwise, tell me to buzz off, and I will go home and face the music for skipping an entire day of school."

Sherlock bit her cheek, looking me over, as if seeing me for the first time. "I suppose I can trust you."

A little late for that, Holmes, I thought. "I've come this far with you. I just want to know what's going on."

She nodded. "Fine. Walk with me. I need to make some phone calls. And then we need to stake out the garage. I'll explain when we're someplace out of the wind."

##

Sherlock made her call, presumably to one of the phone numbers she'd memorized from the banker's mobile phone. She rattled off a series of numbers and passcodes, then asked for some piece of information I didn't really understand.

Listening to the answers from the other side, Sherlock made the appropriate noises of assent, repeated a series of numbers out loud, then thanked whomever she was speaking with, and ended the call.

We walked back in the direction of the parking garage we'd chased our man into this morning. I longingly looked at the near-empty coffee shop as we passed. It was far warmer than a parking garage that was just barely 'out of the wind.' I swore to invest in long underwear as soon as humanly possible, if this sort of thing was to be the norm from now on.

When we reached the intersection just across from the garage, Sherlock almost stepped off the edge of the curb, into traffic, turning right, and onto the street we were attempting to cross. Grabbing her wool coat, I pulled Sherlock back. I could see Sherlock was in thinking mode again--eyes staring forward, but not seeing anything. "I know you're thinking," I whispered with a little more compassion than usual. A line of cars swung around the corner. "But not paying attention here can get you killed."

Granted, city traffic moved much slower than the areas around the ridiculous rows of shopping malls in suburbia, which were two lanes in each direction, turning lanes, people running red lights and generally being the worst drivers in the world. Sherlock would have been dead by 8:30 this morning if we were trying to traverse those suburban blights. But the city was still dangerous where the dense traffic meant no one could move very fast, but idiots always tried to.

We continued toward our destination without a response from Sherlock. No sarcasm. Not even a dismissive glance. Did being exceptionally smart make people inherently weird? I'd never met a certified genius. Just gifted kids who tended not to apply themselves because they really didn't need to, most of the time. Geniuses probably played by their own set of rules. I had guessed that much from the whirlwind that had been the last half a week with someone who was still kind of a stranger. The person I had ditched school (for the first time ever) for. Hell, this was the person I was blowing off my real and actual friends for.

When Sherlock sat on a bus shelter bench across the street from the parking garage where we'd had our unproductive chase, I joined her without question. I watched the other girl's fingers twitch for a few minutes, but eventually curiosity got to me. "Alright. I kept my mouth shut this whole time. Your think time is over."

Sherlock glanced at me, the first sign of responsiveness in ages.

"I didn't give in to my desire to strangle you when you took off without me. I think you'd better start explaining, before another bus comes across the river toward home, and I get on it."

Tilting her head back, a long stream of steam came out of her nose as she sighed. "The frequency of the deposits. Every morning, from an ATM downtown. Who gets paid daily?"

I looked around the streets for an answer, as if that would help. "Drug dealers?"

"It was rhetorical."

I waved a hand. "This is your show. By all means, go on."

"Thank you. Now, they're always deposited from the same ATM. Which is… drumroll…"

"Dramatic effect? Really?"

"It isn't often I have someone to do the big reveal with. Let me have this moment."

Contemplating actually giving her a drumroll on my leg, I decided against it. It probably wouldn't speed things along, and it would probably only encourage this type of behavior. "Moment's gone. Get on with it."

Sherlock scowled. "Well, if you're going to be that way." She folded her arms over her chest and gave a spoiled steamy puff of indignation, staring at the cars that came in and out of the garage.

Shoulders sagging, my head dropped into my hands. Sherlock always knew how to push my buttons. Everything had to be drama and expectation. "Oh, come on. You can't have a buildup like that and just leave it." Because a drama llama couldn't resist an audience.

Sniffing the cold air, she avoided looking at me, taking a sudden intense interest in the ticket-issuing machine, and the man in the booth who wasn't paying any attention to the people with monthly passes leaving one by one. "Can. Did."

"Ass."

"Well, fine. If you insist. They all come from that ATM there." I stared at the machine installed in the side of the building that shared a wall with the garage.

"Okay…" I kept searching for some story from all the mystery novels I'd ever read that would explain this odd chain of events. "We didn't see him deposit anything this morning."

"I know." She said it as if it were some sort of explanation.

"I'm about to get angry. I'm smart but I'm not a genius. You have to start making allowances for us mere mortals."

"So Jeff Blackwell has two accounts. One that he deposits cash into daily."

"Obvious drug dealer," I interrupted, just to be contrary. An older woman passing looked at us with an angry glare from behind the scarf wound several times around her wrinkled and over-powdered face.

"Shut up, Watson. He's not a drug dealer. Don't ruin the reveal."

I held up my hands again. "By all means. Proceed."

Sherlock picked up her head, gesturing toward the ATM with her chin. "The deposits are made mid-morning anyway, we'd never have seen him make it at the time we arrived; we'd faffed off to the corporate building by then," she said, picking up a thread of thought from two or three minutes ago."Deposits daily, he transfers bi-weekly, when he should have been paid. Wife just sees money appearing into the account she can see. Doesn't bother looking further because nothing is amiss. No one actually pays attention to that stuff, if the information they receive is consistent. It's only when there's a change that they look at the details. No one reads their pay stubs, no one looks at their phone bill--if all the numbers are roughly the same every month. So she's not looking for the second account--which she can't see--or the frequent deposits of cash."

"That he gets from drug dealing," I said smartly, just trying to hurry Sherlock along.

"Watson, shut up." This time the order was laced with a bit of humor.

"Money laundering."

"Good thought, but no. He's passing money around so she doesn't notice any difference…"

I couldn't keep from interrupting again. "All of this so his wife doesn't know he's lost his job. I still don't get the subterfuge. Just suck it up and say you got laid off."

"Watson--never mind. The point is--he's not paying himself from a dummy corporation or attempting to legitimize or clean the money in any sort of way. It's just for the wife's benefit. And if it's not laundering or drugs, what is it? Something illegal?"

My compatriot shook her head no, like I should be well beyond such suppositions by now.

233

"Oh, come on, Holmes. Quit dragging it out. It's something so big she is being blackmailed over it. It has to be something illegal. You don't just end up with the same amount of money as you had working a big corporate job from... I don't know." I was still hanging onto the drug dealer thing. Like Sherlock had said last week--they made a lot of money.

"Shut up. You want me to explain it, it takes a while. People hate it when I give up the answer too quickly and think I'm guessing. Or that I'm a magician."

"Fine, fine." I crammed my hands into my pockets. "Carry on."

"I'm not saying it isn't shady. I have a lot of ideas and no data. All I know is that it's not drugs."

I leaned back against the cold wall of the glass shelter. "Oh my god! This was supposed to be the big reveal! I hate you right now! You got me all worked up, then didn't deliver."

She threw her hands up in the air. "We aren't sitting here for our health, Watson! We're waiting for the man himself to come back. I am about to give you a spectacular finish, and you're worried because the lead-up was too long." Her face scrunched up and she wavered, unsure what to do with her angry energy. Finally, she punched me in the shoulder. "Pearls before swine! That's what's going on here!"

Even though the punch hadn't been hard, and there'd been plenty of protective layers between me and her gloved fist, I still rubbed the area. "Ow."

"That didn't hurt. But I'm about to show you something fantastic and you're complaining it isn't over yet. These things take time. And patience. And if I have to come back tomorrow morning and wait for the deposit, I will. But he knows someone is looking for him, and he probably won't put in an appearance tomorrow because he will be too busy lying low."

"And these things also require you wandering around and thinking all day. Now what's your stupid theory that we need more data for?"

Sherlock shook her head, having even less patience for me than usual. "I have to work things out in my head before I pursue them. Or him, as the case may be, Watson. You find out a lot about people by following them. Their daily routine, their habits and idiosyncrasies. Television makes it seem like detection is all about digging through trash and bothering relatives."

I held my tongue. Sherlock didn't seem to be the type to get her hands dirty like that anyway. I considered the possibility that this was what I had been brought along for. Emergency dumpster diving.

We watched a Mustang pull up and press the button for a ticket. Nothing happened. After a long while, the bored and distracted fellow in the booth leaned out and handed him a ticket with the time written on it. A woman clacked past on our side of the street with an enormous case on wheels, her too-big heels striking the pavement unevenly. Two more people stopped at the ATM across the street, which I was now hyper-aware of. Cars came in, cars came out. People moved about the city all around us, getting on buses, old cars stopping at lights next to new ones.

I noticed someone who'd passed twice, probably lost or something. There were too many one-way streets, and streets that didn't go where you thought they would. I'd grown up in the area, and had spent a lot of time downtown with my dad as a kid, going to baseball games in the summer, and the first time I drove downtown I still had gotten lost for half an hour on streets I'd walked over a thousand times when I was younger.

"So," I said after a while, trying to fill the cheek-biting silence. "We'll be able to figure out what he's up to by doing this?" Hopefully before we froze to death.

A car stopped to take a ticket from the machine, but it didn't seem to actually want to release the ticket again. Finally after the angry woman in the rusted-out hatchback Mustang slammed the button a third time, three tickets came shooting out of the machine. I had to smile. There was something about seeing that everyone else's lives were fraught with just as many tiny frustrations as my own that made my life just a bit more bearable.

Sherlock watched the woman in the Mustang until her car turned to go up the ramp and disappeared from view. "Interesting."

I didn't ask what was interesting. I was learning better.

A woman in a skirt far too short for the weather lugged an enormous computer case into the parking garage entrance. The city was filled with so many things that I had never noticed before, but now that I was looking, the world was different and new. And that was, honestly, exciting.

"I used to do the odd bit of dumpster diving," Sherlock mused absently. "It's only marginally effective. And all it did was create arguments with Mrs. Hudson over dry cleaning bills. She's not paying for it, so I don't understand the conflict, exactly. But she takes some sort of offense to me coming home covered in stable muck, or rotten cabbage, or soaked to the bone in river water that stinks of equal portions mold and sewage. Apparently, it isn't very lady-like."

I shrugged. I was the last person to be able to tell anyone what was, or what was not ladylike behavior. I saw beautiful women in beautiful dresses in magazines, and sometimes wanted to look finished and perfect like that--kind of a princess for a day. But then I remembered I was short, stocky, and broad-shouldered. I shuddered to even think about what I'd look like in a prom dress, next to those slim, tall girls in my gym classes who wore tiny shorts to show off their immaculate tans in winter.

I was probably consigned to a lifetime in sweatpants. Well, I did have my current getup. I liked this. It probably wasn't supermodel gear, but it felt nice and grownup, in its own skinny-jean tucked into loose-fitting ankle boots sort of way. Neither of us quite fit the mold, did we?

"At some point she'll give up, right? Trying to shoehorn you into a role you're obviously not suited for?"

Sherlock laughed. "I suspect our levels of stubbornness are comparable to the Cold War. She has nukes that she's not afraid to use. I have nukes that I am unafraid to use. The only thing that keeps us in this constant battle of wills is the inevitability of mutually assured destruction."

"Crap." It sounded exhausting, constantly being locked in tension with someone. "I just have to worry about how every time I forget to do something around the house, my dad freaks out and compares me to my brother."

"That's because he cares."

"He is welcome to find some other way of expressing it, you know? He's paranoid about me doing drugs, or getting in with the wrong crowd. I stayed too long at the main library once. And got grounded. For being at the library. On a Sunday."

"That would get old," she agreed with a tight smile. "But he does care. And that's something. More than something." The last was said with a kind of longing that caught me off guard.

"Mrs. Hudson cares about you, doesn't she?"

Sherlock shrugged. "I honestly couldn't answer that."

I let it go. It sounded like a tough subject, and one I had no experience with, therefore no advice or answers. One thing I had learned--to stay in my lane. Stay away from things I knew nothing about. Of course, I was failing at the moment. But the subject of Sherlock's complicated relationship with the house staff was a landmine I didn't need to step on at this very moment.

Pressing a hand to my nose, I realized how cold my face was getting. Mostly because my nose was officially numb. "You're sure he's going to come back here?"

"Yes. He has to. I think."

I wondered at what point frostbite left one in danger of actually losing appendages. I was about ready to pull out my phone and Google the answer, just so I would know. "Can we wait for him inside?"

I got another smarmy sidelong glance for my trouble. "Getting too cold out here for you, Watson?"

I caught sight of the black Lincoln Town Car that had already passed twice. I could tell it was the same one--the windows were dark, and you didn't exactly see many cars like that hanging around the city, especially when tinted windshields and windows were largely illegal in this county.

The car slowed as it passed us, and I thought of saying something. But it was probably nothing.

"I suppose we could wait just inside. But we'd have to be out of the line of sight of the attendant's booth, because we'd probably get tossed out of the garage immediately."

Looking at the attendant, I didn't see anything about him that would indicate he'd be bothered by much of anything. "Do you think so?"

"We don't look like we'd key or damage cars, or boost them. But you never know."

I made a face. "You aren't opposed to stealing cars. Now you're going to tell me that your sweet and innocent looks preclude you from looking like a car thief? Shut up."

"As I was saying," Sherlock said, charging straight ahead. "Two people hanging around a parking garage are more trouble than they're worth, even if the attendant has no care for what happens in his garage. People look for unlocked cars to steal things. Homeless people come in to get out of the elements."

I pinched the far too expensive jacket that Sherlock had gotten me the night before. "We hardly look homeless." My thoughts went back to the Shakespeare-quoting fellow from the morning and grimaced. "Whatever. We'll keep ourselves out of sight if it means less trouble or work for ourselves, and I manage to get through the day without losing any toes."

With the briefest of smiles, Sherlock slapped my leg, this time roughly. It stung my already-freezing skin. "Good man, Watson."

"Why do you--"

She cut off my unexpressed question by pointing past me, gloved hand barely missing my burning cheeks. "There. By that pillar. We can see who's entering and exiting and the attendant shouldn't be able to see us."

Knowing I'd never get an answer, I crossed the street with Sherlock to our semi-hidden hiding place--between a cement pillar, a boxy grey Volvo, and a guardrail. It wasn't necessarily warmer on my butt than the plastic bench, but it was out of the wind and it made the tingling shivers running up and down my spine dissipate over time.

We sat in silence, watching the cars enter and exit, some with monthly passes that let the gate open for them immediately, and some who had to deal with cash and change, and the unhappy, disinterested attendant who looked like he'd rather be anywhere else. He and I had that in common. But I would see this through. Even if hypothermia was an actual concern at this point.

It was boring and freezing. I glanced again at Sherlock, who had finally put her gloved hands in the pockets of her black coat. But other than that, and a bit of reddening in the cheeks and ears, she seemed completely unaffected. Maybe Sherlock was Batman.

"So… when you're not doing these sorts of uh… case things… what do you do for fun?"

"Hmm." The other girl contemplated. "The cold cases, mostly. Experiments, important data gathering. I have eighty-four types of tobacco ash and sixty-one types of perfume catalogued. I expect to get both well over a hundred by spring break."

"Sounds… awesome," I replied with no enthusiasm. "What do you need to know this stuff for?"

"You never know, Watson. You just… never know."

We went back to the cryptic silence.

After four more cars passed, Sherlock squinted at something. "Watson," she said quietly, never turning her head. "Look slowly. Don't draw attention to yourself."

I followed her line of sight. The homeless man, with his slouched shoulders and duffle bag from earlier in the day.

His face was hidden by his dirty cap and he seemed even more slow-moving than usual.

"Are they going to kick him out?"

The attendant nodded to the man, who saluted in a quick and sloppy gesture, then continued on his way.

"Curiouser and curiouser." Sherlock tapped her bottom lip with her gloved finger.

"What is it? The guy is turning a blind eye and letting someone in out of the cold. I think that makes the guy in the booth a decent human being."

"Your brother was in the Marines, yes? Use your brain and think."

"About *what* exactly?"

Sherlock shook her head, astounded I could be so slow. "His coat. Cold War era. Air Force."

"Yeah, so?"

"That was a half-assed salute that would have been beaten out of him in the first week. Certain things are muscle memory that never go entirely away. While they become relaxed, they never become lazy."

My brain tried to catch up, but before I could process what she was telling me, Sherlock slung her bag over her neck so the strap was across her body, then took off running toward the man.

Chapter 20

Totally unprepared for the sudden movement, it took me an extra few seconds to launch myself into action. Sherlock may complain about her shoes, but she still managed to make some good time in them, because it took me an entire level to catch up with her. When I did, Sherlock was stopped in the middle of the lane for the exit, shaking her head.

"Where the hell did he go?" I called, half out of breath, looking around. There was no one. "We lost him?"

"Yeah, we lost him," Sherlock said in a quiet, still voice as she sucked in cold air. "But I think we have him."

Sure.

Sherlock looked around the garage. At the expensive cars, the older, worn ones... and settled on the white van we'd seen this morning. No windows in the rear, no logo saying it belonged to a telecom company or a plumbing business...

Slowly, quietly, somehow managing to not clack her heels against the cement floor of the garage, she crossed over to the van. Tugging on the fingers of her glove, she pulled it off, then wiped her finger against the side of the van and came back with a thick coating of dark grey pollution and grime. "Hardly good for business, I'd say," she whispered, pulling a cloth handkerchief from her pocket and wiping the mess away.

Next she looked down at the tires. The treads were worn smooth and flat in the middle. But that wasn't what interested Sherlock. She knelt as much as she could in that long, tight pencil skirt and inspected the tire. "They're all like this. Low. Very low. This van hasn't moved from this spot in some time."

"Not following."

"This is why you are the sidekick," Sherlock said with a sigh. She undid the first button on her coat, and reached deep into the inner pocket.

"We are going to discuss the wrongness of that statement later."

Sherlock pulled out a small zippered case. "But that's what this case is all about, isn't it? Secret identities? Villains who know about said identities..." Unzipping the case, Sherlock revealed the contents.

I had seen enough television to know what that was. "Why do you have a lock picking kit? Where do you *get* one of those?" I whispered.

"Locksmith."

"Who just gave you one."

"Borrowed. Long-term loan." She set to work on the lock slowly, not bumping the van or making the slightest noise to be heard by the vehicle's occupants.

She read my mind again, and answered the question I wasn't thinking. "Book from the library." That's how she'd learned to pick locks. "They have everything. Ventriloquism, hacking, cracking, programming, body dismemberment, poisoning, dog training, sandcastle building, and taxidermy." She rattled it all off under her breath, like it was nothing.

A second later, the van's lock clicked open. In triumph, Sherlock pulled hard on the exterior handle, flinging the door open.

And the reveal was... dramatic. So much so that I let out a gasp before I realized it had even escaped me.

There he was---sitting at a long, thin workbench in the back of the van, with a makeup mirror surrounded by bright lights powered by a small battery. The homeless man. But not the homeless man. The hat and wig sat beside him, and the scarring that I had pitied earlier in the day was half-peeled off the man's face. The man himself I recognized immediately. Jeffrey Blackwell.

The man himself had the decency to look stunned. "This isn't what it looks like," he chirped in surprise.

Sherlock looked over the well-tailored suit hanging up behind Blackwell on a hook, still neat and tidy from a day of being unworn. "I think it's exactly what it looks like."

I swallowed the lump in my throat and pushed past Sherlock, shoving her unceremoniously out of the way. "*Why?*" I demanded in a dead whisper.

"Isn't it obvious?" Sherlock muscled her way between us.

I scowled. I did know why. But why this subterfuge?

Blackwell looked back and forth from me to Sherlock and back to me again, his eyes wide like an animal about to become roadkill. "I--I didn't want to tell my wife," the man said pitiably.

Or I would have had pity if it weren't for the painful fire in my chest, my worries about freezing to death suddenly gone.

Sherlock groaned. "It's the twenty-first century, Mr. Blackwell, and the economy has turned to rubbish. There is no crime in being laid off." She looked him over. "Oh. You were fired, weren't you? Still--it happens. Nor is it expected or necessary for you to be the primary breadwinner."

"And you're making your money panhandling. To keep being the breadwinner?" I tried to keep myself calm, but it wasn't working.

"He's good at it, aren't you, Mr. Blackwell? The sad veteran routine--and you had even *me* fooled with the makeup, for which you should congratulate yourself, really. Combined with the Shakespeare--the man of learning down on his luck. How much are you pulling in a day? A couple hundred. At least. Tax free, under the table. Push the money through money orders and a separate bank account and your wife is too busy to notice anything's amiss and you get off scot-free. Almost."

I clenched my teeth together as if that would somehow keep me from unloading. But the man relaxed, as if this were the end of a terrible ordeal, and I snapped. "Except for the part where he is a massive asshole," I interjected. My fist clenched and he was so lucky Sherlock was intentionally blocking my path. I didn't even worry about the inevitable assault charges.

"Who was I hurting?" Blackwell chimed in, as he peeled the silicone scars away from his chin and lip. "People with money who get to feel like they've done something good or useful for society? That's who. They get warm fuzzies for dumping change in the Salvation Army buckets. I capitalize, I get a paycheck, they feel like good people. And I don't have to sit in that god-awful office anymore, pushing paper for corporate scrooges turning down loans for decent people trying to make something of themselves. I never take money from people who don't have it to spare." He held up the fifty-dollar bill Sherlock had given him this morning. Sherlock glanced at it, but did not snatch it back, proving that she really did have the money to throw away. "See, I'm the good guy here."

"I wouldn't go that far." Even Sherlock was disgusted.

I edged closer, my hand on Sherlock's arm.

A cheshire grin spread across Sherlock's thin lips. "My associate appears to be prone to violence. Should I step out of the way?"

"Oh, come on! Because I give people a little culture in this grey, cold place? And they parted with money they had too much of? Don't you think I know who these people are? They're like me. The way I used to be. Stuck in an office, a cog in the machine. The more unhappy they are, the more money they need to assuage their unhappiness and the harder they work. And the unhappier they become. Greed creates a pressure valve; I give them the release. They feel better about themselves and I am free of the rat race. Getting fired was a blessing. For me. For them. I am providing a service."

I shoved Sherlock so hard she bounced off the open door of the truck and I threw myself in, my fist connecting with his jaw. "There are *real* vets with real problems, living on the streets, who don't know how to play it up and get fifty dollars here and twenty dollars there." I grabbed him with both hands by the collar of his dirty flannel shirt, shaking him as a red mark appeared on his cheek. "And then they aren't getting the help they need. You just get on the bus, and go home to your enormous, heated house every night, while they sleep out here, under bridges and in doorways, freezing to death on the street. I hope you rot in a very special place in hell. One reserved for murderers, assholes, and people who hurt children."

I throttled him by the collar one more time. The force of it surprised me; I felt his head snap back, then forward. The way he almost ripped out of my grasp with the force of my own hand made me release him, and I backed out of the van, scraping my knee on the rusting metal bumper.

He didn't say anything. He blinked slowly and rhythmically and might have been stunned from the abuse.

Sherlock put a hand on my shoulder and squeezed hard to keep me from moving. "Get yourself dressed. We'll sort this out someplace warm. And possibly in public so my associate doesn't throttle you to death. Not because I care. But because I find the disposing of bodies to be genuinely tedious."

She closed one of the van doors with her shoulder, then the other with her elbow, never letting go of her death grip just at the edge of my collarbone.

"You don't know where your brother is, do you?"

I looked away, my eyes stinging. "I don't want to do this now."

But as usual, Sherlock didn't need someone else to explain. "No. This is the real reason you're keeping me company. You want to know if I can really find him."

My cheeks burned with shame. Said like that, I was using her. But wasn't I? Testing her to see what she could do for me?

"He served. Did his two years and got out. Your father was so proud, wasn't he? Which is what made it all the worse when he started drinking to dull the images of what he had seen and done."

I breathed in angrily through my nose. I hated that she just knew everything. "Shut up," I spat.

"Nearly killed himself somehow." She continued on, as if I hadn't said anything at all. "Motorcycle accident?"

247

The door handle on the inside of the van twisted, and it cracked open an inch. Both of our hands slammed it closed immediately.

I ground my teeth as she continued. "Which led him to drink more. And another accident. And legal trouble. Your father's pride turned to despair that his son was not the hero he'd envisioned, and he kicked him out. And you haven't seen him since."

"I hate you right now."

Her tone turned gentle. "Most people do hate it when I am right." Sherlock smiled gently, and she bumped my chin upward with her finger so we were eye to eye. "I have a lot of experience in being the family disappointment."

Somehow, those words softly spoken told me just how much Sherlock understood. Despite the disparaging difference in our lives, we had the same shape of disappointment and loss marked on them.

"You're kind of a decent person, Sherlock Holmes," I told her, sniffling hard, trying to hold back both mucus and tears.

She nodded, grabbing hold of the door handle of the van again. "Please don't allow anyone to hear you say that out loud. I have a reputation to uphold." With that, she ripped the door open again. "Are you dressed? Good. It's time we have a little talk."

In his suit and dress coat, red welt slowly turning blue on his jaw, the man hunched on the bench, looking entirely deflated. "Don't tell my wife?" he pleaded.

"Oh, we are so far past telling your wife. It's not her that you need to worry about. It's the professional blackmailer who is demanding a tremendous amount of money to keep your little enterprise from ruining her budding political career.

And I have not ruled out the possibility of allowing my associate to continue punching your face. Repeatedly."

Blackwell seemed confused. He looked around the van which more resembled a stage actor's dressing room than an automobile, as if it would somehow contain the answers he sought. "They're blackmailing Eva? Because of this? No one knows about this. Except for Richie. The lot attendant." Who'd waved him in when he'd entered. "I give him a cut. He doesn't report the van as being abandoned. Everything's fine."

"Mostly for Richie," was Sherlock's dry and salty response. "Your blackmailer pays obscene amounts of money for information. Not only was your friend getting money from you, but from the blackmailer as well. For a parking attendant, he is doing quite well for himself. I applaud his resourcefulness in plying the information trade. Perhaps he will be of use to me at some point."

The man licked his dry bottom lip. "So what are we doing about this?"

Sherlock looked him over in bland disinterest. "I don't know. It's up to your wife if this information is worth the price it will cost you both to keep it silent. Odds are, she will come up with the funds to save herself the embarrassment and the end of her political aspirations. You, on the other hand, may want to find a divorce lawyer."

"But I love her! That's why I didn't want to tell her! We have to find some way of fixing this!" His desperation had gone to groveling in a single sentence.

Readjusting the strap on her messenger bag, Sherlock then redid the top button of her coat, making it clear she was done with this. Taking out her phone, she began texting rapidly with both thumbs. Sending the message, her phone made a 'swoosh' sound, and then she looked up again. "We were employed to discover what Charles had on you. We did that. I believe this concludes our involvement in the case. You're on your own, sir. Good luck."

She turned on her heels, the bottoms of her shoes scraping on the cement, and walked away, no longer caring about the clacking that her heels made as she moved.

I stared at Blackwell for a moment. The man's face was scrunched in personal agony, brow furrowed and lips twisted as he contemplated just how far his life had fallen, and what would happen with the sudden and inevitable stop at the bottom.

"Just so you know," I said in a quiet, cool voice. "I think you are a piece of shit. You had the talent to do a lot of things, and this is what you chose to do. I hope you get what's coming to you." I turned and stood a bit straighter, something in the confrontation changing my carriage, and marched forward to catch up with Sherlock.

It was getting dark, and some of the street lamps were coming on. "I trust you don't need a lawyer?" she asked, sending off another message to our 'client.'

"Not this time. I'm saving my one bailout for later." Because with my dad, that's all I'd get. "I suddenly understand why Mrs. Hudson quizzes you when you get home every day, if this is how your life normally goes."

Sherlock grinned. "I'm not saying the answer to her questions will always be no. But every day that goes by when I can answer them that way, she considers her job to be a success. It's a service, really."

"I'm freezing. Can we get the hell out of here?" I was pretty sure hypothermia was coming for me.

Nodding, Sherlock looked down the street, then at her phone. "Toby should be on his way to pick us up right now.

He's not happy I was not at school when he showed up at three."

I could imagine it. Especially if the whole purpose of Sherlock being transported to and from school was to make sure she actually attended said school, I could see where her driver would not be pleased with having to retrieve us from a part of the city twenty miles from where the school in question was.

The black Lincoln with the tinted windows passed by again. "You know, that's the fourth time I've seen that car today."

Sherlock watched it turn sharply around the nearest corner. "Interesting. Did you get a plate number?"

"Wasn't exactly at the forefront of my mind. I'm lucky I noticed the car making multiple appearances throughout the day."

"Next time, Watson. Don't just see. Observe."

"If there is a next time."

Sherlock laughed and nudged me with her shoulder. "Oh, there'll be a next time. In fact... I suspect 'this time' isn't over yet."

"Ok. So we're going to die of pneumonia or consumption or something, and that will be how the Case of the Begging Banker ends?"

An actual fond look passed on Sherlock's usually serious hawk-like face. "'The Case of the Begging Banker?' That's what you're going to call it? And no one dies of consumption anymore. Don't be melodramatic. It's called tuberculosis and we've both been immunized."

"Consumption sounds... more romantic."

A silent chuckle quaked the other girl's chest. "Romantic? There's not a damned thing romantic about coughing up blood and bits of your own lung. However, I will give you points for 'The Case of the Begging Banker.' When you sell the story to Collier's Mystery Magazine. I expect a signed copy."

"Riiiight. I have lower expectations. Let's start with the school lit mag and then move on from there." Yet another anonymous contribution from someone half the school insisted was a dude. I wasn't even sure how I felt about that.

"Don't sell yourself short. It's a perfect story for a mystery magazine. The serial numbers filed off and the names changed to protect the guilty, of course. And I will proofread it for you. To make sure you got all the important bits right. And don't overly romanticize--oh."

A car stopped in front of us. Not just a car. *The* car. The Lincoln with the tinted windows. It was probably too much to ask that the dark and mysterious vehicle belonged to Sherlock's 'people.'

"I sense this is not-good," I muttered.

Sherlock tensed, prepared for what was sure to be an unpleasant encounter. "I suppose you could always sell your story to a spycraft magazine," she said absently as the back door of the car opened.

"I'm not a real writer," I answered in a rush of nervousness as a familiar heavyset balding man leaned out of the car. In fact, any fantasies I'd had about ever actually getting around to the writing portion of being a real author were slowly fading if these were the types of life experiences it was necessary to gain in order to put words on paper.

The man looked us over. By the sneer on his fat lips, he found us wanting. "Get in. Now." Obviously not a request.

"I'm not allowed to take rides from strangers," Sherlock said, looking at her phone. "And my ride will be here in like… ten minutes. But thanks anyways." She slid her phone back into her pocket.

The man smiled, slow and menacing. Like a Bond villain. "I have ways of persuading people to give in to my requests." In a long, drawn out gesture, he produced a small caliber pistol with a silencer from his coat pocket.

I raised my hands slowly. "I just decided I don't wanna be a writer anymore."

Chapter 20

Augustus waited until we were all situated in the car. He sat behind the driver, facing away from him, Sherlock and me on the other bench seat. He lowered the gun slightly, but still kept it at the ready. "Please, don't try anything, the driver is the only one who can unlock the back doors. I am wearing a stab-resistant vest. And bodies are annoyingly difficult to dispose of, in this day and age. Besides--this isn't about anything as coarse and plebeian as murder."

"This is about blackmail," Sherlock supplied. "I know. And you're quite good at it. Some would say the best."

The man shifted with pride, the fur of his long fur coat rippling. "I'm glad my reputation precedes me. Even if it is with children and small pets." An eyebrow arched as he glanced at me in amused skepticism.

I almost retorted, but decided it was probably not in my best interest. The man did, after all, have a gun that was not yesterday's little Derringer. What did I have? A cute new haircut and out-of-date mace.

Sherlock had that air about her, where nothing seemed to bother her at all. "So what is it to you if Eva Blackwell knows and understands exactly what she's being blackmailed over?"

Good question. Because I couldn't figure out why the big man in the fur coat had bothered to stalk us in a department store, all around the town, and culminating in a slight case of abduction. This wasn't a game, but it felt like it was being played like one.

We crossed over a bright yellow bridge, out of the city's center, and headed west, in the opposite direction of our homes.

"Emotions, Ms. Holmes."

Sherlock nodded, understanding. "She discovers what he's been doing, decides--rashly--to let him hang. She's ruining her future political prospects. And she's being set up to take the retiring senator's place, isn't she? But she won't think about that in the heat of her rage. All she'll be thinking about is her humiliation and the burn of betrayal, and then your information is worth nothing, because she will ruin herself. Which would be fine. You probably don't need her money. But you will lose her future political influence." There was none of the normal Sherlock pride in that assertion. Just the seriousness of cold, hard fact.

I supposed it all made perfect sense. In context. It was a much bigger scheme than I thought. But Sherlock wasn't surprised and must have been expecting it. If this guy was the best, he'd done it to others. And if he had, he'd amassed a fortune and untold influence in who knew how many arenas. Business, politics, and I didn't have the imagination for the rest.

"Ahh. I think your friend's mind is... expanding. Or imploding. I cannot tell."

"Joanna's generally pleasant but a bit slow on the uptake. But she gets there eventually," Sherlock said, patting my leg twice, then sitting back.

Sherlock and Augustus stared at each other, locked in some discussion in which words were not needed.

"You know who I am." Sherlock broke the silence. "You know who my family is. You wouldn't have picked us off the street, in broad daylight, if you didn't want your hand shown." She smiled tightly. "Good news, Joanna. We're now pawns in a larger scheme. My compliments for seeing an opportunity and taking it."

I didn't know anything at all about Sherlock's family, other than their total absence from her life. How important could they be? "So Eva Blackwell is old and busted and we are the new hotness?"

"Your friend doesn't quite get it. Do you wish to explain it, or shall I?"

"It depends on which of us is more obsessed with melodrama."

Augustus gestured to the gun in his hand. "I think I have the drama covered. I will leave the denouement to you."

"Denouement? Yes. You do have the drama covered." She turned to me, shifting slightly, making the leather seat creak. "This isn't about the money. Well, it is. But he has that sewn up. And a future senator. If she had any ideas about not running, Augustus will persuade her. And back her. And control her. So we are just an annoyance, really. Fortunately, one of us is worth something in the grand scheme of things."

Augustus sighed in wistful longing. "Ah. You see the world as I do, don't you? The magnificent turning gyres--the cogs and gears that move the world. And how, if you can find the right one, you can make it turn in your own favor. The intense beauty of the machine."

Sherlock took her time pulling the gloves from her fingers, one at a time. "I do. I see how the pieces fit together. How easily they are manipulated. And those that don't," she glanced pointedly toward me, "are fools." She smiled politely. "I have waited all of my life to meet someone like you, sir. I consider today to have been well spent."

"I appreciate that you appreciate my talents and skills." The smile didn't make it as far as his eyes, which made it terribly menacing. "My apologies for yesterday's... department store debacle."

Sherlock smiled politely. "We had to feel each other out."

"I don't find you wanting."

Sherlock sat back. "Good."

My jaw clenched and I had to sit on my hands to keep from doing something rash and stupid. This whole thing--this case--whatever it was--it had been something other than I'd thought from the beginning. And apparently Sherlock had been, too. Well. Didn't I feel like an idiot.

Sherlock grinned with the same maniacal energy as when she'd attempted to strangle me on the second day of our acquaintanceship. Apparently it was raining kittens and rainbows in Sherlock's head right now, and we'd be hard pressed to bring her back from her happy place. "I'm a student of the greats. And you, sir, are one of the greats. Of our own time, at least. And historically... well, perhaps historically as well. Allow me to congratulate you on a chess game well played."

##

We passed through one of the tunnels that led out of the downtown area as fast as the other cars around us would allow. Which meant we ended up going around sharp bends at around seventy miles per hour, even though the speed limit was more like fifty-five.

Several townships and boroughs passed by until the rush-hour population of cars thinned down to something more manageable and less likely to give me a heart attack. I'd had my license for less than six months, and I still didn't want to drive on the highways in this town. Namely because everyone drove like a maniac, and being on the road with them felt like I was constantly on the verge of being stomped to death by horses.

Even though I was sitting in a car with men with guns and a lunatic friend, I really didn't need anything else giving me heart palpitations.

I stole glances at Sherlock occasionally, hoping for some indication that this was all part of some plan or something. But she just sat there, leather bag in lap, gloves folded neatly on top, unaffected by everything around her. She might have been completely content with the situation for all the unreadability of her face told me.

I tried to pull the phone out of my pocket once and surreptitiously attempt to dial 9-1-1, but, firstly, it was way harder to dial on a touch screen without looking than I'd have anticipated and secondly, Augustus had raised the gun and reminded me he had no trouble killing, even if he disliked it. I started putting the phone away, but Augustus ordered me to hand it over.

Which left the odds of rescue, or escape, or, well... whatever, to be much lower than before.

"Where're we going?" I asked finally, to break up the despised silence.

"Airport," Sherlock muttered, looking out the window absently.

"Why?"

"My brother is in DC. Which is a very tedious four-and-a-half hour drive from here. Why have just a senator when you can have a senator and other miscellaneous and sundry figures in non-elected government positions at your disposal?" She sighed, as if it were boring now that everyone's hand had been played.

I looked down at my knees and rubbed them with nervous energy, trying to think of something--anything.

Sherlock frowned. "Or I suppose there's Switzerland. My father…"

Augustus laughed. "Your father. Don't take me for a fool."

That caught Sherlock off guard. She flinched. Not really. But it was that same shirking back eye-twitch that Sherlock had given me in the bathroom after the public strangling incident. Augustus knew something Sherlock didn't. Something big.

"You are adorable," Augustus said. "You are certainly no Sherrinford." Sherlock flinched for real this time. "But you are adorable. And… moldable."

"Don't say her name," Sherlock said with force.

"There's no harm in saying her name. It's just a name. Macbeth. Lord Voldemort."

Sherlock looked confused by the second.

"Children's books," I supplied. "I'll make you watch the movies later."

"Macbeth, Voldemort… Sherrinford Alice Theresa Holmes, born January sixth, two thousand and…"

The look Sherlock gave him was filled with rage and agony.

He had the good sense to shut up. "I'll let it be for now. For now. We shall see about later. Relative value in this one?"

Sherlock sniffed, then straightened up, her face moving back to passive. "Well, she can drive, which increases her relative value to me, of course. And good for a tumble. Good for a scrap--"

A tumble? Sherlock and I were not tumbling anywhere. "What?"

Augustus waved a hand dismissively. "Well, I did say relative value. But not to you. In the grand scheme of things."

"Father's a cop. If she went missing... Well, there'd be a fervor. I'd be under investigation. But there'd be nothing they could actually pin on me." Sherlock stared off into space, seeming to weigh her options. "I'd like to keep her. But if I can't, I understand."

Well, wasn't I just a comfortable, well-worn t-shirt with a giant hole in the side.

"Done. I hate making a mess. Fortunately I have people to do that for me." Augustus looked to his man in the driver's seat.

My eyes went wide and I glared at Sherlock. "What just happened?"

Sherlock slouched in her seat just a little. "You'll probably be killed. You're pretty worthless."

I glanced at my reflection in the glass window. "Great."

"You know what I mean," Sherlock corrected. "In the grand scheme of things."

"Thanks, again."

"I just mean..." Sherlock sighed, already tired of explaining it. "Seeing the trees for the forest. You're worth nothing for ransom, you have no big players politically or industrially in your family, so there's no leverage in keeping you alive. It's a shame. I was rather liking the thought of maybe having a friend."

I stared out the window, looking at the mile markers as they passed. When I felt more composed, I finally opened my mouth to reply. "Just make sure, when this is all over with, that you inform my father that I'm dead because you are a psychopath with an ego the size of a small Latin American country."

The chuckle that came from beside me was eerie and emotionless. "Oh come on, Joanna. Give me *some* credit. It's not *that* big. Think more like… Luxembourg."

##

"I don't want to die," I said absently, watching the cars in the oncoming lanes pass us by. "I mean--nobody wants to. But I'm not ready yet. Is there anything I can do to save my own skin? I mean, while we have all this honesty going around, regarding everyone's relative worth."

"Probably not," Charles Augustus said honestly. "And your friend was so apt to point out… you're far too low on the social ladder to be of any use to me."

"My dad's a cop."

Augustus chuckled. "I will give you credit for trying. But I only play with the big boys. Local cops are small potatoes. Hardly worth the trouble, when you can have a captain or commissioner willing to look the other way on your behalf."

Sherlock rubbed her lip. "Like the Linden case?"

"You really *are* a fan of my work,, aren't you?" Augustus flashed a quick look of pleasant surprise. "That was a long time ago."

Sherlock nodded once. "Cold cases are a hobby of mine."

"That one is very cold."

She shrugged. "No statute of limitations on murder."

"No, no. I suppose there's not." Augustus grew thoughtful. "You know, I like you. If we had more time, we could have some tea, and a nice sit-down, and I could play you my greatest hits."

"We might. It depends on how my brother feels about me. We haven't exactly spoken in a few years. After we do whatever we're doing with Joanna, we should swap tales. You could tell me what you had on Linden, and what went so horribly awry that his brains ended up splattered across his dining room wall. I can tell you about the time I got my dean fired for necrophilia."

That was not what I had been told at all. Sherlock had informed me that there had been some sort of scandal involving the dean of her old school, yes, but that there'd been lovers and lovers' lovers involved. Not… dead lovers. Or dead lovers' lovers. I hoped to god that it was a front meant to impress Augustus and that something creepy involving dead bodies was the bait. But then, at this point I had no idea what was true and what was embellishment when it came to Sherlock Holmes. If any of it had ever been true.

Augustus laughed so loudly and heartily that the entire car shook with the force of his amusement. "Necrophilia."

Sherlock nodded with pride and affirmation.

"I believe we have time for a tale or two. I almost wish I could keep you. You'd make an admirable protégée." Sherlock and Augustus were cut from the same cloth. It was unsurprising they'd get along.

I rested my elbow on the door and rubbed my forehead. A stress breakout was forming just under my skin. I heard morticians could cover that kind of thing with putty or something. If I got an open-casket funeral.

Sherlock leaned forward, nearly bouncing with excitement. "So, go on. Tell me. Christopher Linden. Were you making an example out of him? So that subsequent marks would know that you mean business? I mean--you've blackmailed at least three hundred people in the fifteen years since the Linden case."

The faintest of smiles pulled at the man's fat cheeks. "Three hundred? The legal establishment far underestimates my reach. And not just this country. I've branched out. I have my fingers in many pies. And in many governments. I'd say it's well over a thousand."

Sherlock leaned still closer with her enthusiasm. "But the Linden case. That was a warning, right? I've read all the files. Fifty times, at least. I have copies of the pictures in my bedside table. Did you do it? Did you have other people do it? How did you get away with it?"

Oh, great. Sherlock was a fangirl. There was an excited intensity in Sherlock's eyes. They shimmered in the low light of the car. There was something feral and hungry about the upward turn of her lips which showed her too-white front teeth, stopping right at her canines. She looked like she could rip a throat out and enjoy every moment of blood and gore and death right now.

Maybe this was the real Sherlock.

Charles Augustus chuckled and I realized the man was staring at me. "I think your questions are too much for your friend's stomach."

Sherlock waved a dismissive hand. "You're killing her anyway. Why would I care if she got a little upset?"

Augustus regarded her for a moment. "You're clever. Not as clever as me. Or as clever as Sherrinford. But clever. Your disadvantage, however, is that you are a psychopath. That will hinder your progress in this field, you know. One needs a clear head and to be devoid of the need for criminal enterprise. It should be a want. Never a need." Augustus sighed, looking out the window for a moment, seeming lost in memories. "Fifteen years. It's a long time ago, when you think of it. And not. When you think of it. Time moves too fast and too slow as you age. Enjoy your youth." He rubbed his chin.

Now I had to listen to him wax philosophical. As if this driving to my death thing couldn't go any worse.

"Linden. That was before I had minions, you know. Minions, lackeys. Whatever you want to call them. Is there a proper term? I've never thought of it much. Anyhow. Believe it or not, that was all me. And..." He leaned closer to Sherlock. "It was an accident. Well, not really an accident. Linden wouldn't pay. I got tired of listening to him whine, and I shot him. It wasn't until I was stuffing him into the freezer in the garage that I really thought about how a dead client was one you'd never see money from, and I vowed not to do it again. However, if my clients had enough rope to hang themselves, and chose to..." He shrugged. "But it did what you said, clever girl. It sent a message that not only was I not joking about playing my hand with blackmail, I was not afraid of getting my hands dirty. It's actually been rather smooth sailing since. I've not had to kill anyone else. And if someone doesn't pay, or disbelieves the seriousness of my claims, I simply make their dirtiest secrets public. They're destroying themselves. I'm simply... Freeing the information."

Sherlock nodded, taking it all in. "So it's not blackmail, really. Information wishes to be free. And you are merely releasing it into the wild. Unless you are paid an appropriate sum."

"The cost of information brokerage, Ms. Holmes. It's simply the cost of doing business."

I looked away from them in disgust. "I can't believe you two. These are lives of actual real human beings you are ruining."

"So?" Sherlock and Augustus asked simultaneously.

"Oh for godsakes." Anger pushed up past the bile. "If you're going to kill me anyway, just do it now. So I don't have to listen to any more of this. Christ, Sherlock. I thought you were--I thought you were--" The rest of the words caught in my chest.

"I'm just a girl who likes solving puzzles," Sherlock said, not even bothering to look me in the eye. "And I do really love a good mystery." Her eyes narrowed. "We should probably pull over there at the old drive-in movie theater. If you kill her up there, they won't find the body until spring. Of course, there are large-enough prey animals up that way that they may not find her body. Or all of it. Just bits and pieces here and there."

I had read about how in crisis situations, sometimes people's minds and emotions shut off, leaving them feeling empty and blank. I couldn't imagine that feeling, until now. I was going to die, and the girl I'd had coffee and muffins with this morning was giving my murderer the best location to do it in. And I felt... nothing. I had lost all intense feelings on the matter the moment it had become inevitable. "Fine. Just make sure it's fast." It wasn't really a request. I knew I had no leverage. It was just something that I hoped for.

"Mmm. I'm going to miss you," Augustus muttered, squeezing Sherlock's leg as he leaned forward to talk to the

265

driver. Sherlock tensed visibly, but Augustus was too busy giving new instructions to take the exit that lead to the Nostalgiaville Drive-In Theater, which was obviously closed for the winter.

The last time I had been there with my family, we'd been an actual family. I had been young. Grade school, maybe. My mother still lived with us. My brother was in high school. We'd gone to see a double feature of something--there was no hope of recalling what. I'd fallen asleep in the back seat of my dad's tiny Toyota before the trailers had even ended. When I woke, I was being carried into the house by my father, and tucked into bed. My mother appeared a minute later with a warm washcloth. Apparently Harry had scrawled a mustache on me with purple marker while I'd been asleep. Oh well. At least I'd have good memories to think of, in those final moments.

Sherlock rubbed her lip again thoughtfully as the car traveled up the dark, unlit road to the theater. "You know, Joanna, we could have been great friends. If things had been different."

"If you weren't deranged?"

"Well, yes. There's that. But, in other circumstances. In other lives, maybe. You'd have been an accomplished doctor. I'd have been a great detective. Instead of pawns." She sighed, sitting back. "I don't like the idea of being a pawn. You get done up execution style, and I get traded for my brother's cooperation in whatever sort of espionage thing Augustus has going on. It's all a bit tragic, really."

Still devoid of emotion, I stared out the window, unable to see more than the thick rows of trees and they went up the hill. "Yeah. And if we'd have been friends, what would we have done?"

"Solved crimes, of course. Been great together. Brains, brawn. Proper spelling and grammar. We'd have had it all."

"And instead you're sacrificing me to cold logic, aren't you? I'm of no value in Uncle Chuckle's scheme, so I'm just going to be disposed of."

The car rolled to a stop at the gated entrance to the theater. There was a chain with a lock on it that needed to be dealt with. The car's headlights shone brightly on the barrier as the driver put the car in park. "I have a crowbar in the trunk," he reported, unlocking all the doors with a single click.

What? Sherlock was not going to show off her lock picking abilities to Augustus? Why the sudden modesty?

The gun, which had been stowed during the majority of our ride, magically reappeared, trained on me. "Get out."

I opened the car door about four inches, then stopped, head stooped in thought. "Before we do this, I just want to know. Why me? Of everyone in that school, why drag me into this mess?"

Sherlock didn't take the bait. "Just get out of the car, Joanna." She shoved my arm, and I practically fell out and onto the ground, and she got out on my side, just behind me. Sherlock grabbed my arm with a rough, tight grip and pulled me to my feet. "Though I will tell you this," she said as Augustus came around the car, gun in hand, leaning toward my ear. "Al Capone was never convicted of bootlegging, racketeering, or murder. He was convicted of tax evasion and mail fraud," she whispered. "Now move." She pushed me toward the gate.

The driver, in comparison to Charles Augustus, was a lean, tall man in a heavy wool coat. He grabbed the crowbar from the trunk and moved in a handful of long strides to the gate. This wasn't his first turn with illegal activity, because he jammed the narrow end of the crowbar into the U-shaped portion of the lock with relative ease. Using the gate as leverage, he pushed against it only once and the lock snapped. He grabbed the chain and yanked it from the gate, letting it fall to the ground in a snaking, clanging thunk, since there wasn't a soul around to hear.

Sherlock shoved me in the center of my back. "Hurry up. You need to die quickly so we can get to the part where we negotiate for my safe return."

I didn't respond, I simply obeyed. All four of us walked past the ticket booth, the gravel and frozen grass crunching beneath our feet. The individual speakers for each car sat on posts, all equal distance apart, in rows that reminded me more of tombstones in a national cemetery than a movie theater. In the darkness, the moonlight reflected off the giant white screen in a way that was eerie and disturbing. This was the movie of my life. And instead of being played by someone taller and thinner, with long dark hair and matte red lips, I was being played by my own foolish self. Not how I had wanted things to end up.

Sherlock pointed ahead to a small cement building that housed both the restrooms and concession stand. "Over there. Leave the body on the side facing the screen and no one will see it from the road when they check in on the place. They won't find it till spring."

"You've thought about this," Augustus said, impressed.

"Always have an exit strategy. I think about murder a lot. They say the average teenager thinks about sex once every three seconds. That's how often I think about murder." She glanced over at Augustus with hopeful eyes. "Do you think maybe I could…?"

The driver reached for a gun in a holster just beneath his coat, but Augustus held up a hand, telling him to stand down. The driver's hand fell to his side, but was still tense and at the ready. "You want to kill your friend," he said incredulously.

Sherlock gave a hopeful smile of girlish innocence. "Please? And I never said she was my friend."

Augustus took the request seriously. "Have you ever done this before?"

"I've always wanted to try. I've imagined it so many times. A shot to the chest--the heart exploding. The spatter. Or to the head. Brains and bits of skull blowing out the back. I've read all about it in books. I want to see it firsthand. For science." She held her hand out for the gun. "Just think. You'd have the ultimate blackmail material on me. You'd have my brother by the you-know-what."

The idea intrigued Augustus, who looked from the gun to Sherlock to me. I could do nothing but stand there, helpless with my hands in the air, wondering when this would all be over with. New students who showed up mid-week and mid-semester were trouble. I obviously should have maintained my conviction on the matter.

Augustus smiled, slowly. "Alright. But take your gloves off."

"Ahh. You want my fingerprints on the murder weapon. I like it." She nodded and obeyed.

Augustus unloaded the revolver, dumping the bullets into his gloved hand. "And the shells, if you please."

Sherlock grinned and shivered, nearly giggling with delight. "Oh, you're smart. So smart. A man after my own heart." She held out both hands for the weapons and bullets.

"And you, my dear. If you weren't so obviously deranged, I think we could have been great friends." He handed everything over to her. "I trust you know how to use this?"

She slid one bullet into the chamber. "I've read about it loads of times in books. I'm sure I can figure it out." She continued loading with steady fingers.

"God in heaven, save us from the book-learned." Augustus shook his head and gestured toward his driver. "Syl is here to make sure you don't try anything. I can absolutely guarantee that he can draw faster than you can aim and fire. Are we clear?"

"Can we please shoot me before I freeze to death," I asked in all politeness.

"I do enjoy bravado. It's a nice touch, Joanna," Sherlock said, slowly sliding the last bullet into the gun. "Let me enjoy this, ok? It's my first kill."

I looked around me in hopelessness, in search of some way out of my predicament. "Sorry for the inconvenience," I grumbled, scowling at my soon-to-be murderer.

Sherlock finally finished loading the gun, and pointed it at me. But then she paused, lowering it before turning around. "The safety's this bit right?" She held up the gun and pointed to something that I couldn't quite see in the darkness. Hell. I was about to be killed by someone who knew nothing at all about guns. It was insulting, really.

"Amateurs," Syl the driver grumbled. "Yes, that's the safety. And remember to cock the damned thing. Can we get this over with?"

Sherlock grinned. "Thanks!"

In a single gesture I almost missed, Sherlock pulled the safety and fired at the man, hitting him in the shoulder of the arm he'd used to reach for the gun earlier, then spun, lowering the gun just a bit and firing twice, into Augustus' knees.

Syl the driver dropped to the ground with a groan, but rolled onto his side to reach for his weapon with his other arm.

Without thinking, I launched myself at Sherlock, knocking the other girl to the ground, hard, just as a bullet whizzed by us, so close that I could feel the heat as it flew by. I suspected the only reason it hadn't hit home was because the man was firing with his non-dominant hand.

I ripped the gun out of Sherlock's hand and fired at the man, all in one motion, like in those super-cool movie action sequences. The bullet hit him in the other shoulder. I had no idea if I'd been aiming for his shoulder or his chest. I didn't want to think about where or if I had been aiming at that moment.

Rolling off of Sherlock, I scrambled to my feet, training the gun on Augustus and the driver alternately, both of them still on the ground, groaning as they tried to hold back cries of abject pain, and quickly losing their will to fight back due to blood loss.

"Do either of you want to try anything else?" I demanded, my voice echoing off the battered old movie screen. "My father's a cop. My brother's a Marine. Do you think they didn't teach me how to shoot? Try me, assholes!" I shouted the last, jumping up in flamboyant excitement.

Adrenaline rushed through me and I felt like I could go after a hundred more of them. I felt like one of those

Hollywood antiheroes, and it was a hell of a lot more of a rush than playing sports.

Heart still pounding, I took a few steps forward and helped Sherlock to her feet with one hand, the other still moving the gun between the two men, making sure we were safe. For her part, Sherlock was still struggling to draw breath, and I knew I'd hit her with a rugby tackle hard enough to knock the wind out of her. It'd be a few more minutes before Sherlock could do more than stand there, crouched over, with her hands on her knees, trying to suck in air.

"You ok?" I asked, trying to look her over for injuries, the way the Red Cross First Aid Training had taught. Head, torso, limbs…

Sherlock nodded, her face flushed and puffy from the lack of air, and the force with which I had knocked her to the ground.

I didn't feel too bad about it, after how she'd treated me in the car. "I don't care if it was all an act," I told her sternly. "You're still kind of an asshole."

"It's ok," Sherlock gasped. "I know." She pointed to Charles Augustus, lying in the dusty, broken gravel, unconscious. "His pockets. Our phones," she huffed.

"Yeah, I guess I should call an ambulance for these two, or something." It was the right thing to do, blah blah blah. With slow, cautious steps, I made my way to Augustus, keeping an eye on both of the men.

"No," Sherlock managed, finally standing up, an arm wrapped around her chest. "My phone. Was recording. Since before we got in the car." She sucked in a few more painful breaths.

I crouched and carefully slid my free hand into the fat man's pocket, trying not to look at the bloody aftermath of two blown-out kneecaps. If I did, I would just keep staring. I did have a sick fascination with that sort of thing, after all.

I grabbed both phones and saw that Sherlock's was, as she'd said, engaged. Thank goodness Augustus had missed that. Probably in the midst of all the well-intended but amateurish fumbling with my phone, if I had to guess.

I noticed the gun arm was a bit stiff, so I slid my own into my pocket before I tossed Sherlock hers, which she fumbled. It hit the ground but it was probably OK, I decided. It was in a leather case. And I was sure she could afford another, and another, if need be.

Walking over to Syl, I saw he wasn't moving. Gun still ready, I checked for a pulse in the man's neck. It was there, and steady, if a bit fast from blood loss. His heart would just keep trying to pump what he had left faster through his system. And out the wounds, of course. I supposed we should put pressure on them. But I wasn't completely sold on the idea.

Putting the safety back on the gun that had previously been Augustus', I slid it in the waistband of the jeans Sherlock had bought me. The adrenaline was wearing off and my arm seemed to be cramping up, but I made sure I wasn't going to shoot my ass off. Letting out a deep breath, I forced my hand to grab hold of Blond Tall Syl's gun and likewise secured it. Gun safety was important, damnit.

I let out a deep breath, everything going painful and sluggish as that last bit of chemical rush fell out of me. I stared at my breath, fascinated with the way it billowed and curled in the darkness. "So what's next?" I asked Sherlock, who still had her phone to her ear.

She pulled the phone away, ending the call. "I called some... people to deal with these two. As for us, we're going to get out of here before the authorities arrive." She looked over at the car. "See, we really do need someone in this partnership who knows how to drive."

"That's all you think about, isn't it? How to use people." You'd think I would be used to it by now.

Sherlock grabbed my shoulder and held me still. Not bright when I was still holding the gun. In fact, I was loaded right now. I almost giggled. "What?"

Gently, Sherlock pulled the fabric away from my arm, then used the flashlight function on her phone to illuminate the hole in the brand new coat. And the magnificent tear of flesh--through muscle, maybe almost to the bone. We both stared at it, oddly fascinated by the texture of the muscle and thin bubbly yellow fat sticking out of the edges of the wound, blood oozing around it.

"Well...crap," I muttered. That bullet that had zipped past us hadn't exactly missed, now had it? "I wrecked a good coat." I didn't know how drycleaners did with blood. Now I noticed the smell. There was so much blood around us, the humid, metallic smell hanging on the cold.

Sherlock slid my good arm around her neck for support. "Yeah. I figure we better get you somewhere before you go into shock and can't drive."

I blinked slowly. There was no way I was fit to be behind the wheel. I didn't even like driving on the highway if I didn't have to. "Seriously. You're going to have to drive."

"I don't drive."

"I kind of hate you right now. First thing, when this is over, is solving this whole rich entitled girl who gets driven around thing."

Sherlock scowled, pulling off her scarf and tying it around my arm so tight it made me gasp. "I'm not allowed to drive."

"What the hell did you do, that you're not allowed to drive?" I yelped when Sherlock tied the second knot to prevent further blood loss. "Who the hell did you hit and kill?"

Sherlock gritted her teeth, her nose flaring up as she started maneuvering me with a kick of her leg and the push of her bony hip toward the car. "I'm not allowed to drive because I'm fourteen."

I blinked repeatedly. "I'm sorry, I must be going into shock now," I said calmly, keeping myself together by sheer force of will. "Because I thought you just said you were fourteen."

Looking down and away, Sherlock answered in a firm and quiet voice, repeating her previous answer. "I'm fourteen."

"You're fourteen," I repeated sly. "You're a junior and you're fourteen." Of course she was. The universe hated me.

"I've skipped some grades, ok! Don't judge me. Do you want to see my birth certificate? I can't drive because for some ungodly reason Tobias refuses to teach me to due to 'laws' and him being fired or some such." She pushed me up against the passenger door behind the driver's seat, holding me upright.

I stared for a moment, waiting for the punchline. "Oh god. You're freaking serious."

Sherlock licked her lips, eyes darting around in nervousness. "I've read about it. And I can hotwire a car. But I can't actually drive one because there are some things you really can't learn just from reading, ok?" She let out a huff of indignation. "If you think you're going to pass out or go into

275

shock, or whatever, I guess we should stay here. But do you really want to explain why we shot those guys?"

"Or why I have a gun stuffed in my jeans like a TV badass?" I did giggle that time. I didn't want to explain to my dad how I'd gotten mixed up in political intrigue and blackmail, and had skipped school. There was no way I would get out of that conversation alive, much less intact. "I kind of hate you right now," I reiterated, keeping myself upright while she opened the car door.

"Well, I wiped our prints off the gate. I can take care of the guns." Once the door swung open and bounced on its hinge, she slid in next to me, supporting my weight again. "I'm sorry about letting on like I was going to kill you."

"You should be." I took a deep breath, thinking out how to twist myself around to get into the car. "I didn't think you had a plan." That's how convincing she had been. I slid my back against the car and just pretty much fell into the seat, dragging my legs into the footwell and letting Sherlock close the door for me.

Sherlock slid into the passenger's seat and slammed that door as well, jostling my arm so hard it sent a shiver down my side. "I kept calling you by your given name instead of your surname."

As if that should have been all the clue I needed. "Right." I managed to turn the car on with my left hand and put it into drive. I pulled into the gate and turned around inside the theater, then slowly drove it back down the hill. "We seriously need to work on our communication skills. Before one of us gets killed."

"So does this mean you're willing to do this again with me sometime?" the other girl asked hopefully, practically batting her eyelashes at me.

"Someone needs to make sure you don't get killed." I turned onto the highway, having no idea what direction I was going in, and not really caring. It was the highway. And it had just started snowing with big fluffy flakes. "How are you not dead yet?"

"It's... complicated. Or I'm very lucky. One of the two." She held up a hand, reaching for the wheel with concern. It hovered there, but she didn't grab it. "Um... I think you're supposed to keep it between the lines, not drive it down the middle, like it's an aircraft carrier."

I concentrated as hard as I could until the next exit. There was a gas station and two chain family restaurants. I pulled into the far end of the gas station lot, away from the building itself, and shut off the car. "Ok. I'm done driving," I muttered. "I'm either going to pass out, or go into shock now. I haven't decided which." I was cold and clammy, a sweat forming across my face and shoulders, and I had forgotten what that meant.

Sherlock's face contorted with concern. "Do you have a choice? Neither is good. Maybe you could do neither. Stay awake and don't go into shock."

"It's just a flesh wound," I quoted quietly, the words beginning to run together.

Sherlock grabbed my sleeve and pulled at the scarf. "Are you kidding? You have a little more than a flesh wound."

I grinned, leaning back on the headrest, eyes beginning to droop. "It was a joke. But it was kinda cool looking, wasn't it?"

"You're going to be a great and unsqueamish doctor someday," Sherlock said, running her fingers over my hair.

I closed my eyes. "Thanks for probably not being a psychopath," I muttered, enjoying feeling fingers so close to my scalp.

"And thanks for tackling me and probably breaking all of my ribs," she joked.

"Melodramatic," I muttered. Opening my eyes a little, I could see the snow was really coming down. The globby flakes hit the hood of the car and melted immediately. It was going to be wet and gross soon. I was glad not to be driving in it anymore. "Can I ask…? Who's Sherrinford?"

I don't think I got an answer. If I did, I didn't remember.

##

I had some weird memories of what happened next-- strong flashes of things, but nothing that actually connected together coherently. There'd been some young guy. Paramedic? Doctor? I couldn't remember if he'd been attractive or homely or tall or short. I just remembered he'd been wearing a white shirt that hadn't been white when he was done.

By the time my brain finally came back online, I'd been carefully stitched together in a shady motel room near the airport that smelled of lingering tobacco and dry rot. I wasn't entirely sure how I got there, nor did I care to ask.

When the man handed me a paper prescription for painkillers and antibiotics, and a photocopy of instructions for wound care that looked like it had come from an actual emergency room in the area, I took it, knowing not to question things. Those three sheets of paper were a ticket out of trouble with my father.

Still hazy, I looked from the papers to the sign on the door that ordered guests that there was to be absolutely no cleaning of game in the room.

Eventually, Sherlock touched my leg, then gestured to the papers. "If anyone asks, we were playing with my father's sword collection and things got out of hand. Mrs. Hudson will not even second-guess it, and Toby will confirm he drove us to the emergency room. They couldn't get hold of your father, so they did the work anyway, since you're nearly of legal age. The end."

"Tidy story," I muttered. "I thought Toby was in charge of keeping you on the straight and narrow?"

"We negotiated. I get two lies a month." The doctor, or whoever, was already gone and I had been so preoccupied I hadn't seen him leave. It felt like I should have thanked him or something. "Where'd... he come from?" I gestured to the door.

Sherlock shrugged and blushed a little. "I have a lot of numbers in my phone. Sometimes you have to use up a favor or two."

"What'd you do for *that* guy, that he'll just show up and put someone's arm back together?"

"It wasn't really that deep. But oh! Look! It's swelling already!" Sherlock stared down at it with hungry eyes. "Can I take pictures for comparison? Day of, two days..."

I slumped and sighed. "As long as it's for science and not for some sort of sick game or something."

"Define sick game."

I looked around the room with a frown. "Take a guess."

Sherlock's face twisted up. "Well, we weren't really given toys as children..."

279

I thought about the two little clay animals with nicknames carved into the bottom that I'd seen in Sherlock's room, but I didn't say anything. Sherrinford. "Yeah, I guess that must be it."

Sherlock hopped to her feet and snuck a look outside the curtain. The snow was lying heavy and wet. "Toby should be here soon. He commended me for getting around him, but I'm pretty sure I'm in long-term trouble." Sherlock thought it over before giving her professional opinion. "You'll get grounded for two weeks. I'll be grounded for three. But we'll find some way to circumvent the punishment." She pulled out, and then held up a photocopied sheet of blue paper with scratchy pen drawings on it, announcing a club for that misunderstood and too often maligned segment of the population: redheads. "Because we're investigating this as soon as your stitches are out."

"Fantastic." I took the paper with my good hand and looked it over. "Nothing could possibly go wrong."

"That's statistically--"

"Sarcasm, Sherlock. I need pain killers now before I think better and tell you to go deal with this red-headed league on your own."

Sherlock clapped with bright-eyed glee. "You'll never think better, Watson."

I sighed. "I probably won't."

THE END

About the Author:

T.L. Garrison is a librarian who works with young adults. She has been a Sherlock Holmes fan since the tender age of 7, when *The Return of Sherlock Holmes* (1987) aired on CBS, and Margaret Colin became her first Watson. She has lived everywhere in the eastern half of the United States from Western Kansas to Chicago and Connecticut, but Pittsburgh, Pennsylvania will always be home.

She lives with her husband, four cats and dog on the Kansas/Oklahoma border on a farm with chickens, goats, and far too many grasshoppers. She has a master's in Library Science from the University of Pittsburgh, and a BFA in theater studies from DePaul University.

Also from MX Publishing

MX Publishing is the world's largest specialist Sherlock Holmes publisher, with over two hundred titles and one hundred authors creating the latest in Sherlock Holmes fiction and non-fiction.

From traditional short stories and novels to travel guides and quiz books, MX Publishing cater for all Holmes fans.

The collection includes leading titles such as _Benedict Cumberbatch In Transition_ and _The Norwood Author_ which won the 2011 Howlett Award (Sherlock Holmes Book of the Year).

MX Publishing also has one of the largest communities of Holmes fans on Facebook with regular contributions from dozens of authors.

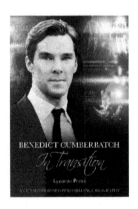

www.mxpublishing.com

Also from MX Publishing

The Missing Authors Series

Sherlock Holmes and The Adventure of The Grinning Cat
Sherlock Holmes and The Nautilus Adventure
Sherlock Holmes and The Round Table Adventure

"Joseph Svec, III is brilliant in entwining two endearing and enduring classics of literature, blending the factual with the fantastical; the playful with the pensive; and the mischievous with the mysterious. We shall, all of us young and old, benefit with a cup of tea, a tranquil afternoon, and a copy of Sherlock Holmes, The Adventure of the Grinning Cat."
Amador County Holmes Hounds Sherlockian Society

www.mxpublishing.com

Also from MX Publishing

The American Literati Series

 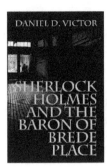 

The Final Page of Baker Street
The Baron of Brede Place
Seventeen Minutes To Baker Street

"The really amazing thing about this book is the author's ability to call up the 'essence' of both the Baker Street 'digs' of Holmes and Watson as well as that of the 'mean streets' of Marlowe's Los Angeles. Although none of the action takes place in either place, Holmes and Watson share a sense of camaraderie and self-confidence in facing threats and problems that also pervades many of the later tales in the Canon. Following their conversations and banter is a return to Edwardian England and its certainties and hope for the future. This is definitely the world before The Great War."
Philip K Jones

www.mxpublishing.com

Also from MX Publishing

The Detective and The Woman Series

The Detective and The Woman
The Detective, The Woman and The Winking Tree
The Detective, The Woman and The Silent Hive

"The book is entertaining, puzzling and a lot of fun. I believe the author has hit on the only type of long-term relationship possible for Sherlock Holmes and Irene Adler. The details of the narrative only add force to the romantic defects we expect in both of them and their growth and development are truly marvelous to watch. This is not a love story. Instead, it is a coming-of-age tale starring two of our favorite characters."
Philip K Jones

www.mxpublishing.com

Lightning Source UK Ltd.
Milton Keynes UK
UKHW022248110123
415160UK00010B/1465